To Sia

Curries Colours & Chaos

(A journey of friendship and discovery)

Lots of Love

10th Nov'24

Curries Colours & Chaos

(A journey of friendship and discovery)

Jhimli B Saha
Suman Mukherjee

PETALS
PUBLISHERS

PETALS PUBLISHERS & DISTRIBUTORS
KIDWAI NAGAR MARKET,
LUDHIANA – 141008
E-mail: mail@petalspublishers.com
www.petalspublishers.com

First Edition: September 2024

Curries Colours & Chaos
Edited by: Parminder Kaur
Illustrations by: Durvesh Daryapurkar

Printed in India

A Special Thanks To,

Rajat Sikder for his indispensable guidance in recounting the anecdotes of our teenage years, without which this book could not have been written.

Amitabh Patney for instilling the idea in my mind to write about our childhood days.

Durvesh Daryapurkar for the illustrations, without which the book wouldn't have been complete.

Index

It was a time of innocence, wonder, and love. It was also a time of arrogance, annoyance, and punishment. It was a time of ambition, obsessions, and discovery. But above all, it was a time of glorious nonsense.

1

Chandan Chandola

Chukchuk Nagar, Lucknow, 1974

Chandan Chandola stood in the middle of the road in broad daylight, pulled down his half pants, and, with his legs wide apart, started to urinate, oblivious to the chaos around him. He elicited an amused smile from the bystanders, bikers, and motorbikers who looked at him and zoomed past in their vehicles, enveloped in the marriage of sounds from the wheels of the machines to the chattering of each person in the booming crowd upon the street.

He was immediately forgiven for this indecent exposure, not because of the act but because of his duration on planet Earth. He was four years old.

His mother, however, was not so forgiving. She turned around while buying vegetables when the vendor pointed his finger at Chandan while he had succumbed to nature's call, ran up to him, pulled up his pants, and then gifted him with a real, tight slap. Chandan started to cry with his mouth wide open, swaddling all the other sounds on that busy road and the entire neighbourhood. By the time he reached home with his mother with his mouth still open, the whole neighbourhood was overwhelmed by compassion and sympathy for this poor kid whose bawls, howls, and squalls echoed through the neck of the woods.

Chandan had arrived in Lucknow the previous year. His father, Amrit Lal Chandola, who worked for the Indian Railways in Calcutta, was transferred to Lucknow, where he joined the National Research and Design Organization, also known as NRDO. The organisation was the technical advisor and consultant to the Railway Board of India. His mother, Jaya, a teacher in a primary school in Calcutta, left her job and joined her husband and son on their new journey. NRDO had a township for its employees known as Chukchuk Nagar Railway Colony.

The quieter, more peaceful railway colony of Chukchuk Nagar, surrounded by lush greenery on all sides, stood as a stark contrast to Calcutta's fast-paced bustling metro life. The change in scenery was evident as the Chandola family exchanged the swell of humanity, an unholy accumulation of sweat and smell, and a claustrophobic swirl of people flowing like rivers in Calcutta for open spaces and rhythmic clatter of the train tracks in the Chukchuk Nagar colony. Their new home, a little block overlooking a well-maintained garden with beautiful flowers, offered a different kind of tranquillity. The distance chugging of trains passing through the nearby quaint little railway station known as Lau Path Gamini or LPG Railway Station offered a sweet melody that replaced the constant whine of a metro city. Chukchuk Nagar was about a slower pace, serene simplicity, and a sense of community where neighbours became friends, and every face had a story to tell.

Though originally from Dehradun, Amrit Lal Chandola and his wife Jaya had spent their entire lives in Calcutta.

Their respective parents arranged for their marriage-ready son and daughter to meet with potential spouses with an accepted right of refusal. They didn't have to search far and wide. Neither were there any refusals. Amrit Lal and Jaya were destined to be man and wife on the first day of their search, formally and legally consummated in the summer of 1966. Their daughter, Phuchki, followed a year later. She was their wordless definition of joy.

But then, a day after her first birthday, Phuchki died. The doctors couldn't find a reason. She slept at night after celebrating her birthday and didn't get up the next morning. Amrit Lal and Jaya Chandola didn't cry. Even when Phuchki was decorated with flowers, her eyes shut, that smile still intact. Even when she was taken out of the house. Even when she was cremated. Even when prayers, condolences, and rituals followed. There were no tears. They, however, quickly learned how to hide the pain but couldn't escape the pain of isolation. They clung to each other, trying to find solace in the shared grief, yet they lived with an incomplete soul in search of Phuchki. The scar never healed or faded away. There was always a certain numbness, a state of emotional anaesthesia. And when Chandan arrived in the summer of 1970, he could do nothing about their shattered world. His parents had peeled all emotions, and it took him a long time to understand why his birthday was never celebrated.

At the moment, however, he was going through extreme emotional and physical pain after the slap. He cried his heart out, but his mother was unperturbed. He had discharged his watery yellowish fluid in the middle of the road, flanked on one side by the Cooperative store, which was the main market of Chukchuk Nagar, and the Polyclinic on the other, which was the only healthcare centre for the employees and their families. To make matters worse, the bus stand was just a few meters away, making the place a bustling hive of activity, right from bus passengers to doctors to patients to salesmen to shopkeepers, to fruit and vegetable vendors, to *paanwalas*, to cycle mechanics, to bike repair mechanics, to rickshaw pullers and occasional beggars, all carrying on with their duties of the day trying to create value for themselves and others. Even though the boy was only four, to urinate under the staring eyes of the inhabitants of this 'vibrant in its own way' place was not only unacceptable and unforgivable but also unthinkable. And there was no scope to escape punishment.

Chandan:

I don't remember. I don't remember at all. Maa said we arrived in the new city in January of 1973. Papa says it was February. I don't care when. I was too little to care.

But they put that red fluffy coat on me. It will be your shield, they said. Shield from the cold. It's a new city, not the old one. 'Lukno' is cold, they said.

I saw colours and butterflies over and over in the garden. I remember. Colours and Colours. Delicate grace and fluttering wings. There was no garden in the old place—only dust. Here, tall trees swayed in the breeze. And flowers, so many of them. I went to pluck one, but Papa said no. They are still growing.

I remember the slap—tight and hard in the middle of the

road, straight on my cheeks. Maa was angry—very angry. Everyone was looking at me, smiling, pitying, and both. I began to cry, and Maa pulled me aside.

'Why did you slap me?' I asked years later. She didn't say anything. Maa and Papa spoke little. Only their eyes talked. With their mouth, they spoke only to Phuchki's photo. And no one else.

Mother said the slap was required. I did something terrible, and I needed to be disciplined. What will people say?

'What will people say?' I asked.

She said nothing, walked away, then turned and looked at me.

'For mothers, love often collides with pain,' she said.

I looked at her eyes. Swelling with tears, and this time, she voiced her words orally.

2

Spice of Mischief

Chukchuk Nagar colony was a celebration by itself with its green spaces, gardens, tree-lined avenues, fruit trees, flowers, and refreshing pleasant air. The colony comprised various types of residential quarters based on the grade and position of the railway employee, their job roles, and seniority. There were four schools to cater to the educational needs of the children, a Polyclinic or dispensary to provide healthcare services, an auditorium to provide recreational services for the overall well-being and quality of life of the residents, the Cooperative shopping centre to ensure easy access to essential goods and services and a bus station for convenient access to other parts of the city that made the lives of the residents quite convenient. There was also a community centre, the Capital Hall, where people gathered to celebrate various festivals. However, it was the community that provided real meaning to the lives of its residents.

Chukchuk Nagar was not just a Railway township but a close-knit community where the employees lived like extended families. Neighbours shared not only walls but also their lives with each other, celebrating joys and shouldering burdens together. In times of need, there was never a shortage of helping hands or comforting words. There was love and respect for each other, which transformed the colony into a warm, familial haven amidst the bustle of daily life. The residents were straightforward, easy, and uncomplicated people with simple dreams and desires. They came from all over India and resided with their families in this township away from their native places. They left their kinfolks behind to join the Indian Railways, seeking a new life on a road to adventure with a degree of fog and chill. Their harmonious blend of tradition and camaraderie fostered an atmosphere of acceptance and shared enchantment.

The residents of Chukchuk Nagar treated each other as their own, as one's flesh and blood, bonding with laughter, love, and trust. They were open-hearted and full of soul, creating a natural bonhomie. Every community event was attended, which made the neighbourhood special and joyful. There was always a party. And everyone was welcome. Every festival was celebrated with joy, good humour, high spirits, and cheer. From Holi to Easter, to Pongal to Onam to Basant Panchami to Eid, to Durga Puja to Diwali, and finally to Christmas- it was celebrated with pomp and mingling by the old and the young alike, commemorating each festival with laughter and joy. The residents of Chukchuk Nagar colony navigated life together like joyful fish, vibrant in rainbow colours, transforming the happiness of unity into a warm and radiant glow.

Chandan Chandola, however, was interested in something other than these festivities. His only attraction and focus were the chocolates and ice creams he received (or gifted) during these festivals. His round face, dimpled cheeks, long curly hair, and sunshine smile were a clear-cut incentive for such gifts. Be it ice creams, chocolates, *samosas*, or footballs, all were a part of that incentive. Quickly, he gained widespread attention. His smile, curly hair, nose, lips, and eyes became a part of the colonial chatter.

'Such a handsome child,' someone remarked.

'Yes, he is Chandan. He was the one who pissed near the Cooperative store. You know, he had an elder sister. Unfortunately...' and Chandan used to shut his ears with his fingers and run.

Chukchuk Nagar colony boasted clean roads and a ubiquitous green cover resembling a mini forest. From Eucalyptus to Mango, to Jackfruit to Guava, the place was enamoured with lots of diverse flora and fauna along with *Gulmohar*, *Peepa*l, and *Sheshum* trees encompassing the evolutionary and ecological processes that sustain life. Cows and buffaloes roamed freely and aimlessly, grazing around the colony between their lazy afternoon naps. Cats and dogs ran around, the birds sang their songs, and the squirrels and other rodents ran up and down the trees, nibbling at fruits and vegetables grown in the front and backyard of almost every block or whatever they could lay their hands on.

But it was the monkeys that troubled the residents of Chukchuk Nagar. The monkeys used to visit the colony from a nearby forest in groups. They caused utter destruction, dismantling everything that came their way, tearing down the leaves and branches of fruit-laden trees, plucking and then eating both the ripe and the unripe fruits, smashing and shattering the window glasses, breaking water pipes, tearing up the clothes hanging outside for drying and occasionally biting the residents who revolted. A monkey once entered a house, picked up a six-month-old baby while the baby's mother was busy with household chores, and then sat on the edge of the roof with the baby on its lap. There was complete pandemonium as the gathered crowd shouted, threatened, and begged for mercy. But the monkey didn't move an inch. It was only when the baby, enjoying all the attention of the crowd below, giggled and started to poke her finger in the monkey's nose that the animal, fed up with this childish act, kept the baby on the terrace and left.

Chandan tried without success to climb the mango tree in the backyard, the juicy mangoes swaying along with the leaves in the summer breeze, mocking and daring him to get hold of them and freaking him out on his futile attempts, and then, one day, fell from the guava tree just when he had managed to climb and was very close to pulling it off. He fell with a thud, and his mother came running towards him. Chandan, covering his cheek with both his palms to protect himself from another onslaught, ran inside the house, his mother dropping the chase when a guava fell on her head. He was convinced it was the same fruit he was trying to pluck.

'Come back, Chandu. Take the guava.'

But those were the rare moments when he saw his mother smile, one of growing happiness like the opening of a spring flower. On most days, she would be cold and indifferent, and as he grew older, he could see the irreversible damage inflicted on her by her firstborn and wished to see her smile every day, inside and out.

His failed attempts to climb the trees didn't deter him from trying. With a combination of agility and persistence, he managed to climb the trees and eventually pluck the fruits at will, in the morning, in the afternoon, and sometimes late at night, even though he was convinced that there was a ghost who perpetually lived under the jackfruit tree and stared at him with its eyes popping out of its sockets whenever he tried to climb the adjacent mango tree. But he always managed to brush that thought aside and clamber up the tree, accomplishing his desired aim, cradling his bountiful harvest, indulging in the ripe, juicy mangoes, and savouring the taste of victory with each delicious bite.

However, one fateful day, he was terrified not because of the ghost but of the presence of Partho Sarkar, his immediate neighbour who was more than double his age and who came and stood in front of him with his clenched fist.

'You want some juicy, sweet stuff?' Partho asked.

'Yes.' Chandan responded.

Partho slowly opened his palm and showed Chandan the 'sweet, juicy' green chillies.

'I have plucked them from my garden. Sweeter than any toffee. Want it?'

'Yes.'

Partho handed over two green chillies to Chandan.

'Bite it and then suck the juice.'

Chandan did as he was told. In less than a second, he was on fire. His mouth, nose, eyes, and ears were all on fire. He choked. He coughed and then gasped with a high-pitched whistling sound. Tears swelled in his eyes, and he wagged his tongue like a mongrel before fleeing in agony.

'Watr. Watr. *Paani*.'

Partho laughed.

'Wait. Want another?'

Hearing this chaotic din, Partho's father, who was reading the newspaper sitting on an easy chair on the verandah of their block, came out and saw Chandan's situation. He immediately rushed towards Chandan. Partho, panicked as he saw his father, ran in the other direction and hid behind the jackfruit tree. Partho's father raised an alarm. In a few minutes, almost the entire neighbourhood gave Chandan water, sugar, and jaggery to soothe the pain.

'It's not okay, Mr Sarkar.' Chandan heard his mother say to Partho's father.

'I am sorry, Mrs Chandola. Partho is turning into a brat.'

'He is already a brat. The other day, he repeatedly pinched my three-year-old daughter on her cheek. Her face was red and swollen, and she cried the entire night.' An angry neighbour gave vent to his feelings. 'You should do something about him.'

Partho was now trembling. He was at his wit's end. This time, he was silly and had gone too far. How will he face his father now? His father had seen it all, and there was nothing he could hide. He was trying to contemplate his next steps when two monkeys on the top of the jackfruit tree were quarrelling over a big booty. They had gotten hold of an enormous jackfruit and were supposedly arguing about who should own the fruit. In the process, they lost their balance and fell right on Partho's head along with the fruit. Partho was horrified. The animals were flustered. Both stared at each other. As an animal instinct and as an outlet to their defence mechanism, they dropped the fruit, slapped Partho hard on his face, and ran. Partho, totally bewildered by the happening around him, was about to regain his composure when he received a hard kick on his bums. He turned around and saw his father and a few other neighbours enraged, fuming, and raving at him. He tried to get up, but his father, this time, slapped him, which sent him rolling towards the guava tree.

'The monkey was Lord Hanuman. He punished you for troubling a child,' one neighbour remarked.

'There were two. One was Hanuman. Then who was the other?' Partho managed to ask even in that unfathomable circumstance.

'Sugreev.' His father gravely uttered, followed by another blow with a kick.

The monkeys must have been divinely powerful. Three months later, Partho's father was transferred to a remote railway post in west Rajasthan. As Chandan watched the family bid goodbye to their colonial neighbours, Partho approached him and whispered, 'You want some toffees?'

'No, No.' Chandan responded quickly, convinced that the 'toffees' would again set him on fire.

But Partho took his arm forcibly and put a few 'real' chocolates on his palm.

'I am sorry for the chillies,' he said, then turned and left.

Chandan didn't say anything. That was the last time he saw Partho.

The Sarkars vacated the block, and the Chandolas were without an immediate neighbour for the next few months. Then a new neighbour came, and that neighbour changed Chandan's life forever.

Chandan:

I was too young when I arrived at Chukchuk Nagar colony, so I don't remember much from those days. But I remember the flowers, the trees, and the garden. I remember the jackfruit tree, the guava tree, the mango tree—and, of course, the juicy mangoes. I remember the monkeys. And I remember my neighbours always smiling at me, giving me toffees and ice cream, and affectionately pinching me on my cheek.

I do remember the chilly 'toffees' Partho forced on my palm. They were a mix of red and green. I chewed, and it was like a fire inside my mouth—burning red hot. I was crying and howling. It was very painful. Mother was angry with Partho that day. Father was furious, too, when he came back from the office. They didn't say much, but I know they love me.

I remember that red truck loaded with their belongings. Partho's mother hugged my mother and wept. Maa said something—some consolation, I think—and then Partho's mother stopped crying. They were friends. Then she left with Partho and his father.

I don't know where Partho is now. Someone told Maa that he was in a faraway land and kept playing with fire. Playing with fire? I didn't understand that at all.

I am sure there was a ghost beneath the jackfruit tree. I saw it on many nights, but then no one believed me. Such folly, I tell you!

3

The Demon

The summers in Lucknow were hot. Real hot. The radiant sun wrapped all in its brilliant rays. Hot winds blew, sucking up every drop of water or moisture, blowing dust in the eyes. Cracks grew deep in the barren, parched soil baked hard. The water in the nearby *Naher* or water canal evaporated, turning it into a trickle. The earth was neither grey nor brown nor beige and resembled the no colour of the dead. Birds and animals were exhausted. Many animals died, and the leaves turned yellow. Streets were deserted in the afternoon. People avoided leaving the house during the daytime and came out only after sunset. Ice and cold drinks, apart from *lassi* and *nimbu paani*, were in high demand.

In Chukchuk Nagar, the middle of a summer day was a time of siestas and lazy restfulness—not for the employees but for their families. There was no air conditioning, very few water coolers, and the electric fan was the only saviour. Chandan's mother used to take blissful naps in the scorching summer afternoons while his father braved the heat at his office.

One day, Chandan wanted to visit the *Naher*. He had heard his neighbour, Mrs Titli Basu, who lived in the adjacent quarter opposite the block where Partho lived, talk to his mother about how the *Naher* had gone dry due to the summer season. Her husband used to visit the place for fishing, which was both his hobby and meditation. After he had caught his fill, he had time to decompress and was fit for family life. Of course, the fish were cooked and eaten too. But now, with no water in the *Naher* and no fish to catch, his newly developed favourite pastime was to quarrel with his wife for no rhyme or reason whenever he was at home, making him unfit for family life. Their elder son, Monu, was upset with his father's snappy behaviour, which coincided with the level of water in the *Naher*, and the younger one, Sonu, didn't care.

Chandan came out of the house one afternoon while his mother was taking a nap, slowly closed the door behind him, and then started to walk towards the *Naher*. It was scorching hot; the streets were all quiet except for a cat that ran for its life, chased by a dog. Chandan reached the water tank near his house and saw two men drinking *lassi* and chatting, enjoying the comfort of the shade of the adjacent pumphouse, which used to be relatively cooler and more relaxed due to the thick iron pipes that encircled the building and pumped water from the tank back and forth. The tank was meant to supply clean drinking water to the neighbourhood twice a day, in the morning and evening, and there were a few more of those structures in the entire colony.

He walked and lowered himself on one of the pipes. He could hear the hollow gurgling sound of the water inside, a relentless force coursing through the metallic arteries. Despite the scorching heat, the iron pipes were as cool as a cucumber, retaining a refreshing coolness mirroring the temperature of the flowing water within. He sat on a pipe for a few minutes, stood up, and walked towards the men.

'Where is the *Naher*?' he asked.

The men looked up at this little boy and pointed towards the right. 'That way. But why do you want to go to the *Naher* now?'

'I want to catch fish.'

'There is no water there. It has dried up. Maybe you can go after the rains.'

'But I want to go now.' Chandan stamped his foot on the ground.

The men looked at each other.

'You can go, but you may not come back,' remarked one of them.

'Why?' Chandan asked.

'Because the hungry and thirsty demon is not getting enough water nowadays. So, he is eating up kids your age.'

'What demon?' Chandan was alarmed.

'Oh! You don't know? A demon resides there. When the *Naher* is dry in summer, it eats up children to quench its thirst. You can go, but if you get eaten up, then you will not be able to see your parents again. Are you okay with that?'

'No.'

'You still want to go to the *Naher*?'

'No.'

'Then go back home.'

Chandan turned around and ran like the wind. He reached his house, opened the door, and was relieved to see his mother still asleep. He closed the door, went to the kitchen, filled some water in a glass from the earthen pot on the table, sat on the sofa, drank the water, and fell asleep.

When he woke in the evening, he saw his father, who was

already back from office, quite agitated, talking to his mother, 'I don't know what's happening to this colony. They found the body of a little boy near the *Naher* at the same spot. It's no longer safe here. Two murders in a month. That too of kids. Unbelievable!'

'Maybe the killers are from Nakshal Khera, not our colony. That place is full of goons,' his mother said while sipping tea.

Chandan went numb. He had no idea where Nakshal Khera was, but he was sure the demon resided there.

'We need to keep an eye on Chandu. He shouldn't go out alone. Times are bad,' his father warned before venturing into the garden.

That was around the time the President of India proclaimed a state of National Emergency on June 25, 1975. Chandan's father was right. The times were really bad.

Chandan:

Papa said times were bad, but for me, the demon was bad. How can he be hungry all the time? How can he eat little boys like me? It's sad that the *Naher* had dried up. Otherwise, the demon wouldn't have eaten the boys.

I loved the thick water pipes at the pumphouse. They were always calm and cold. I could hear water inside—gurr...gurr. Sometimes, I sat on the pipes, and sometimes, I lay down on them. They were super cool.

There was this big tank—a big, big tank. Its roof touched the sky. My friend told me one can go straight up to the sky if one jumps from the roof of the water tank. I don't understand.

How can you go up while coming down?

Papa was telling Maa that there is some 'emgemcy'. He needs to be punctual in the office. He also said trains are running timely. He said there's a lot of discipline. He said all looks good now. But still, he says, the times are bad. A mix of good and bad. Very confusing to me! This 'emgemcy'.

Basu Aunty is a chatterbox. Talks and Talks. Maa only listens. Basu Uncle goes to the *Naher* to catch fish. They eat fish. Chee, chee!

I don't go out alone now, but I will go once it rains and the water fills the *Naher*.

4

Mona Mishra

Chandan Chandola was the first outside her family to see Mona Mishra naked.

Their eyes had met for the first time. They widened with curiosity as Mona's mother carefully lowered her into the water, ensuring a gentle and gradual immersion as she cooed and giggled in her tub outside in the courtyard, amused at the water splashing at her face. Mona continued to splash and swash with her tiny fingers as if trying to swim.

Her mother used a soft washcloth to cleanse her delicate skin, starting from the face and working her way down to her tiny toes. Mona responded with contended gurgles and happy kicks, enjoying the sensation of being clean and refreshed. But after the cleansing ritual was complete, and as her mother carefully lifted her out of the water, she screamed so loud that the neighbours thought that, indeed, something terrible had occurred. The baby wanted the ritual to continue.

Mona had just turned two.

Jitendra Mishra, Mona's father, had been transferred from the Northeastern railway zone in Varanasi, where he was an officer in the zonal headquarters. He joined NRDO over a month back and stayed in the officer's guest house before his family joined him. His wife, Malti, had remained in Lucknow for a while when she was a kid before her family moved to Bhopal. Now, she was back in the city where she had spent her childhood.

Unlike Chandan's mother, Malti was extremely talkative, outgoing, and friendly. She could talk about absolutely anything and everything. Within a few days of their arrival, she knew the neighbourhood residents by their names. She was loquacious and would talk about Mona, her husband, her relatives, her neighbours, her friends, the news aired on the radio about the Prime Minister, the President, the world, and everybody she knew. The neighbours would listen to her in utter silence even though they knew she was as clueless in politics as a cat at a chess tournament. But she always had something interesting to say, which either amused or shocked people, depending on the subject. Whenever she saw Mr Basu going towards the *Naher* for fishing, she shouted from her balcony.

'Where Mr Basu? To catch fish?'

'No. To catch elephants.' Mr Basu gave the curt reply.

Malti roared with laughter.

'Catch many elephants today. And eat them with curry. We are vegetarians, but I would like to see how many you catch.'

Mr Basu just nodded and hurriedly cycled his way towards the *Naher*.

And to Chandan's mother, 'Come on, Jaya. Let's go to the movie. They are playing *Sholay* at the Krishna Talkies at Alambagh.'

Chandan's mother would politely decline the invitation.

Mona was now Chandan's new neighbour and resided in the same block vacated by Partho's family. Chandan had not seen them in the morning while getting ready for school. A month ago, he was admitted to St William's Convent, one of the four schools in Chukchuk Nagar, after much deliberation by his parents on whether he should go to the nearby Montessori school or the Kendriya Vidyalaya or the Chukchuk Nagar Railway School. Finally, they decided on the Convent school so their son could be conversant and fluent in English. It's a different matter that Chandan had difficulty grasping the language and later cursed Shakespeare, Milton, and Wordsworth for making his life miserable.

After he returned from school that day, he saw their new neighbour, with their daughter, taking a bath in a tub out in the courtyard. A truck stood by the road, and a few men unloaded the furniture and other belongings.

By the time Chandan was in the second standard, he had made quite a few friends. Lavanya, Rocky, Bholanath, and Daksh were in his inner circle. Anshul and Nayantara were in the outer circle. But Balveer, Balvant, and Banjeet were kept away from any circle. The reason? They stayed near Nakshal Khera, the home of the demon.

Then, there were Diksha, Chaitanya, and Chakradev, whose positions fluctuated between the inner and the outer circle, depending on Chandan's mood. All of them were a part of the neighbourhood except for the boys near Nakshal Khera. They saw each other quite often, in the streets, in the playground, in the Cooperative store, and more frequently in the Polyclinic, which they used to visit to cure a cough or cold or fever or, later, more regularly to stitch up a wound sustained during a cricket or football match at the Unity Club or from falling trying to climb a mango tree or both.

But Mona was neither in his inner nor outer circle. She was in his soul circle. And in that circle, there was only Mona and no one else. Mona's energy filled him with vibrant tones of innocence and laughter in the stark dichotomy of the grim solitude of his home, where his parents spoke little, coupled with the quiet desperation of being a single child.

Since he first saw Mona, his little soul discovered a connection that surpassed the ordinary. Chandan, a quiet but curious boy, found himself drawn to Mona, whose sparkling eyes mirrored the glow of the fireflies that waltzed in the evening air. This childhood fascination unfolded like a story, written in the stars, sprinkled with magic, and woven with threads of a fairy tale. Their bond, forged in the magical crucible of childhood, remained an enduring witness to the extraordinary nature of human connections that bloom in the heart of both the real and the unreal world.

After returning from school, Chandan would throw his bag, drink a glass of milk, and rush to Mona's house. Mona used to wait for him near the gate, and as she saw Chandan, she would jump with joy, clapping her hands, reaching out to him with outstretched arms, and shouting, 'Chandu, Chandu.' He closed his fingers around her hand as he was too small to pick her up, as he did every morning, evening, and night whenever he was with her.

'Chandu, finish your lunch first,' his mother used to shout.

But by then, Chandan was already handing Mona the *churan* he had bought from Laddu ki Dukaan (Laddu's shop) near his school or, much later, sharing the *samosas* from Dewalal's shop with his pocket money of two rupees every month. He looked down at her pink, round cheeks and grinned while she was fully focused on her *churan* or *samosa*, occasionally trading furtive happy glances at each other.

From the time she stepped into his life and as his neighbour, their friendship grew inside their soul and then sparkled through their eyes. She was cute, sweet, and adorable, with long hair up to her shoulders and eyes that spoke so much. For Chandan, those eyes exuded a sense of home and a sense of belonging. Though they seldom exchanged words, even when they were together, their friendship was always of a silent understanding that needed no words.

Chandan:

I don't know how and when Mona and I became friends. She was two years younger than me, and I remember the first time I saw her. She was bathing in a tub and giving her mother a difficult time, splashing water everywhere with her tiny fingers.

My parents spoke little. Chandu, yes, Chandu, no. Don't do that. Don't go there. Lunch and dinner are ready. Those were the frequent words. As I grew up, Papa sometimes inquired about my marks in Maths and English. And that's all.

My home was still, and all was quiet. The rooms were empty, and the sound of emptiness was louder than any noise. Papa returned home from the office and would have dinner and listen to the radio before going to sleep. Maa knitted or read a book. All in silence.

There was not much laughter but occasional smiles, occasional hugs, occasional ice cream, occasional chocolates, occasional cakes, and many other occasional things, but no birthdays.

Mona broke that silence with laughter, love, joy, chatting, talking, giggling, jumping, and everything else. My mother saw her Phuchki in her—her dead Phuchki, back to life in another form.

Mona's innocent giggles provided a certain warmth and hope. With this newfound life as our neighbour, we started to bloom—my parents and me, I mean.

She was first a friend, then became my best friend, and then we were inseparable.

Mona:

Chandu always teases me, saying that he had seen me naked while I was bathing. I asked, who takes a bath wearing a frock, skirt, or bell bottoms? I was only two years old at that time. He doesn't say anything but laughs. His mother and father love me so much. Whenever I go to their house, they give me lots and lots of chocolates and pastries. Chandu brings *churan* from school to me every day. It's so tasty. Yesterday, he brought *samosas* and potato chop. They were so yummy!

Chandu loves me more than anyone else. I love him very, very much.

5

Neighbourhood Curries and the Healing Hands

Chandan's immediate neighbourhood consisted of around ten blocks. Mona and her family came from Varanasi and were his immediate neighbours. On the block opposite Mona's resided an important and famous man, a homoeopathic doctor, Dr Ramulu. Dr Ramulu, originally from Andhra Pradesh, was not only a great doctor but a gentleman to the core, loved and respected by all. On the block right of Dr Ramulu's was the block of Mrs Titli Basu, who was forever fighting with her husband and lived with her two sons.

Opposite Mrs Basu's quarter, Mr Ratan Chopra (who had come from Delhi) lived with his family. His house had a beautiful garden with blooming flowers. He was a plant enthusiast and would often host gardening workshops. He was also a frequent visitor to the nearby nursery. He would participate in the flower festival every year and often receive the first prize. His son Daksh was Chandan's classmate.

In the block opposite the Chopras resided the Iyers, who came from Coimbatore. Mrs Sheetal Iyer was a Bharatnatyam dancer. Though she couldn't devote much time to dance after marriage, she continued practising her dance, bringing a sense of art and creativity to the neighbourhood. After her husband, Ganesh, persisted she should continue with the art, she started to teach students. She helped them participate in dance competitions in and around the colony. Lavanya, her daughter, was Chandan's classmate. She was dusky, pretty, and quite close to Chandan.

Mr Gopalakrishnan, from Mysore, lived with his wife, Janki, and son, Chakradev. He was a trained guitarist who played his guitar at home and during get-togethers and festivals. On weekends and holidays, his house used to be filled with music, as all his friends and neighbours would gather for a cup of South Indian Coffee and enjoy his performance, followed by chatter, laughter, and occasional dancing. His son Chakradev had no interest in music. He was into sports and was Chandan's classmate.

The Singh family from Amritsar lived on the next block. Jaswinder Singh, a Sikh, and his wife Tajinder Kaur were artists and created murals. Jaswinder Singh joined the railways through the sports quota as he had played and captained his hockey team in Punjab. In his youth, he was a brilliant player and was about to be selected for the Asian Games when he broke his leg. He couldn't pursue the sport, so he joined the railways. He could occasionally be seen in the stadium coaching players who aspired to play hockey for the state or their country. The couple painted on the plain walls of their home and even helped some schools in Lucknow design the murals. Their only son, Anmol Singh, was an army officer. Anmol occasionally visited his parents whenever he got leaves and shared lots of stories of his adventures in the army with his friends and neighbours. He was currently posted in Siachen.

Mr Chandraprakash Nayyar, from Patiala, lived with his wife, Sushma, in the next block. He was a teacher at one of the schools in the colony. He loved children, and the children loved him. On Sundays and other holidays, the children would gather at his home. He would tell them stories mostly about mythology and also gift them comics. After the narration, the children were given chocolates. Mr Nayyar had lost his son to typhoid. He and his wife treated all the children in the neighbourhood as their own.

Mr Ravindra Nair and his wife, Parvathi, lived with their daughter, Diksha, and son, Chaitanya. Diksha and Chaitanya were twins. They were both classmates of Chandan. As they were the immediate neighbours of the Nayyars, people mistook them as being from the same family due to their similar surnames. Mr Nair had a doctorate in Physics and a passion for technology. He built his air cooler and a little air conditioner, the first of its kind in Chukchuk Nagar, using nuts and bolts and basic scientific principles.

And then there was Mrs Nupur Chatterjee from Haldia, an entrepreneur who bought ladies' garments from Bengal and sold them in the Colony; Lokkhi Das and her family from Dibrugarh; Urvashi Iyengar from Madras, the mother of Nayantara. Nayantara was Chandan's classmate.

Anshul's parents, Mr and Mrs Deshmukh, were from Pune. Rakesh Sood, known as Rocky, lived with his parents, was their immediate neighbour, and belonged to Chandan's inner circle. Anshul and Rocky were also Chandan's classmates.

Finally, there was Mr Arun Chauhan. He was originally from Udaipur, unmarried, and lived alone. He loved animals and often participated in pet-care events. He had two dogs with bright eyes and tails in propeller spin. They never barked at anyone and always seemed happy.

Chukchuk Nagar colony was like a cosmopolitan metropolis. Life was simple and stress-free. The men would go to their offices at nine in the morning and return by six. After completing their household chores, the women would visit their neighbours in the afternoon for a chitchat. The bond with the neighbours was strong. One could hear the laughter, chatter on the streets, and the rumblings of trains on the nearby railway tracks. These neighbourhood sounds bonded everyone as readily as fish in clear waters.

But Amrit Lal Chandola and his wife preferred privacy. They stayed away from most gatherings or festivities. Their interactions with neighbours were limited to polite nods and the occasional exchange of greetings. They were not unfriendly, though. They were always there to help anyone in need. However, most invitations by neighbours were denied, and attempts at making closer connections were met with polite but firm resistance. There was always a haunting silence of grief, even after Chandan's birth. Phuchki never left them, but once Mona arrived, she largely nullified the gloom of the Chandola family.

But the Chandolas gave their son full freedom. There was discipline but no real restrictions at home. They always attended Chandan's school events, celebrated achievements, and shared tender moments through the numbness of their own hearts. They always tried to shield their son from the sadness that raged within them. As he grew up, Chandan participated in almost every function, festivity, and celebration with Mona. However, Chandan couldn't ignore the subtle undercurrent of melancholy in his home, which contrasted sharply with the laughter and joy that filled Mona's house.

It was Dr Ramulu who came to his rescue when, in the middle of a wintery night, Chandan gasped for air. The doctor was in deep slumber when Chandan's father banged at the clinic door in panic, waking the exhausted doctor who had just gone to sleep after seeing his last patient. Dr Ramulu came running to his house, put the stethoscope on his chest, and could hear the air moving through Chandan's bronchioles, making sounds like weird instruments. It was a squeaky wheezing sound. Chandan felt as if his airways had been blocked and concrete had been poured over his airways. He panicked, and the lack of air drove him to start gasping as if the oxygen had been sucked away from his lungs. By this time, the entire neighbourhood was in the room by the grace of Mona's mother, who had knocked at every door but had forgotten Dr Ramulu's block. Dr Ramulu ran to his clinic and, within a few minutes, was back with an inhaler and asked Chandan to take a puff. Chandan did as he was told. The breathing eased, Chandan, now relaxed, went to sleep, and so did his neighbours, who had spent a frightful night with him and his parents. Dr Ramulu gave him a few medicines the next day, and Chandan never had an asthma attack again.

Though he was never troubled by asthma, he was frequently tormented with other ailments—severe stomach ache, fever, cough, toothache, measles, mumps, and chicken pox. And every time a visit to Dr Ramulu would cleanse him of the sickness.

As a reward for being the doctor's most frequently visited

yet lovable patient, Chandan was given the privilege to sit in Dr Ramulu's brand-new Fiat car, probably the first purchased car in the colony as soon as it came out of the showroom.

During all his illness, disease, and disorder, Mona was always at his side. Even during his measles and pox attack, wherein no outsider was allowed in his room due to the infectious nature of the disease, Mona would drag a plastic stool from her house, keep it near the window of Chandan's bedroom, climb on top of it, and then peep through the open window and see Chandan on his bed, sick and weak and ask, 'Are you okay?'

'Yes, get down, or you will fall.' Chandan would respond meekly, turning over on his bed.

Dr Chakraborty, the head of the Polyclinic, was another saviour in the colony. If patients visited Dr Ramulu for chronic illness, Dr Chakraborty, an allopath, was more adept at handling emergencies. An accident, a fracture, high fever, vomiting, and loss of bodily fluids and their cure was his domain, and he excelled in that. His patience with patients was legendary as he kept calm in the patient's personal storm. This steadiness came at a cost to his health and his ability to give the same to his own family. There is no rest for the good, and Dr Chakraborty exemplified that.

And then there was Dr Arora. Another doctor, another gentleman. He didn't have to prescribe too many medicines. He spoke with such love in a voice that soothed and showed so much emotional warmth that the patients felt better immediately, convinced they were in safe hands.

These doctors of Chukchuk Nagar were highly respected.

They knew their job well and had built a personal connection with not only their patients but all residents of Chukchuk Nagar.

Chandan:

Dr Ramulu, Dr Chakraborty, and Dr Arora were my superheroes. They had one thing in common- their magical healing touch. I am sorry. There were other things in common: wisdom, gentle smile, boundless energy, and their spectacles perched on the bridge of their nose. They were friend first and doctors second. Dr Ramulu and Dr Arora prescribed the sweet white pills, which I immensely enjoyed. Dr Chakraborty stitched up wounds and gave me bitter pills that I reluctantly swallowed with water.

I often fell sick those days, and they were always there for me. I had it all: measles, mumps, chicken pox, stomach ache, and whatnot. But one day, I couldn't stop hiccupping. My mother tried every remedy she knew, then Mona's mother tried, followed by Basu Aunty, Arora Aunty, and then all the neighbourhood aunties. Even Mona tried, but my hiccups wouldn't go. Finally, they all took me to Dr Chakraborty.

Dr Chakraborty asked me to lie on the bed to inspect my stomach. He pressed his fingers on my tummy. Then he gave me a spoonful of sugar and instructed me to eat it while hopping on one leg. I got up and started to hop around the entire clinic on one leg, trying to balance myself. Everyone laughed, and the hiccups vanished.

Whenever I was ill, Mona would be by my side. She

refused to go home. So, my Papa got a small movable cot for her to sleep in my room. She used to get the class notes from Nayantara or Lavanya and read them to me without understanding anything. She used to ask Daksh, Bholanath, Rocky, and Chakradev to come and see me, and they used to show up unannounced with some chocolates and fruits, sharing stupid jokes that would make me laugh. And then she used to get me lots and lots of comics and borrow the Amar Chitra Kathas from Lavanya to keep my spirits up. Lavanya herself would visit my place quite often.

It was I who was sick. And it was Mona who weathered the storm of my sickness.

Mona:

I worried about Chandu, who often fell sick those days. I watched him lying on the bed, pale and thin. But I never wanted him to be alone in this fight, so I stayed with him. Chandu used to sleep most of the time, weak and helpless. His mother and father were always worried. The doctors used to come and go all the time. There were countless sleepless nights I had spent by his bedside along with his parents. The fever and the harsh coughing fit made us nervous. The doctors, however, said we need not worry. He would be fine.

They were right. Chandu is solid now.

6

Wheels of Freedom

Four events of sufficient dimension and importance took place in 1977. The Janata Party defeated Congress in the elections for the first time, electing Morarji Desai as the fourth Prime Minister of India. In the Chukchuk Nagar colony, Mona received a gift in the form of her little brother. She, too, got admission to St. Wiliam's Convent that year. And Chandan got his first new Hero bicycle.

That was also the year Chandan and Mona, hand in hand, visited the Cooperative store on their own for the first time, without their parents accompanying them. They saw children playing and shouting in the playgrounds, laughing, fighting, running, hiding, and whatever they could do. They heard the temple bells as people gathered near the temple for the evening aarti. They listened to the cheers and the greetings of those who lived on those streets.

A year later, they could gather the courage to enter the Chukchuk Nagar stadium further away from the Cooperative store, staring in awe at the green blanket of the football field, the basketball courts, the cricket pitch, and the clear view of the Capital Hall and the Temple as they sat on the stairs of the stadium, surrounded by the bright yellow flowers of the Amaltas and the Gulmohar trees amidst the bounty of clover and sun-strengthened grass, the blossom's song ringing in their ears.

'Shall we go there?' Mona asked, pointing at the Capital Hall building.

'Some other day. It's getting late. Let's go home.'

With the gift of seasons past and the promise of the seasons to come, Chandan, now on his bicycle with Mona sitting on the back carrier or in the front, entered the Capital Hall one afternoon. The building had a peculiar shape; neither a square nor a rectangle, neither a triangle nor a rhombus may be close to a trapezoid. But Capital Hall gave emotional structure to the colony and, over time, became etched in the psyche of Chandan, Mona, and the inhabitants of Chukchuk Nagar.

Capital Hall was not only the community centre but also the celebration centre. Festivals, parties, and marriage ceremonies were all organised in the Capital Hall. It was not just a building; it weaved the colonial people together like the most magnificent clothes.

Mona and Chandan stood in front of the building for some time. Then, they walked up to the main entrance and entered the building. A spacious entrance led to the main hall flanked on either side by large doors and windows. The ceiling was quite high, with an elevated stage on one side. Designs of apsaras (celestial nymphs) were carved into the moulding, with vases of blossoms at each corner. They were surprised to see boys and girls playing badminton inside the main hall and others trying to learn karate on the stage where, just a few months back, the idol of Goddess Durga was placed during Durga Puja and the Dussehra festival. The Durga idol was finally immersed in the *Naher* on the tenth day of the festival as per the ritual.

They walked towards the back of the building, flanked by *peepal*, tamarind, Eucalyptus, and mango trees. There lay a defunct, dry, and disused swimming pool, now covered with dry, dead leaves and proliferating mushrooms. A few years earlier, the swimming pool was in use, as many residents would visit it on weekends and enjoy their swim.

They walked around Capital Hall for some time and exited it. Then, they visited the adjacent temple, *the Sanatan Dharam Mandir.* They removed their shoes and went inside with folded hands to seek the blessings of the Gods, which they received in the form of a sweet *prasadam*.

While paddling back home that day, Chandan and Mona felt their first sense of freedom. Together, they explored the world of Chukchuk Nagar, cycling from one end of the colony to the other. They smiled and laughed all the way back home. It was a time of innocence, wonder, and discovery. They felt a certain joy. And in that happiness, their friendship defined the magic of growing up together as they turned ordinary days into extraordinary adventures.

That was the joy they found in their childhood connection.

Chandan:

I vividly remember the day I accompanied Papa to Aminabad market to buy the bicycle. 'This is a gift,' he said.

'Gift for what?' I asked.

'You have been a good boy,' he smiled. I was thrilled.

I learnt to ride it quickly—all by myself. I wobbled and

fell. I got up and tried and tried again—bruises here, bruises there. I wobbled and fell again. I had scraped knees and a heart full of courage. And finally, the victory.

Chukchuk Nagar colony with its vast spaces. Broad and empty roads. Cycling wasn't too tricky.

And it gave me my first taste of freedom!

From my school to Kendriya Vidyalaya to the Cooperative store, to LPG Railway Station to Capital Hall, to the temple, to the powerhouse, to the Bank, to the Post Office, to the stadium, to Milan Club, to the auditorium, and even to Nakshal Khera-every street of Chukchuk Nagar was explored.

And then, one day, while going to school, there was a direct clash with a rickshaw. I had stitches on my knee as I kept a brave face in front of Dr Chakraborty and Mr Dubey, the compounder at the Polyclinic, as they stitched the wound. I smiled in their presence and then howled after reaching home.

And then, very soon, I was paddling everywhere in Chukchuk Nagar with Mona. She sat on the back carrier and sometimes on the front tube. From indulging in Dewalal's *samosas* to sweet betelnut and *churan* from Laddu's shop to devouring *masala chaat* and *golgappe* from Dixit's, we sampled a feast the colony could offer. Our adventures knew no bounds as the intense feeling of freedom swept over us like a wild gust of an untamed wind.

By the time I cycled out of Chukchuk Nagar for the first time to Alambagh market, Mona's brother Mihir was three years old, Mona was already in the third grade, Prime Minister Morarji Desai had lost the elections, and Mrs Indira Gandhi had come back to power as Prime Minister but unfortunately lost her younger son in a plane crash. That was 1980.

Mona:

Riding on Chandu's cycle, every moment felt like an adventure. I clung tightly to him as we circled Chukchuk Nagar. At that moment, nothing else mattered, just the thrill of going round and round the colony. I felt more alive, more connected. With Chandu by my side and the wind in my hair, I felt unstoppable, as if the entire world awaited me to explore. It was surreal.

That was freedom for me.

7

Shadows in the Dark

Power cuts in the evenings, particularly in the hot summers, were common in Chukchuk Nagar. But the children eagerly waited for the darkness to surround them. There were reasons for their excitement. During the entire duration of the disruption of the power supply, they could come out in the courtyard or the lawn and play. A prolonged power cut was a perfect excuse to escape studies and homework. It used to be extremely hot, even at night. The parents understood the unbearable conditions at home and allowed a temporary respite for their children from their studies.

With each power outage, the children in the neighbourhood breathed a collective sigh of relief. The cuts were like an unexpected vacation. The adults would come out of their rooms and gather on their lawns or balconies, fanning themselves with handheld fans and chitchatting while the children ran outside to play.

'Dr Rajendra Prasad, our first President, used to study under streetlights, and you want an excuse to evade studies whenever there is a power cut.' Amrit Lal Chandola rebuked his son, who, as soon as the supply was cut, ran outside to play with his mates, who were already starting to gather in front of his house.

'But there are no streetlights, Papa. It's all dark. You see,' he responded, pointing at the stillness of the dark street, his face illuminated by the faint glow of the candle. 'Otherwise, I too would have...'

'Studied under the streetlamps.' His father completed the sentence.

'Yes, Papa.'

'Okay, I understand. You now go and play. The other Presidents and Prime Ministers are waiting for you.'

Chandan dashed out of the house and saw Mona standing near the front lawn when the others joined her.

'What are we going to play today, Chandu?' Mona asked.

'Hide and Seek,' was Chaitanya's prompt response, who was with his sister Diksha.

'Who would be the seeker?' Nayantara asked.

'Pugan Pugai, the way we do every time.' Chakradev answered.

Everyone placed their palm one over the other and then removed it quickly. They had to face the palm either up or down. If the player faces their palm opposite to the others, then he or she becomes the seeker. Mona, being the youngest, was spared from this activity as Chandan had put a lot of pressure on the group and put his foot down for her.

'Mona will never be the seeker. She is too young, and I can't let her be alone to find others.' Mona giggled and hugged Chandan for protecting her.

Anshul held his palm in the opposite direction and became the seeker for that night. He went into a corner, looked the other way, and started counting to twenty to give the others time to hide. The sounds of crickets and rustling leaves added an enchanting soundtrack.

He started to count... 1, 2, 3...

The children ran in all directions. Chandan and Mona hid behind the jackfruit tree along with Lavanya. Diksha took shelter under the mango tree. Chakradev hid behind the pillar of the porch. Nayantara hid in the lawn's corner behind a bush. Daksh and Rocky settled on the side of the staircase. Chaitanya climbed the guava tree. Everyone held their breath, as they didn't want to be spotted.

Anshul turned around and started his search as Chukchuk Nagar stood dark and still without electricity.

He first turned towards the neem trees in Mr Arora's block. The yard was cast in shadows, and there was absolute silence.

'They wouldn't be here.' He thought.

He walked towards Dr Ramulu's block and searched the backyard, looking around the curry tree. Someone must be hiding there, he thought. But no. There was complete silence. He went to Lavanya's block and then to Chakradev's quarter. He found nothing there.

He left the block and walked into Chandan's backyard. The jackfruit tree stood tall with its gnarled branches, their leaves rustling in the whispers of an unseen breeze. Even the moonlight struggled to penetrate the foliage. The distant chirping of crickets created a haunting symphony reverberating throughout the neighbourhood.

Anshul saw some movements and was convinced it was either Chandan or Rocky. He tiptoed toward the mango tree. 'I will get both of you.'

He tiptoed in that direction. Just then, someone tapped him on his back. As he turned around, he found himself face to face with a pair of gleaming eyes in the moonlight, which was definitely not Chandan's or Rocky's.

Anshul couldn't believe his eyes. He was so shocked that he lost his balance, stumbled backwards, and fell while the monkey, unfazed by the disturbance, continued to stare at him with a curious tilt of its head and a mango in its hand.

Anshul was terrified. 'Help, Help.' He cried. The urgency in his plea spurred the others to come out of their hiding spots and race towards the source of the distress call. In the shadow of the moonlight, they saw a trembling Anshul lying on the ground with the animal sitting beside him. The monkey saw the children, ran, and jumped on the mango tree, utterly confused to see this crowd. The neighbourhood residents sitting on their lawns and verandahs also came running and joined the children when they heard Anshul's cry for help.

It took some time for all to understand what had happened. They laughed at the absurdity of the situation.

'One monkey meets another today.' Anshul's father said, ruffling his son's hair.

Anshul, who had turned white as snow, regained his composure, got up, and joined in the laughter.

'No more hide and seek for me. I am done with it,' he announced. The promise was kept for less than a day.

They invented another game. During power outages on a full moon night, they used to get thread and a needle from their mother. Holding the end of the thread between their thumb and index finger, they would gently guide it through the eye of the needle under the full moon's glow. The one who completed the task most quickly was rewarded with a chocolate. Diksha used to win hands down every time.

Then, Chandan would tell the story of the ghost, who he believed lived under the jackfruit tree. The gang would eagerly listen to his spine-chilling tales.

As the power came back, the children returned to their homes, unhappy that they had to stop their games and sit down to study again. They enjoyed the power cuts as they ran around in the neighbourhood playing *chupan-chupai* (hide-and-seek). The night, though powerless, gave them the power of freedom—the freedom they would remember for the rest of their lives.

That was the life of the children in Chukchuk Nagar—a life filled with adventure, pranks, joy, and laughter.

And a life that could never be replicated elsewhere.

Chandan:

Power cuts in the evenings in Chukchuk Nagar were gleeful chaos. It was so hot inside, so no studies. Ghost stories, hide-and-seek, or needle-and-thread games. Gathering of friends at my house or sometimes at their house. Running, Jumping, and Chatting. Fun. Fun. Fun.

Anshul had turned white that day—haha. He looked like Snow White on the black night. He said that he feared nothing, but then that night, he feared everything...ha ha ha. Monkey Anshul again played hide-and-seek the next day. He broke his promise.

Mona:

I liked holding the lighted candle during power cuts—

the shadows. My father's head looked like a football in the shadow, and my brother's a pumpkin. Then, our flashlight game. We searched for insects and worms with our torches. Then, lo and behold! One day, we saw a snake. A slithering serpent was going to its den. Chandu pushed me aside, and then we ran.

But then Chandu's story of the ghost that lived beneath the jackfruit tree, our hide-and-seek and moonlight needle thread games, were the best.

8
Buzzing Danger

Amrit Lal Chandola had never hit his son. But when he did, when he smacked his son's face hard and then thrashed him on his ears, tears swelled up in Chandan's eyes before he started shedding them and then burst into sobs.

It was not Chandan's idea, though. It came from someone in the group. He couldn't remember whether it was Chakradev, Daksh, or Chaitanya. Or was it Rocky, Lavanya, Diksha, Nayantara, or Mona. He couldn't remember.

They all had visited Nayantara Iyengar's house to celebrate her birthday. The birthday was celebrated in the afternoon as Nayantara's father had to go on an official tour in the evening, and she wanted her father to be there no matter what. Nayantara was Chandan's classmate and always stood first in the class. After the party, someone in the group first thought and then proposed the idea of climbing the water tank that stood tall at more than eighty feet just opposite Nayantara's house. From her balcony, the first structure one could see, apart from the greenery around, was the water tank and the pump house.

They agreed. Mona was the youngest in the group, but she, too, nodded. They had often played near the water tank but could never gather the courage to climb it. They all came and stood near the tank, then sat on the cool water pipes, pondering how to execute the plan, looking skywards at its circular dome hovering over them. A spiral stairway led to the top of the tank, which the maintenance department workers often used to clean and repair.

Unknown to them, on the inner walls of the dome, another community—the community of bees—was thriving and busy building its homes. Large and small beehives were on either side at the top of the tank.

'Who will go first?' someone asked.

'Me.' Daksh responded quickly.

Daksh took the lead, followed by Chaitanya and the rest. They started climbing the stairs slowly, holding the side railing for support. They heard the occasional happy buzzing sound as they moved further in silence. As they had crossed the halfway mark and were forty feet above the ground, watching the surrounding trees sway in the swarming breeze and the rumble and burble of the flowing water inside the pipes, Diksha felt a sharp sting in her hand and saw a bee flying away. She rubbed the skin near her elbow as a painful swelling appeared with a red bulge on her arm. Instinctively, she let out a loud groan but continued to climb along with the others. They must have moved a few steps higher when suddenly, a swarm of bees attacked, provoked by this unforeseen disruption, the low hum gradually intensifying into a menacing buzz. First a hundred, then a thousand, and then it felt like a humming, buzzing, and stinging dark cloud cover fluttering furiously at the climbers. Panic ensued in the group as they tried to evade the attackers with their arms and legs or whatever part of their body they could use. Mona was the second victim after Diksha of this voracious attack, followed by Lavanya and the rest. A hurried and mad scramble followed by screams and wails echoed in the neighbourhood as they turned around to escape this assault. Nayantara slipped in their panic-stricken state while hurriedly coming down the stairs. Her one foot went out of the railing, dangling in mid-air as she tried to hold on to the iron parapet for support. Chaitanya misstepped and fell on her but managed to hold on to the handrail at the last moment. Daksh, trying to take two steps at a time, fell on Rocky and Chandan as they somehow managed to hold on to the railing. They could hardly open their eyes as the bees continuously bombarded them with their poisonous sting, the excrescence now all over their exposed faces and limbs.

Mrs Sheetal Iyer came out of her room to check the clothes hung to dry in the sun. She heard the screams coming from the direction of the water tank and glanced at the structure. She was horrified! Her loud, piercing scream was enough to wake the whole neighbourhood even at midnight—and it was still early evening.

A crowd gathered below the tank, and the children were rescued, one by one. Though the incident was traumatic for all, for Chandan, a more profoundly distressing experience was the smack he received across his face from his father. As his face burned and he lowered himself down on the bed at night, he didn't understand whether it was due to the bite of the insects or the man whom he called his 'Papa'.

Mona, whose face, like others, had bulged like a balloon, sat with Chandan on his bed that evening, wiping his tears with her favourite yellow and pink handkerchief.

The trio of Dr Ramulu, Dr Chakraborty, and Dr Arora intervened again to get rid of their bumps and blisters, deracinating the venom injected by the stinging winged insect.

Years later, when Chandan and Rocky met unexpectedly at a coffee shop near Hazratganj, they hugged and sat for a chit-chat. Rocky confessed that it was his idea to climb the stairs.

'I got my first thrashing from my father because of you.' Chandan complained.

They both laughed and then went to Rovers to eat frankies.

Chandan:

I still shudder to think of that day. The bees buzzed angrily around us, and we were all on the brink of falling from the water tank. I understood what happens after a fall. We go straight up in the sky. We were terrified. Iyer Aunty was our saviour. She was the angel. Then the neighbours.

The shock of that slap still reverberates. Papa had never hit me before. It was fear and anger for a father. As Maa said, love always collides with pain. It's always all about love.

It was Rocky's foolish idea. That's what he told me when we met after years. But then he made the day memorable. All our faces had swelled like a big red balloon. But Rocky's was the biggest. I thought he would float away like a helium-filled balloon.

Mona:

Oh! My face was swollen, and I had a fever. It was so

painful. Our faces had turned into red tomatoes. Chandu wept the whole night. His father had slapped him for the first time. I consoled him, but he kept crying. What more could I do?

9

Taste of Temptation

The Dixit Sweet Shop was located at one corner of the Cooperative store, where Mr Dixit, the owner, and his entire family converted a small storehouse to sell snacks and sweets. The shop also housed seven of his family members. It was a grocery cum snack cum sweet shop, and its location in the centre of the colony made it quite convenient for the residents to visit the shop. He ran the shop with the help of his wife and brothers.

Mr Dixit was a middle-aged, warm, and friendly man. The shop had everything from everyday necessities to snacks and sweets. Dairy and baked products, biscuits and bread, eggs, cigarettes, matchboxes, *samosas,* sweets, and *golgappas* were all available. The *golgappa* were hollow, crispy fried balls that were filled with potato and chickpeas and flavoured water, usually tamarind, and popped into one's mouth whole. People were drawn towards Dixit's shop as the tantalising aroma of the snacks and sweets persuaded the young and the old alike to indulge in the *chaat, tikki, golgappe, samosas,* and sweets. Apart from its gastronomic delights, the shop was also a hub for chitchat and friendly conversations.

Mrs Dixit, the 'Managing Director' of the shop, was a plump lady with a rounded face and characteristically just the opposite of her husband. Her stern expression intimidated many, particularly the children. She discouraged casual conversations and would shout if someone loitered aimlessly around the shop, gossiping and smoking cigarettes. She was loud, and her voice carried a sharp, commanding tone, scrutinising young and old customers. Her responses were curt and to the point. Though her overall impression was that of an unfriendly person, her husband made up for her lack of warmth and a more welcoming retail environment. But deep within, she was very kind and empathetic, lending a listening ear or offering a comforting word to someone who needed it most.

On Sunday, Chandan's mother asked him to get some biscuits from the shop. Mona was on her lawn playing with her little brother.

'Where are you going, Chandu?' Mona asked.

'Going to the Dixit shop. Maa wants some biscuits.'

'Wait, I will come with you.'

Hand in hand, they walked down the path, laughing and looking up at the water tank, which had been the site of an impending calamity a few days earlier.

Chandan kicked a stone, which hit a dog. The dog barked and ran away with its tail between its legs.

They both entered the shop. They saw a robust-built man with a thick moustache sitting at the counter.

'Where is Aunty?' Chandan asked the man, enquiring about Mrs Dixit.

'The family has gone to attend a function. They will come back tomorrow. I am her brother. What do you want?' the man responded, sternly looking at Chandan.

'Biscuits. One packet.'

'Which one? The salty or the sweet?'

'Sweet one.'

The man handed Chandan a pack of biscuits. 'Two rupees.'

Chandan handed him the amount and turned towards Mona.

'Do you want anything, Mona?'

She grinned. 'One toffee.'

The man opened the lid, took out an éclair, and gave it to Mona. 'Ten paisa.'

Mona unwrapped the chocolate and then tried to break it with her fingers.

'What are you doing?' Chandan asked.

'I am trying to break it. To give the other half to you.'

'No need. I will have the biscuits.'

Mona nodded and happily popped the chocolate in her mouth.

Chandan removed the wrapping and found that all the biscuits were broken inside the wrap.

He turned around at the man.

'These are all broken.'

The man thought for a while and then smiled.

'They are not broken, beta. That's the design of the biscuits. Nowadays, they come in this new design only.'

Chandan was shocked but didn't know what to say. Mona thought for a while and pulled the toffee out of her mouth, the sticky caramel stuck to her teeth and gums, and tried to return the partially eaten chocolate to the shopkeeper.

'Chee, Chee, Chee...' the shopkeeper sprang to his feet. 'Throw it if you don't want it. I can't take it back.'

'It's neither broken nor chewed, uncle. It's a new design, and I'm not fond of it. You must take it back, or I will shout.'

The shopkeeper was horrified but understood what she meant and immediately gave Chandan a new pack of biscuits. While returning home, they both burst into laughter. The shopkeeper didn't even ask to return the broken pack of biscuits.

But a few days later, Bholanath was caught in a dire situation at the same Dixit shop. They had all gathered in the shop to celebrate his birthday. Bholanath, though their classmate, lived in a neighbourhood a bit far from theirs. He would walk from his house to play with his friends in their neighbourhood and celebrate birthdays. It was his birthday, and the best way to celebrate it was with the sweets and *golgappas* at the Dixit shop.

The children stood around the vendor as the man (Dixit's younger brother) expertly crafted the hollow spheres with his fingers, filling them with mashed potatoes and tamarind water. The children devoured the *golgappas*, and because of their spicy and tangy flavour, they kept asking for more.

Then suddenly, disaster struck. One large *golgappa* went down Bholanath's throat but in the wrong pipe. He panicked as he gasped for breath, as the *golgappa* lodged in his throat obstructed his airway.

Struggling for air and unable to dislodge the stubborn *golgappa*, Bholanath turned pale. His friends gathered around him, but they didn't know what to do. With each passing moment, Bholanath's breathing became more laboured, his face turned red, and his eyes widened in fear and panic.

Chandan rushed towards him, lifted Bholanath on his shoulders, and rushed towards the Polyclinic across the road. The others ran after him. The people witnessing the scene were shocked and horrified as Bholanath's life hung in the balance.

'Call his parents.' Chandan instructed his friends as he scuttled inside the Polyclinic. Daksh and Chaitanya turned around and ran towards Bholanath's house. Mona, Lavanya, Diksha, and Chakradev put Bholanath on a stretcher as the ward boys quickly wheeled him into the emergency room. Panting heavily, Chandan dashed to Dr Chakraborty's cabin, where the doctor was examining a patient.

'Uncle.' Chandan could hardly utter a word, gasping for breath. The doctor looked up at him.

'Chandan, why are you here?' the doctor asked.

Dr Chakraborty's eyes widened in shock as Chandan explained the *golgappa* mishap.

The doctor sprang out of his seat and dashed towards the emergency room. Chandan ran after him and saw two nurses and one compounder already trying to stabilise Bholanath. Within a few minutes, Dr Chakraborty removed the *golgappa* with precision. Bholanath, extremely exhausted yet now relieved, could breathe normally. By the time his parents, who were still in a state of shock and completely traumatised, reached the Polyclinic, Bholanath was off the stretcher and was standing again on his own two feet, smiling.

'Thank you, Doctor,' his father said while his mother wiped her tears as relief washed over her face. They thanked Dr Chakraborty and his team for successfully pulling out

Bholanath from an almost fatal disaster.

'Not me, that guy.' The doctor pointed towards Chandan. 'And all of them,' he said, pointing towards the rest. 'Thank them.'

Bholanath's father's eyes were filled with tears as he wept uncontrollably. He hugged Chandan tightly. That embrace formed an unspoken bond between them.

Years later, when Bholanath's father passed away, Chandan stood by him with his hand on Bholanath's shoulder, offering support in every possible way he could. Over the years, they developed a genuine connection, which evolved into a lifelong friendship. After all, it was the *golgappa* incident that brought them closer.

That evening, they all returned home quietly, stunned by this sudden emergency. It took time for them to return to normalcy.

Chandan:

The Cooperative store had many shops. Behind the Dixit Sweet shop was the Munna's mutton shop. I never visited his shop. We are vegetarians. But I could see the meat hanging there as Munna meticulously sliced through them. Rocky and Daksh used to frequent the shop mostly on Sundays, and I occasionally accompanied them, though I never entered the shop as the odour inside was unpleasant. I stood outside and watched. However, the shop's front wall slogan told a different story, 'Veggie's envy, Munna's mutton pride'.

The corner shop was called 'Buddhe ki Dukaan' (old man's

shop). I don't know why it was called such, but the owner was an old man, and that could have been the reason. The shop was for stationery: pens, pencils, notebooks, paper, and chocolates. He always smiled and gave me a free chocolate whenever I visited the shop. One day, while speaking to a customer, he collapsed. That was the end of his tenure as a shopkeeper and a father. His sons took over.

Then there was Kapoor's dry-cleaning shop. The aroma inside was very pleasant as if everything inside was clean and tidy. The clothes were neatly hung and carefully folded. Mr Kapoor was a gentleman, always smiling. He was busy during the winter months, refreshing our coats and sweaters. But then, one day, Mr Kapoor suddenly closed the shop. I don't know why. After he closed the shop, we had to go to Alambagh market to dry clean our clothes.

Sharmaji's grocery shop was also there. It was the go-to place for everyone in the colony to buy groceries. His shop was stocked with everything, from spices to grains to eggs, bread, biscuits, and many more items. At one end of the store was a cooling machine neatly stacked with bottles of Gold Spot, Campa Cola, and Duke's, the famous brands of beverages. Adjacent to that, there were bottles of Rasna Cola and Kissan jam. Packets of Campco chocolates and Poppins were displayed on the front shelf. Baby food items like Farex and Lactogen were stacked on the other side of the store. Soap brands like Rexona, Breeze, and Binaca toothpaste adored the rear shelves.

I received quite a few free chocolates from Sharmaji, too. That was always the focus: free chocolates.

There was Meena Tailor and Rajendra Book Depot, a

barber shop where I indulged in head messages after a haircut, a Khanna scooter repair shop, an Atta chakki, and many other shops catering to the day-to-day requirements of the residents of Chukchuk Nagar.

I could never figure out how the *golgappa* got stuck in Bholanath's throat. Come on, it's just a crispy *golgappa*. Or maybe he was trying to gulp two at once. Bholanath said no, it was only one. Anyway, he somehow managed that day. Somehow.

Thank God. And thank Dr Chakraborty.

And what can I say about Mona? She always protected me. I still remember the shopkeeper's horrid look as she pulled the half-eaten chocolate out of her mouth. The second pack of biscuits was completely free.

Mona, my friend, my guardian angel!

Mona:

The incident will be etched in my memory forever. It still sends shivers down my spine. Bholanath was laughing loudly, and we all joined him. In an instant, the mood changed from jovial to frantic as I watched Bholanath suddenly clutch his throat. I will never forget the sheer terror that gripped us that evening.

Chandu was quick. Bholanath is heavy, so carrying him was not easy. But Chandu always does what others can't.

Bholanath didn't eat *golgappa* for a few days, but then, yesterday, he gulped a few again.

Boys will be boys!

10

Tug-of-War

There was seldom a cat that was legally domesticated in Chukchuk Nagar. But they were loved, for they belonged there, and the colony looked after them. That also gave them the independence and ample freedom to move, eat, drink, sleep, and procreate. They were entitled to certain privileges that even the residents, particularly the children, were deprived of. They could roam freely at any time of the day and night, eat and sleep at any time they wished, and even sneak into any block without much adverse repercussion except the occasional shout. They had full knowledge about the neighbourhood, the target houses, the friendly ones, the ones with dogs, the ones to avoid completely, basically the cat haters. It was normal for them to sneak in through open doors or windows to find opportunities for their hunt.

Mrs Titli Basu was busy with her daily chores. She was happily singing an awkward tune; some of the high-pitched notes were enough to deter anyone from their mission.

Mrs Basu was taking care of the clothes on the washing line. Her husband was at the *Naher* to catch fish, and her two boys, Sonu and Monu, were out on the ground to play football. Mrs Basu marinated the fish her husband had caught the previous day for cooking later that afternoon. It was a bright, sparkly spring morning. Everything was pleasant, apart from the occasional out-of-tune record of Mrs

Basu's singing.

A cat, which was aimlessly passing by, first heard the tune and then detected the smell. With its white and black furry body, gleaming bright eyes, and a nice bushy tail, she quickly singled out her target—Mrs Basu's kitchen.

The cat crept inside the house through the kitchen window in her phantom silence. Her over-sensitive whiskers had helped her locate her food. Her chatoyant eyes glistened even brighter as she pounced on the largest piece of marinated fish lying on the plate. With her mission accomplished, she clenched it between her incisors, jumped off the kitchen counter, wagging that proud tail of achievement, and started to make her way out of the kitchen.

She was in the dining room when, suddenly, her gaze met another pair of eyes staring at her in disbelief. In front of her stood a plump, pot-bellied lady with her mouth wide open as if ready for a huge scream. Mrs Basu stood still like a rock, with a massive pile of clothes on her head, shoulders, and arms, flabbergasted to see this little beast holding her favourite dish in her mouth.

She dropped the pile of clothes in a flash, closed the back door, and pounced on the beast. The cat, alarmed and shocked at the same time but still holding the fish tightly in its mouth, took a few steps back to avoid another assault. Mrs Basu was quick. She dropped down and grabbed the dangling fish from the cat's mouth. Her instincts were faster than those of the animal.

The beast did not anticipate that. A serious pursuit commenced, with Mrs Basu at one end of the clenched cold-blooded vertebrate and the feline on the other.

Nobody was ready to let go.

For the first time in her life, Mrs Basu was confident that no matter what, she wouldn't give up. She pulled the fish with all her might, force, and power.

It was her favourite fish and the favourite dish of her entire family, and she was very serious about not letting it slip away from her so easily.

The cat arched her furry body, tail all puffed up, paws clawed for resistance, whiskers on high alert. She, too, wasn't ready to let go of her afternoon hunt after all.

She retraced her claws, digging them. "Screech...!" came the deafening sound of scrapping and scratching the floor, and her cracked pads tried with full force to resist.

A tug-of-war.

Eyes locked and narrowed, teeth clenched, claws unsheathed and dragging through the cement floor, creating a loud screeching noise.

No mechanics of a man or woman have the shock-absorbing power of a cat. Neither the beast nor Mrs Basu conceded defeat.

But alas! The fish gave up. It split in half.

Mrs Basu found her ground and controlled from stumbling and falling over, one-half of the fish in her hand.

The cat, too, found her footing and, in a flash of the moment, with a tiny prize still in her mouth, turned and ran towards the kitchen, jumped and escaped from the open window. She never looked back, her bushy tail still on high alert. She was sure never to forget this house or this lady she had just battled with.

When the echoes of the tussle had died, there was only a colossal pounding of her heart. Yet, Mrs Basu, proud of her achievement, took the piece in her hand to the kitchen, washed it thoroughly, fried it separately, and ate it that afternoon. It was now her favourite dish and a satisfying win after the scrimmage, even though she was half victorious. She didn't let that bushy little thief steal everything that belonged to her.

By afternoon, almost everyone had heard about Mrs Basu's courage, agility, and stunts, which had earned her reverence from the entire neighbourhood.

That evening, the bell rang at Mona's house. She knew what it was about. She suddenly heard a roar of laughter from the living room.

Mrs Basu was unique. A few days later, her neighbours found it amusing when she lovingly fed a cat with milk. But then, milk was never her favourite drink.

Chandan:

Basu Aunty was an exceptional character. Restless, talkative, erratic, yet comforting. She talked so much; her words poured forth like raindrops. Her tongue always wagging with no moments of silence. Her thoughts were like light and its speed. She was the only one who gave a tight competition to Mona's mother. In talk competition, I mean. But there was an undeniable charm to her endless chatter. Her presence left a lasting impact on all who had the privilege of knowing her. I have never seen a kinder and more compassionate person in my life.

I heard about the cat story from Mona, who had heard from Iyer Aunty and who, in turn, had heard from...the list goes on and on. But I was not surprised. Basu Aunty was quite capable of either fighting or feeding a cat.

Mona:

I laughed and laughed when Iyer Aunty told my mother about the fight between the cat and Basu Aunty in my presence. Iyer Aunty had heard it from Sood Aunty, Rocky's mother, who had heard it from Chopra Aunty. I don't know from whom Chopra Aunty had heard, but I think it was from Chatterjee Aunty. She and Basu Aunty were quite close. I wish I had been there to witness the scene. Despite her quirky mannerisms, Basu Aunty's sharp mind never failed to impress those around her. She was always so helpful.

I love Basu Aunty.

11

Summer Delights & Mango Magic

Summer vacations were the time for fun. Chandan learned swimming that summer along with Anshul, Bholanath, Daksh, and Chakradev under the guidance of Mrs Basu's husband, who temporarily paused his fishing activities and taught them to swim in the *Naher*. In two weeks, they had all learned how to swim. Swimming not only taught them a new skill but also gave them a new confidence long after leaving the water's embrace.

'So, you are now a fish?' Mona chuckled.

'Like a fish.' Chandan corrected her with a smile.

Then there was the mango madness. From Alphonso to Dussheri, Langra, Chausa, and Totapuri...it used to be a feast. Mango lassi, mango shakes, mango ice cream, and whatnot. Chandan and his friends indulged in mangoes the entire summer.

One afternoon, the gang gathered at Chandan's house, sitting beneath the mango tree in the backyard. On one side, the jackfruit tree was heavy with fruit and stiffly competing with its mango counterpart. They were all there. And they came with the sole purpose of chitchat and eating mangoes. Birds and squirrels flitted up and down the branches, the bees buzzed busily, and a dog slept under the cool shade, oblivious of the cat staring down from a branch of the guava tree. A gentle breeze blew as they gathered around the water tap near the mango tree. The water from the tap was used for watering the plants in the summers, rinsing the fruits and vegetables, and cleaning the hands and mouth after indulging in a mango feast.

Mona composed and rendered her first poem.

Oh! Sweet Mango,

You are the golden glow,

We eat you, but you steal the show,

Mango, Mango, Mango,

You are such a delight,

Chandu's face is ripe and yellow,

Oh! What a sight!

And they all clapped and laughed.

They chatted amongst themselves for a while. Then Daksh stood up and addressed his friends.

'Dear Friends, I have something to say. Would you like to listen to me?'

'Yes.' They chimed in unison.

'Wouldn't you love to enjoy delicious ripe mangoes daily?' he asked.

'Yes. Absolutely,' his friends responded eagerly.

'I have a plan. Listen carefully.'

The children leaned in attentively as Daksh unfolded his strategy.

'My father will be bringing a lot of semi-ripe mangoes all the way from Malihabad tomorrow. They will fill three large boxes, which are kept in the kitchen. Last year, too, he bought the mangoes, so I know.'

The children listened intently.

'My mother meticulously counts each mango. No one is allowed to eat them without her permission. But since there are so many, some end up rotting after ripening. That's a waste. Last year, she had to throw away a lot of rotten mangoes.'

There was a pin-drop silence as he continued.

'We could enjoy the mangoes without her ever finding out,' he proposed.

Daksh's friends exchanged meaningful glances.

'I will inspect the mangoes daily once they arrive. I will press each mango to estimate their ripeness. I will then choose a ripe one and puncture a small hole on each ripe mango. Those mangoes will be shared with you all, my dear friends. We can then squeeze it out and enjoy its sweet flesh.'

The silence continued.

'Now, this is the tricky part. After eating the mango, we have to blow air back into it and seal it with one of these small green stickers to keep it from deflating for some time. I will keep the fruit back in its place. It will appear like any other ripe mango for my mother.'

He retrieved some small green stickers from his pocket.

All eyes exchanged glances with each other. No one spoke.

'This is not right. This is theft.' Chandan protested after the silence.

'No, my dear. I am just trying to avoid any wastage.' Daksh responded confidently.

They all thought for a while.

'What if we get caught?' Nayantara asked.

'We will not, Nayana, provided we blow the air and seal the hole nicely.' Daksh persuaded.

This time, the silence was more prolonged than Daksh had anticipated.

'Let's vote.' Chakradev announced after a long silence.

They voted. Chandan and Mona were the only ones against the plan. And they lost badly.

The mangoes arrived from Malihabad the next day.

The plan unfolded flawlessly. Every day, when his mother was out at the neighbour's place, Daksh would get a few ripe mangoes out of the carton, share them with his friends, which they wholeheartedly enjoyed, then blow air, seal them as per the plan with the little green tape, and keep them where they belonged. Mona and Chandan were not a part of this adventure, though they watched eagerly while their friends hungrily indulged in devouring the fruit every afternoon.

However, after a few days, a serious complication arose. Daksh was in his room in the evening trying to study without much success as his mind was on the football field. He suddenly heard his father talking to his mother.

'Let me take one box of mangoes to Mr Bakshi's house. He has reminded me more than a few times in the office today. After all, he had paid for one crate, and it had been stupid of me to delay handing it over to him. After all, he is my boss.'

Daksh's mind was now neither in his studies nor football. He was terrified. He didn't know what to do as he saw his father pick up the same box whose contents had been used up quite thoroughly for the past few days. He dashed out of the room and stood before his father, who was now holding the pack.

'Why don't you take the other box?' Daksh asked, pointing

towards the adjacent carton.

'This one feels lighter. It will be easier to carry,' his father responded, even without looking up at him.

Daksh's father picked up the carton, tied it with a rope in the back of his motorcycle, and rode to Mr Bakshi's house. Daksh helplessly watched his father depart.

Every day, Daksh checked on his dad after he returned from work to ensure everything was all right. He felt no cause for concern. The month went by peacefully, though the pilferage and the subsequent taping, stickering, and blowing air had ceased.

But three months later, when his father was transferred for a year to one of the remotest corners of the Northeast, where he had to go alone without his family, Daksh immediately understood the reason behind the relocation.

That day, while his father packed for his journey, Daksh felt a pang of guilt and sadness. He hugged his father tightly.

'Did Mr Bakshi like the mangoes?' he asked his father tentatively.

'He absolutely loved them, son,' his father replied with a beaming smile. 'Who knows, the mangoes played a part in my promotion? I feel bad that I will be away from you and your mother for a while, but it's just a year.'

'You have been promoted, Papa?'

'Yes, of course. Otherwise, why should I agree to go to the remote Northeast when my family is here? The promotion was an incentive.'

He hugged his son.

As he watched his father board the bus to the railway

station and wave goodbye to him and his mother, he felt a heavy burden lift off his shoulders, leaving him light and relieved.

While returning home, he asked his mother, 'Can I have some *golgappa* at the Dixit Sweet shop?'

'Okay, but only one plate.' His mother responded.

Daksh jumped across the street and dashed towards the Dixit shop, feeling as light and crispy as the savoury *golgappas*.

Chandan:

I used to water the garden every evening during the summer, sprinkling water on the lawn so that the grass would stay cool, green, and lush. Afterwards, I would unfurl a bamboo mat for my friends who would come at any moment. Mona arranged the water bottles and some glasses. We all used to feel hungry and thirsty all the time during summers and vacations.

They all used to be there. Anshul, Rocky, Lavanya, Nayantara, Daksh, Diksha, and Chakradev were regulars, while Bholanath and Chaitanya occasionally joined. Chaitanya enjoyed spending more time smoking near the *Naher*.

We all used to lie down on the mat, side by side, gazing at the night sky. The scent of jasmine and mogra, which I had planted, filled the air with a certain muskiness and an enchanting fragrance. A cool breeze whispered while the gentle glow of the moon illuminated the garden with its soft, silvery light. Daksh would occasionally bring his little Murphy radio. We would listen to the 'Mann Chahe Geet', the film songs broadcasted by All India Radio, like *'ruk jaa raat tahar jaa re chanda...'* a plea to the night to pause and the moon to stay back a little longer, sung by Lata Mangeshkar and was always our favourite.

A distant sound of a passing train would gently break the melodious silence. It was like another holy music.

We lay there motionless, the gentle rustle of the leaves, the distant whistling of the train, and chatting neighbours all merging into a soothing piece of music.

And then up in the sky, the twinkling stars, the *Saptarishis, Arundhati* and *Vashistha*, the celestial couple, *Rohini, Marichi, Pulaha*, and many more.

And then there were conversations—primarily gossip. Rocky used to take the lead. He knew everything. Who was having an affair with whom? Who broke up? Juicy details of romantic encounters, crushes, admirers, love triangles, everything. He even delved into the personal lives of his teachers. He was convinced that one young teacher who had newly joined the school had started developing feelings for him. However, he had a secret crush of his own, which he was not ready to disclose, leading to a misunderstanding with his young teacher, which resulted in a big 'zero' on one of his exams, which, according to him, was a clear act of revenge. He knew who got into trouble in school and for what. He knew who ate what in their breakfast, lunch, and dinner. And he knew which one of his friends was going to have a little brother or sister soon. With his vast knowledge, he was the colony's All India Radio.

I liked Diksha. She also possessed vast knowledge, like

Rocky. But in a different way. She knew everything. But the real thing. She was like a human encyclopaedia. She could tell all the names of the Saptarishis. She could talk about Barbarika and Yuyutsu in the Mahabharata and Jabali in the Ramayana, names which I had never heard of. She could teach you Physics and Maths, Geography and Sanskrit, History and Chemistry at any time of the day, at any time of the year, even in her sleep. She was undoubtedly gifted.

And then there was Bholanath. He spoke little, but his conversations centred around food when he opened his mouth. He utilised his summer vacation to learn how to cook from his mother. He had already mastered Pulao, Matar Paneer, Rajma, and all types of *daal* and pulses and was now learning the art of making mango pickles. Bholanath was chubby from an early age, and he, undoubtedly, lived on this planet to eat and not the other way around. The other day, he somehow survived the *golgappa* ordeal.

Chakradev was interested in nothing except sports. He played every sport and won, hands down. He played everything from basketball to cricket, hockey to football, and participated in marathons and gymnastics. He was a gifted sportsperson. When we once made the impulsive decision to leap from the mango tree one afternoon, where the highest branch jumped from would determine the victor, Chakradev won easily and broke both his arms.

Lavanya was the second closest to me after Mona. She was a quiet girl. She preferred to lend her ears more than her voice. She attentively listened to everyone. She was funny too. Her one-line jokes were witty and comical. She had learned to play the violin and frequently assumed a central role in many cultural activities in the colony. Lavanya was the wisest of us all. She was kind, helpful, and respected by all who knew her in the colony. To have a friend like her was a blessing. More than a friend, I always had a crush on her.

Nayantara was the most competitive among us. She worked hard in her studies and strived for excellence. She excelled in debating skills and was a good singer. She was a friend to only those not competing with her. She was close to Chakradev as they never encroached upon one another's domain. He was never into academics, while she distanced herself from sports. I maintained a slight distance from her, fearing that if I were to achieve a higher grade than her, it might strain our friendship. Luckily for us, that didn't happen, and our friendship continued.

And then there were Daksh and Anshul. They were clever, street-smart boys, yet balanced. To this day, Daksh's parents are unaware of what he did to those mangoes. And Daksh himself could never solve the puzzle of how Mr Bakshi couldn't figure it out.

We played cricket everywhere: the park, the gully, the lawn, the terrace, near the water tank and the stadium. I was good at the game, but Chakradev was better.

Those were my friends. Some evoked laughter, some had depth, and some blended both. Together, we celebrated. Together, we mourned. Together, we danced and laughed. Together, we shared our experiences. And together, we created lasting memories.

Mona:

Lying down in Chandu's garden, listening to old Hindi film songs, was sheer magic. It would be more fun during power cuts—all of us chatting and Rocky with all his stupid stories. There used to be something about those summer nights. Later, in school, we read 'A Midsummer Night's Dream'—our nights with the full moon glow, the soft breeze, the chirping of crickets, and the fragrance of the jasmine flowers felt like a dream, too. It was some magic whispering to the soul.

I can still feel the caress of the soft grass on my skin and smell the jasmine of Chandu's garden.

Then the rains after the summers. The first drops as we rushed outside to immerse ourselves in the joy as the cool droplets pattered against our skin. Rocky and Bholanath went to the terrace, Chandu, Lavanya, and me in the garden, and the rest stood on the balcony—that little pool of water, splash, and frolic. Daksh and Chaitanya made paper boats, and we ran towards the pool of water near the tank to sail the boats. That scent of damp soil, fresh fragrance, and monsoon rhythm. The lightning, the thunderous roar, the grey clouds. The coolness of the raindrops drenched us from head to toe as we chased each other around. Monsoon was magic. And our childhood? Magical.

Chandu blushes whenever Lavanya is around. Lavanya always smiles when he looks at her. The other day, they stood hand in hand on the terrace, getting soaked by the rain. Something is going on between them. Hehehe.

12

Mihir Mishra

Mihir was not a part of the gang. He was too small—five years younger than Mona—and had his own gang and group of friends. However, he often visited the mango tree and met Chandan's friends.

At home, there were conflicts. Both Mihir and Mona demanded attention, which led to clashes between the brother and his sister. He would snatch her badminton racket, which Mona had been gifted, and would not return until he was treated with sweets. He used to hide Mona's books, which would really make her angry. After his birth, more attention was paid to him, which made Mona somewhat jealous of her brother.

'Mona, you need to be more responsible,' is what she often heard from her parents whenever they fought.

Mihir would run around the house and scatter things around the house. He often mimicked Mona's activities, whether in studies or badminton, to gain recognition from their parents. Mona often felt that her younger brother invaded her personal space.

'Mihir is such a dumbo.' Mona used to complain to Chandan.

'Forget it, Mona. He is your younger brother. Forgive him. He will understand once he grows older.' Chandan would advise Mona.

Mihir interrupted her conversations whenever Mona

wanted to share something with her parents. When Mona enrolled in the badminton class, Mihir threw a tantrum, insisting he wanted to join too. Then there was constant bickering on who gets to watch their favourite TV show. He fought over Mona's teddy bear and threw it away. It was then that he received a tight slap from his mother, much to Mona's satisfaction. They complained about each other to their parents, exaggerating each other's mistakes to gain their approval and recognition. Pushing and shoving became common, and it quickly transformed into physical fights requiring interventions from either their parents or Chandan on numerous occasions.

One day, quite excited, Mihir shouted, 'Diamond. Diamond in my garden. Come and see.' His mother dashed out of the kitchen along with Mona. Chandan, who also heard him shout, joined them. They quickly realised that what Mihir had mistaken for a diamond was simply a dew drop glistening on a leaf.

And then, one day, he handed a piece of paper to his teacher.

'Love letter from my father to you.'

The teacher was shocked to hear that from a six-year-old.

'Your father has written me a love letter?' she exclaimed.

'Yes, I have tummy pain.'

'Oh! A leave letter?' she said, controlling her laughter.

'No. A love letter. I will not come to school tomorrow.' Mihir persisted.

When he was around eight, his English teacher asked him about the superlatives of the word 'tall'.

'Tall, Taller, Tallest,' he replied.

'And superlatives for good?'

'Good, gooder, goodest,' was Mihir's prompt reply.

When he was around ten, his teacher posed a question to the students,

'Where is the only place in the world where nothing grows and is barren?'

Mihir raised his hand and stood up.

'My grandfather's head. It's bald and barren.'

And then, after watching Zakir Hussain say, 'Wah Taj' on the television, he used to mimic sipping tea from an empty cup and roar, 'Wah Taj.' He once smeared his face with shaving cream after watching Kapil Dev say, 'Palmolive *da jawab nahi.*' (Palmolive is the best shaving cream)

Chandan loved Mihir, and Mihir loved him back. Mihir was like a younger brother he never had. Chandan allowed him to join them in their meetings beneath the mango or jackfruit tree despite objections from the other members, including Mona. 'What will this kid do here?' they would ask. But Chandan always welcomed Mihir into their gatherings whenever he visited them.

Chandan would take him to the Dixit Sweet shop for *samosas* or sweets. He gave Mihir a lot of chocolates. He also lent him his bat and ball whenever Mihir wanted to play with his friends. Chandan patiently taught him how to tie his shoes. Their bond deepened as they spent more time together under the mango tree and elsewhere. And when Chandan wrapped his arm around Mihir, pulling him close in a tender embrace, they both realised the depth of their bond and friendship.

Chandan:

I love Mihir as I love Mona. His laughter, his smiles, his mischief, and those curious eyes fill my heart with warmth and joy. He always gifts me with mangoes and many other things. That other day, his mother made paratha, and he shared it with me. I feel a responsibility towards him. He is growing up. He is an intelligent boy and plays cricket well. He has many friends. I see them coming and going out of his house all the time. I tell him not to watch too much television. And he listens to me. I know I am a source of comfort and security for him, and he is the same for me. There is a special bond between us that words cannot express. I love him.

Mona:

There are moments when Mihir drives me absolutely crazy with his constant and countless questions, especially when I am trying to focus on my studies. He borrows my things without asking. That makes me angry. He is utter chaos but laughter, too. He reminds me of the innocence and wonder of childhood when I was his age. I used to complain about him to Chandu. But now I don't. They get along very well, and Mihir loves him. He listens to everything Chandu says. Sometimes, I wonder who is Mihir's natural sibling. Chandu told me I was the elder, so I needed more patience. Despite our disagreements, I love my brother. I love him very, very much.

13

New found Toy

The cacophony of an early Saturday morning. It was a holiday, and Mona's little block seemed to burst with life. The sound of the children running helter-skelter, Malti's animated dialogues with the utensils in the kitchen, and her husband noisily parading up and down the living room created a turbulent ambience.

Malti was in her element in the kitchen cooking breakfast, a ritual she embraced wholeheartedly that was almost becoming a tradition for every Saturday, excited and talking. With her boundless enthusiasm and penchant for chatter, she didn't need anyone particular to talk to. With her little understanding and uncertain temper, she could go on and on. From instructing the children about the food to sharing titbits about their school adventures and her updates on her newfound information to bombarding her husband with tales of dubious relevance about which he most certainly had no interest. 'Are you listening!?' she would occasionally check without expecting much response.

As for her husband, though more or less a pedantic middle-aged man, he maintained his devout gentility. He had his way of handling his wife with more or less a quiet composure that he had mastered over the years. Yet today, his mind was somewhere else. He was parading up and down, waiting for the delivery.

Mona was playing ludo with Mihir and Chandan, utterly unaware of the surprise.

Mona had been coaxing her father for some time to buy a television. It was the latest talk of the town, and she wanted it so badly. Her father stood in a queue for half a day to order the TV. The television used to get delivered after another long wait.

In 1982, the demand for a TV had grown because of the Asian games hosted in India, creating a pressing need for Jitendra Mishra to buy a set for his daughter. Now, providence finally smiled upon him.

Around 11 am, a delivery van stopped in front of the quarter. Two men stumbled their way with a huge box to Mona's house. As they opened the little iron gate, Mihir danced around, alerting and announcing to the whole household.

Mihir was mischievous and insatiably curious about the giant box that the men delivered. As Mona's father stood by the door talking to the men, Mihir prompted, 'Hi! I am Mihir. I am 5 years old. Is this box for me?' No one seemed to budge. He continued for some time, asking nonstop questions to the men doing paperwork after the delivery.

By this time, almost everyone had gathered around. Mona's eyes gleamed with anticipation as she heard the news about the package. Overjoyed, she gave her father a tight hug.

'Chandu, that's the TV I have been waiting for a long time,' Mona remarked.

'No, that's for me,' Mihir immediately clarified.

'That's like the same TV we saw in Dr Ramulu's house.' Poor Mihir's words were almost sidelined; Mona's eyes sparkled as she held Chandan's hand tightly.

In the meantime, Malti, too, had dashed out from the kitchen, hearing all the commotion.

'Could you bring something to help with the unpackaging?' Mona's father asked his wife without looking up, his eyes glued to checking the details.

Malti disappeared and returned like a bolt of lightning with all the equipment she could find handy.

The box was quickly cut through, and out came the huge television. Malti had already cleared a table for the television to be placed. It was very religiously placed on the altar.

The children had gathered, and so had the neighbours. Mr Gopalakrishnan hurried from his block, clutching the newspaper, with his son Chakradev tagging behind. Moments later, Daksh arrived, followed by Lavanya and her mother. Nayantara and Diksha joined them all, running to the gathering.

'Wow! That looks absolutely like a huge toy box,' exclaimed Mona.

Chandan whispered, 'Do you know who invented the TV?'

Mona looked from the corner of her eyes and nodded, 'No idea.'

'Philo Taylor Farnsworth used electronic signals to produce images on the video screen,' remarked Mona's father. 'That's an excellent question, Chandan. I'm proud of you.'

The television was a huge brown box.

The men first took the antenna and showed Jitendra Mishra how to put it on the terrace to help them catch a signal.

After setting that up, they came to the eagerly waiting

audience for the rest of the demonstration.

One of them explained, 'The screen is protected with brown shutters that need to be drawn back shut after every use.' Then, the men started explaining the details to everyone. 'These are the knobs on both sides that are for controlling the different functionalities, like sound, brightness, and channels.'

Everybody was just as happy with the television as they could be. It was the most desirable toy not only for the owners but also for the neighbours. Over the years, television has become another attraction for neighbours to gather and celebrate together. Weekends usually became a planned event: a movie night, a match, news, cartoon shows, or the movie song-based program called 'Chitrahar'. The colony needed a reason to assemble; this was just an add-on.

A schedule was set when the kids would come to watch the shows, and in the afternoons and weekends, they would gather to watch movies and cartoons.

Mona's father was glad his mission to watch undisrupted Asian games with his daughter was fulfilled. The evenings were filled with aromatic snacks, tea, and drinks around the television. It was mesmerising how they could be visually connected to the rest of the world, a clear advancement from the radio era.

One afternoon, Mona, Chandan, Rocky, and Lavanya were sitting beneath the mango tree playing ludo when they saw Mrs Basu, one of the ardent visitors for any musical shows, lost in her reverie, coming their way.

As they saw her approaching, Rocky, the naughtiest of the lot, started hollering to Mona, so much so that Mrs Basu could overhear, 'Mona, do you know if you go up to the terrace and sing to the antenna, you can be seen on TV?'

Mona's eyes widened, and she raised her eyebrow, but as Rocky winked, she gave a big nod in acquiescence, 'that's so amazing ...' she beckoned with another wink. They exchanged smiles as they glanced at one another.

As Mrs Basu overheard them talk, she hastily retracted her steps and darted back to her house.

The children were curious about what might be going on in her mind.

To their surprise, after a few minutes, Mrs Basu emerged, fully decked up, as if going to some function: a bright-coloured red sari, dark lipstick, and full makeup.

Seeing the botched makeup, the children giggled with their palms pressed against their mouths. Mrs Basu dashed to Mona's house, peeked through the window of Mona's room where her mother was cutting vegetables, and remarked,

'Malti, I am heading to the terrace. I will be on your TV, so could you please switch on the TV and check?' She hurried confidently to the terrace.

Malti Mishra was at her wit's end and couldn't understand what Mrs Basu was talking about.

Mrs Basu reached the terrace as the children tiptoed behind her. Standing in front of the antenna, she started singing loudly. As loud as her inharmonious scale and notes could take her.

The children couldn't hold back their laughter while Mrs Basu continued singing.

Hearing all this commotion, the neighbours started

gathering. Even the neighbourhood cats and dogs assembled to witness this crime against music.

Malti impetuously emerged and was astonished to see Mrs Basu singing loudly to the antenna on the terrace.

'Titli, what are you doing?' she yelled louder than the deafening singing.

Startled by the alert, Mrs Basu looked down and said, 'Malti, I will appear on TV. Just switch on your television.'

The children couldn't suppress their laughter anymore, and the whole gang joined them. Daksh, Nayantara, Diksha, and Anshul continued to enjoy this rare spectacle.

Malti, with a smirk on her face, understood who was behind this mischief.

It took a long time for Mrs Basu to comprehend her folly.

Adjusting the antenna for TV reception was a synchronised activity. Malti would be watching on the TV reception, Mona by the window, Mihir bouncing up and down the verandah screaming the final relayed instruction to his father, who would be adjusting the antenna almost hanging at the edge of the terrace. 'Not yet...a little bit more to the left...yes, yes, a bit to the right...ya, ya. Now stop.' But Malti would instruct Mona, 'No, a little bit more to the left...' Mona would holler to Mihir, who bellowed the same to his dad as loud as he could. Mona's father, following the instructions, would adjust the antenna. This would continue until the television finally caught the desired reception.

The joy of overcoming trivial difficulties was priceless in those days. Life in Chukchuk Nagar flowed easily, and memories of serene simplicity were cherished forever.

As the happiness of the newly purchased television grew and the Asian games drew to a close, another game started brewing up north of the country in Punjab. Jarnail Singh Bhindranwale, a Sikh militant, was getting ready to occupy the Golden Temple.

That was the beginning of an end.

Chandan:

Nowadays, Mona has no time for me ever since the arrival of the new television. She has suddenly disappeared in her own house. So, I have to go to her house to meet her. Her little bed in front of the television is her permanent residence now. She eats, sleeps, and studies there. Malti Aunty keeps complaining about her as she watches too much TV. But she is in her world of cartoons and movies. The other day, I saw her watching a farmer's debate. Can you believe that? What will she do with farmer debates? Make fertilisers? Or plant wheat? Her brother is always running around the house. Gave me a mango yesterday. Sweet little boy!

Basu Aunty has stopped visiting us. Her son Monu tells me she was too embarrassed to come out after her singing episode on the terrace.

Mona:

I know Chandu is angry. Rocky, Daksh, Lavanya, Diksha, Chakradev, and even Bholanath. All annoyed with me. They say I regularly miss meetings under the mango tree as I am always glued to the television.

But television has given me a new world. My life and ideas

started depending on it.

It was much better than Mummy's boring music on her tape recorder. She still listens to the radio.

It has started having a significant influence on our lives. The style, fashion, and how I looked at the world changed.

It made us dream. Better, bigger, and clearer.

We started watching movies and developing an interest in film stars. We were all starry-eyed. Now, we had our favourite actors and actresses. The other day, I watched Amitabh Uncle sing with Jaya Aunty. They are also real husband and wife, like my Mummy and Daddy.

Our clock for homework, studies, or other non-essential activities revolved around our favourite TV shows.

I disliked doing Maths, and the icing on the cake was a perfect bright Sunday morning when my father would call me to practice Maths while my favourite Sunday morning cartoons were on. Can you believe it? How wonderful my life was! I complained to Chandu about this, and he said it's the irony of life. My Maths improved after Chandu started tutoring me. He is so good at Maths.

Mihir got away with everything being younger to me, and I wouldn't say I liked it.

Age started to show on our TV set sooner than we had expected. First, the shutter started giving away due to overcleaning and overuse. Mummy ordered us to clean the TV twice a day.

Then the sound started vanishing. Switching it on and off didn't help. Turning and twisting the sound knob was completely useless.

Frustrated, Mihir banged on the TV, and suddenly, the sound returned.

This torture on the poor TV started becoming a norm. Only the intensity of slaps and punches increased.

Sometimes, Chandu, Mihir, and I would laze around and watch something. Suddenly, the sound and the picture would disappear like a signal vanishing in a dark tunnel. Chandu and Mihir would roar with laughter.

We would end up screaming for Mummy's rescue. She would be busy in the kitchen and come out all charged up, her face all red, either from the heat or the anger.

She would come with a kitchen tool in one hand: a saucepan or a rolling pin, depending on the luck of the TV.

And, BANG!!!

The picture and sound would come back again.

Mummy would return gladly to the kitchen. It was always best to submit to her.

But the television had started to cause more drama than the shows it broadcasted. It frequently caused trouble and demanded attention. So, after a while, I returned to the mango tree meetings, and my friends welcomed me with open arms.

Was television a blessing or a curse? I would say both. And what about spending time with friends beneath the cool shade of the mango tree? It's always a blessing.

But this newfound toy would become a turning point for centuries to come. That's my prediction.

14

Tears of Tragedy

The 1982 Asian Games, hosted by India for the second time after 1951, had come to an end. They provided a unique combination of excitement and camaraderie, an experience that united the people in the country as well as in Chukchuk Nagar. It was just another common ground and interest to share.

Mona's house used to be buzzing, providing a live theatre. The neighbourhood gathered at her home every evening (and in the mornings and afternoons of every weekend) to watch the games on the television. Apart from Dr Ramulu, no one in the neighbourhood owned a television set until Jitendra Mishra acquired one.

Mr Basu took a break from quarrelling with his wife and his fishing expeditions to watch the games. Ratan Chopra, Daksh's father, put a hold on all his gardening workshops and accompanied his son to Mona's place for the games. Mrs Sheetal Iyer, with her husband Ganesh, a sports enthusiast, would attend in the evenings with their daughter Lavanya. Chakradev was there the whole time after school, though he also spent some time with Chandan and Mona. Chaitanya accompanied his father while Mr Chauhan would arrive with his two dogs. However, Jaswinder Singh remained present throughout the day, even taking leaves from the office. After all, he represented the state of Punjab in hockey and couldn't afford to miss the games.

Mona's mother used to be super busy preparing tea every hour while offering snacks to the guests, her tongue wagging all the time, engaging in lively conversations.

They all found it engaging, and everybody celebrated the country's achievements in the Asian Games together. India won 13 gold and 19 silver, placing fifth overall.

Mona's home and television became a complete lucky charm a year later when India won its exhilarating first World Cup in cricket in 1983. Kapil Dev and his team became national heroes overnight. Chukchuk Nagar erupted in celebration with firecrackers, music, sweets, and jubilation like never before. Jaswinder Singh invited the whole neighbourhood to his home for a feast to celebrate the World Cup victory.

'I know Kapil Dev. He is from Haryana, and I am from Punjab. I am a Sikh, and he is a Jat. I met him many times in Chandigarh. He was a little boy when I first saw him,' he boasted.

But with time, when the sense of bonding and community grew stronger, fate had another story to tell.

In Amritsar, Operation Blue Star unfolded, which led to the assassination of the Prime Minister of India, Mrs Indira Gandhi, on 31st October 1984 by two of her Sikh bodyguards. The country was left in shock and disbelief, marking twelve days of mourning.

While the autumn leaves danced across the empty roads, the aftermath of the assassination had started taking its toll. Sikhs were targeted as violence erupted and spread to different parts of the country. Mobs targeted Sikh homes and businesses, burning down their houses and shops, resulting in thousands of deaths and damage to their property. Sikhs were dragged out of their homes and beaten, while many others were tortured.

In Chukchuk Nagar, all the shops, including the Cooperative store, remained closed as a nationwide curfew was imposed. Every household in the colony had started to feel the effects of domestic scarcities.

That Sunday morning, Jaya Chandola went to the kitchen only to find that she had little to cook with. All the perishable vegetables had run out, and the grocers had stopped coming with their supplies. The Cooperative store was shut, and the vegetable vendors were nowhere to be found.

The days felt lengthy and the nights lengthier.

Along with a national crisis, simple households also started to suffer.

'Chandu, could you quickly visit the Cooperative store to check if anything is available? I am running low on supplies.' Chandan's mother called out to her son. 'But be very careful and vigilant.'

'Yes, Maa.' Chandan was ever so ready. He was bored sitting at home because, due to the curfew, he couldn't meet his friends regularly.

He came out of his room and walked a few steps towards Mona's block.

'Mona, do you want to go for a ride?' Chandan called out to Mona from her living room window. Mona came running out of the room.

'But there is a curfew.'

'They have relaxed it for two hours. That's what Chatterjee Aunty told Maa yesterday. My father and Chatterjee Uncle have gone to Gorakhpur for an official visit. Otherwise, he could have gone to the shop.'

'My father has also gone to Warangal on an official tour.' Mona remarked.

Mona's mother came out and asked,

'You are going somewhere, Chandu?'

'Aunty, I am going to the Cooperative store. Can I take Mona along with me?'

'Ok. But be careful, you both.' Malti asserted.

With Mona sitting in front, Chandan took out his cycle and rode through the almost deserted streets of Chukchuk Nagar. They rode past the closed shops of the Cooperative store.

Wherever they went, there was absolutely nothing available.

'Chandu, let's go to the railway crossing near Nakshal Khera. There are a few shops there. We will come back if those are closed.' Mona suggested.

'Okay.' Chandan nodded.

Chandan paddled through the empty streets as the soft auburn autumn sunlight scattered its rays.

They approached the railway crossing near Nakshal Khera. All the shops were closed there, too. They stood there for a few minutes, trying to figure out what to do: cross the railway lines and check whether any shop was open on the other side or return home. They were contemplating their next steps when they heard a cry: 'Help, Help.'

They dashed towards the railway crossing and were

shocked to see Jaswinder Singh surrounded by a few men with a burning rubber tyre, which they were trying to put around his neck. The men were cursing him. 'You killed Indira Gandhi. You killed. You are a Sikh. Now face the consequence.'

Chandan and Mona froze. It was Jaswinder Singh, their neighbour and the most respected man in the neighbourhood and the entire Chukchuk Nagar colony. Chandan turned towards Mona.

'Mona, do you see the building there? With the yellow and red walls? That's the police station. Hurry to that place and ask the officer to come here immediately. I will go there and check.'

'But Chandu...'

'Now run.' Chandan instructed.

Mona hurried towards the Police station while Chandan dashed towards the men.

Jaswinder Singh saw him and shouted,

'Chandu *puttar*, they will kill me.'

The men turned around and saw Chandan.

'Who are you?' one of them asked.

'I am Chandan Chandola. And Jaswinder Uncle is my neighbour.'

'Oh! Is it?' one of the men remarked with a menacing smile. 'But after today, he won't be your neighbour anymore, as he will be dead in a few minutes.'

'Yes, I know. He will be dead, and all the people responsible for his death will also be dead by tomorrow.'

The men exchanged a swift glance with each other.

'What do you mean?'

'Jaswinder Uncle's brother is the Director General of Uttar Pradesh Police. His sister-in-law is an Inspector General. His other brother is a Senior Superintendent of Police, and his son is an Army officer. If he is dead and you are the cause, then all his relatives who are in the Police force will search and find you regardless of your location on earth. They will pounce on you one by one, and by tomorrow evening, you will be all dead and cremated near the *Naher* along with Jaswinder Uncle. So, do as you wish. I just warned you. I am fourteen years old, and a little boy like me, don't lie.'

Jaswinder Singh was speechless. Apart from his son being in the army, everything was made up. But he kept his mouth shut.

'Is it true? one of them asked Jaswinder Singh.

'Yes.'

They all looked at each other, their face slightly shaken.

'Let's get out of here.'

But as they threw the burning tyre on the roadside and were leaving, a Police jeep came out of nowhere and blocked their way. The officer, along with his men in uniform, stepped out of the jeep accompanied by a twelve-year-old girl and apprehended them. They were handcuffed and taken into custody.

Jaswinder Singh fell to his knees and wept, tightly hugging Chandan and Mona. After they returned home safely, Jaswinder Singh narrated the entire episode to the neighbourhood. Overnight, like Kapil Dev and his team, Chandan and Mona became the stars of Chukchuk Nagar colony.

'But uncle, why did you venture out during the curfew?'

Chandan asked him one day.

'*Puttar*, there was nothing at home to eat. We had been eating bread and biscuits for days. So, I went out to get some groceries and milk from Nakshal Khera as the Cooperative store was closed due to the curfew.'

But the ordeal had not ended. The kitchen had dried up, and the shops were still closed. As a last resort, Chandan plucked the papayas, climbed the jackfruit tree for the ripe and unripe jackfruit, picked the unripe bananas, and ventured into Dr Ramulu's garden for the curry leaves. Jackfruit, papayas, bananas, and sambhar with curry leaves were served for breakfast, lunch, and dinner at the Chandola and Mishra households for the next fifteen days.

A few days later, Chandan saw some policemen around the water tank.

'Why are you all here?' he asked one of the khaki-clad men.

'We received information that some miscreants are planning to poison the tank's water. We are here for vigilance.'

Chandan was shocked, but then, as he learned later, it was just a rumour.

The period was almost like a bad dream. A fog of doubt floated like a ghost over Chukchuk Nagar, testing the residents' loyalty and friendship.

But those dark times had failed to darken the heart of Chukchuk Nagar colony and its entire neighbourhood.

Chandan:

I remember 31st October 1984 being a Wednesday, as my

karate lessons were scheduled for Wednesdays and Fridays. It was a bright sunny morning, and a gentle breeze whispered through the air, carrying the scent of blooming flowers as the birds chirped joyfully in the trees.

A school cricket match was scheduled between the Green House and Red House teams. I was a part of the Green House team. We won the toss and opted to bat first. I had scored 21 runs and had just hit a four over the head of the fastest bowler of the Red House.

It was then that I saw some teachers and staff running towards us.

'Stop the game and go home immediately.'

We didn't have a clue what was wrong. So, the game was stopped, and we all paddled home. Mona was already standing at the school's main gate, and I picked her up. As we reached home, Malti Aunty came running out in a panic.

'Our prime minister, Mrs Indira Gandhi, has been assassinated. I just watched the news.'

By evening, we learned that a curfew had been imposed. Until then, I had never known what curfew meant. Papa was in Gorakhpur, and there was no way to contact him. Maa was worried. However, there was some solace in knowing that Chatterjee Uncle was accompanying him.

Maa listened to the radio. Malti Aunty would come often, as Mona's father was also out of town in Warangal. The curfew used to be relaxed for two hours daily, so I visited Lavanya's and Daksh's houses during that time. Chaitanya and Chakradev came to my place with Nayantara and Diksha. We sat under the mango tree and chitchatted. The school was closed for two weeks. Chaitanya said that Jaswinder Uncle, being a Sikh, was being targeted by some goons, and Chaitanya had gone to his house and warned him not to go out.

That day, it would have been tough for Jaswinder Uncle if Mona and I had not been there. We could have returned home after visiting the Cooperative store, but Mona suggested we check the markets around Nakshal Khera. It was plain luck.

What type of people live in this country? Two men assassinate the Prime Minister of a nation, and others have to suffer just because they belong to the same community. Have we gone nuts? Or were we always nuts?

Chakradev was very angry. He said the looters should be thrown into the Indian Ocean. Why not the Arabian Sea? Rocky asked. Chakradev said that his native place is closer to the Indian Ocean. Chaitanya said that the perpetrators should be thrown in the dirty water of the *Naher*.

We made an important decision beneath the mango tree. Each one of us, by turn, would stay with Jaswinder Uncle for the next two weeks. Uncle and Aunty were pleased and hugged us. They need not go out anymore, as the gang will get their groceries for the entire curfew period.

I think I would have easily scored 50 runs the way I was playing that day. The Red House bowler was fuming red at me after I hit him for three consecutive fours in that over, all over the ground and over his head. Hard luck for me and good luck for him; otherwise, he would have been massacred in his next over.

Mona:

The school was shut down, so I spent much time with

Chandu, and we were all glued to the news. Chandu, Mihir and myself I mean. Lavanya joined us every day. We watched people mourning and crying as Mrs Gandhi's body lay in state. Leaders worldwide had come to pay their respects, and everyone offered condolences.

Daddy always said that Mrs Gandhi was a very strong and powerful leader. Some senior leaders also addressed her as 'Durga'. I don't understand politics, but I would never allow anyone to hurt my Prime Minister. The Prime Minister is our supreme leader. I may have differences with my leader, but I will always try my best to protect them. But how can I protect them? I am only twelve years old. But I will try my best.

Chandu's quick wit saved Jaswinder Uncle that day. Otherwise, God knows what would have happened. Chakradev was very angry about the situation. He was so furious that he forcefully tore down a branch of the guava tree to demonstrate his strength. Chakradev is well-built and muscular. He should be the bodyguard of our Prime Minister.

15

Fangs of Fate

In most households, a day in Chukchuk Nagar began quite early. Most residents were up before six in the morning. The day used to begin with a cup of tea as the aroma of *chai* drifted through the air. Many men and even boys would visit the nearby Nakshal Khera, which had many cowherds, to buy milk early in the morning while others waited for the milk vendor to arrive. Many started their day with yoga and meditation amidst the sound of temple bells.

The most difficult activity, especially for the mothers, was waking the children early since the schools operated in the morning. After a quick breakfast, some students used to walk to the school; some went cycling, while others used a cycle rickshaw. Those who came from outside of Chukchuk Nagar preferred auto rickshaws. Chandan used to cycle to his school with Mona riding on his back, and once Mona learned to paddle, they would ride together. Almost all the children left for school by half past seven in the morning.

At around nine, the men and some women would leave for their office on their cycles, scooters, or motorbikes. The offices were in Chukchuk Nagar and not far from their houses. The women got busy with household chores, cooking, cleaning, washing, chatting with neighbours, and so on. Their husbands returned home for a lunch break around noon before returning to their offices.

Plenty of vendors would weave their way through the streets. Selling fruits and vegetables, ice cream, and even fish, they shouted at the top of their voices, inviting the residents, primarily women, with their goods. Mrs Basu would run outside as soon as she heard the shout of the fish vendor. Then there used to be the ragmen or scrap dealers, cobblers, and many other vendors who roamed the streets frequently to sell their services or commodities.

In the afternoon, the pace slowed down. The children would return from school after one in the afternoon, have lunch, do their homework, read comics, or take a nap. The men used to come home for lunch. The women used to knit, visit a neighbour, or nod off for a while. At around five in the evening, the children used to go out to play or meet under the mango or jackfruit tree in the case of the gang.

The children used to return home by seven in the evening. After eating some light snacks, they would sit down to study and complete their homework. The men would return by six from work, have tea prepared by their wives, go for a stroll alone or with their spouse, read a newspaper, or watch television in case they had one. Otherwise, they would listen to the news on the radio. At around nine, the family would sit together to have dinner. After dinner, the women would watch television serials or listen to the radio before retiring for the day. The children used to study till around eleven before going to bed.

There were some rules and guidelines in Chukchuk Nagar, especially for children to follow.

Boys and girls were expected to be home before the

streetlights came on in the evening unless there was some emergency. They were supposed to tell their parents their whereabouts and when they would return.

Showing respect to elders was a basic expectation, as demonstrated by touching their feet. Verbal abuse or using cuss words meant punishment. Slaps, scoldings, and criticism from teachers and neighbours were acceptable in case of misbehaviour. To show respect towards women was mandatory. Giving up seats on public transportation for the elderly was not only compulsory but was also a responsibility. Frequent disagreements were discouraged.

There was a lot of freedom for the children, albeit with discipline.

Chukchuk Nagar also boasted of three clubs: the Milan Club, where the members were mostly Bengalis, the Recreation Club, and the Officer's Club. These clubs had a library where one could read books and newspapers. The members could take books and magazines home with their membership cards. They visited the clubs regularly to play card games, chess, badminton, or table tennis. These clubs used to organise sports leagues in which many residents of Chukchuk Nagar would participate. A cyclist was invited by one of these clubs to cycle non-stop for nine days in the Chukchuk Nagar stadium. People gathered in the stadium to witness this incredible feat of endurance.

As salaried employees in a Central Government organisation, the income was modest, if not low. But the residents of Chukchuk Nagar were well compensated with laughter, joy, camaraderie, and peace of mind. Their salary was not the major compensation. The real reward was the richness of their relationships and the bonds they cultivated forever.

Life was blissful in Chukchuk Nagar.

One day, however, the bliss was broken, albeit for a short time.

It was around eleven in the morning. The children were at school, the men were in their offices, and the ladies were busy with their household chores. A snake charmer arrived, sat cross-legged in front of Chaitanya's house with a large wicker basket in front of him, and started playing the flute, also known as the *pungi*. The women, hearing the sound of the flute, came out of their house and walked towards the snake charmer to watch the show. The snake charmer removed the lid of the basket and started to sway and play the flute. The snake, a cobra, emerged from the basket with its hood flaring, swaying from one end to the other. The ladies in the neighbourhood stood to watch the spectacle. This went on for a few minutes as the reptile moved its hood from one side to the other. The women cheered and clapped. Suddenly, the cobra lunged at Parvathi Nair, the mother of Diksha and Chaitanya, and bit her on her wrist. Parvathi Nair was shocked. She cried out in pain and then fell unconscious. Panic struck as the women scattered in different directions, screaming and shouting in fear. The snake charmer quickly captured the agitated snake, put it back inside the basket, closed the lid, opened a bottle filled with a liquid, and splashed it on Parvathi Nair's face. She regained consciousness after a few minutes. Everyone gave out a sigh of relief.

'You don't need to worry,' the snake charmer told Mrs Nair. 'The poison glands of this baby have been removed. You were unconscious due to fear, not because of the poison. This baby has no poison.' He smiled as he kept referring to the adult cobra as a 'baby'.

Despite his assurance, a few women took Parvathi Nair to the Polyclinic, where Dr Chakraborty administered an injection and gave her some medicines.

The children, back from school, and their fathers from office, were horrified when they heard what they heard. It was a narrow escape. But then, as Shakespeare once said, 'All is well that ends well.'

Chandan:

I ran to Nair Aunty's house as soon as I heard the news after returning from school. Mona was with me. I saw Nair Aunty lying on the bed surrounded by the other neighbours. Chaitanya and Diksha were sitting on the bed along with Iyer Aunty. Nair Uncle had still not returned from the office for his lunch break. Someone dashed to his office to inform him of the accident.

Nair Aunty was still in shock. After a while, Dr Chakraborty came, checked her pulse, and told her not to worry. He told her to take the medicines he had already prescribed. Then he left.

Aunty's wrist, where the snake had bitten her, had swelled with redness around the entire area. She complained of discomfort, a headache, and a stinging pain in her hand.

We were all surprised to see the snake charmer coming back. He entered the house, sat on the floor, took a pouch from his bag, and opened it. There was some yellow powder with some dry leaves and twigs. He asked for water, mixed it with the powder, and applied the paste to Aunty's wrist. Then he put a few leaves and twigs on the wound and wrapped it with a small cloth.

'You will be fine by evening,' he said with an air of confidence.

And lo and behold! The pain and the swelling disappeared within a couple of hours.

Maa and Mona's mother joined us. Maa told me to go home and have lunch. She said she would come back home a little later.

So, Mona and I came back.

In the evening, Chaitanya told me that the swelling had disappeared and that his mother was fine.

Mona:

I was shocked to hear that a cobra had bitten Nair Aunty. In school, we studied about snakes and how a cobra poison can kill within a few minutes. But thank God, everything is fine now. Aunty has started her evening walks with Nair Uncle, which means she is okay. Rocky said that he once saw a python in his garden. A Python? Can you believe it? Next time, what will he see? A tiger in his bed? Rocky always makes it up in his imagination and dreams.

16

In the Jaws of Danger

It was a bright, sunny Sunday morning. Chandan and Mona decided to go for a stroll. On the way, they met Lavanya and Rocky, who bought *laiya chana*, or spicy puffed rice with various other flavours from the vendor who was lovingly called Chacha.

'Where?' Rocky asked as he saw both.

'Just taking a walk. Want to join?' Chandan asked.

Rocky looked at Lavanya, prompting her to ponder the idea.

'My parents have gone to Indira Nagar. They will be back by evening. Yes, let's go.' Lavanya responded.

'Chalo then.'

They embarked on a casual stroll as vibrant blossoms showcased their full bloom on both sides of the road amidst the crisp winter air.

'Let's take the Kendriya Vidyalaya route.' Rocky remarked.

To their left was the bus stand while a straight road stretched ahead. Elegant bungalows, the residences of senior officers of Chukchuk Nagar stood as dignified patrols on both sides of the road.

'Nowadays, some guys are going to the *Naher* to smoke.' Rocky remarked while popping some puffed rice into his mouth.

'I know. Chaitanya is a regular there. He is mixing with the wrong crowd and has started chewing *paan masala*,' Chandan replied with a hint of concern.

'And it seems Malini and Joy are having an affair.' Rocky continued sharing another piece of gossip.

'How do you know?' Lavanya, now intrigued, couldn't help but ask with excitement.

'The way they look at each other, holding hands while getting into the green bus, sitting together...even a blind man can see.' Rocky responded.

'Malini stays somewhere here, right?' Chandan asked.

'Yes, that bungalow.' Rocky remarked, pointing towards his left. 'She is Dr Chakraborty's neighbour. She was two years our senior, I think.'

'But where does the green bus go?' Mona asked, redirecting the gossip into a new thread.

Rocky stopped midway.

'Mona, we are talking about Malini Bharadwaj and Joy Sengupta. Don't interrupt when such an important topic is being discussed. And the green bus goes nowhere.' Rocky remarked, visibly irritated by the disruption.

Mona's face fell into a sombre expression while Chandan and Lavanya laughed.

'I think she studies in Sacred Heart Convent, and Joy has joined Rishi Mission. But even when they were in our school, they were fond of each other,' Lavanya remarked with a giggle, offering her perspective.

'How can that Joy fellow get a divine angel like Malini? I mean, look at him. He looks like a monster.' Rocky commented, his words tinged with disbelief.

'Opposites attract. Plus, the dog.' Chandan remarked with a smile.

Rocky, now intrigued, asked, 'What dog?'

'She has a pet. And Joy loves it. In fact, he is the one who takes care of the dog.'

'But Joy lives near the stadium, more than 500 meters from Malini's house.'

'Yes, but he jogs every morning from his house to her place. And then takes the dog out for its rituals.' Chandan concluded.

'Devotion despite the distance.' Lavanya chuckled.

'I have to get a pet. Maybe a bulldog.' Rocky's imagination flashed with an image of a ferocious mongrel gnawing at Joy.

He didn't realise whether it was his imagination or if it was for real when a dog's eyes ablaze with aggression suddenly emerged from the side road. Mona hid behind Chandan as the dog bared its teeth and gave a low growl. It snarled and lunged towards Rocky. Lavanya shrieked while Mona screamed. Chandan, with lightning reflexes, kicked the canine on its face. It fell to the ground but quickly recovered and lunged towards Rocky again. Without hesitation, Chandan again kicked with full force on its stomach. The dog whined, momentarily deterred, but gathered itself and launched another attack. Just then, someone wielding a solid hard stick intervened and delivered a decisive blow to the dog's legs. The canine cried out in pain, momentarily subdued, and then ran away.

They all turned towards the young man.

'Hi, I am Joy Sengupta. You all study in St William's, right?'

'Yes.' Chandan responded.

'I was a student there. Now, I study at Rishi Mission. I

topped in St William's.'

They looked at each other, exchanging glances. Chandan was the first one to speak.

'Yes, I have seen you at St William's. Thank you for helping us. It could have been quite dangerous.'

'You are welcome. I can handle canines well.'

No one spoke as Rocky's eyes widened in disbelief.

'Okay, bye guys, will see you later. I need to get Poppy out of the house for a walk.'

'Poppy, who?' Rocky asked, still in shock.

'Malini's dog. Do you guys know her? She also studied at St William's.'

'No...yes...yeah. A bit, I mean. She was our senior.' Rocky could hardly get the words out of his mouth.

Joy Sengupta jogged to Malini's house while the three looked at each other and broke out in a burst of uncontrollable laughter. Rocky sulked, still processing the unexpected turn of events with a mix of surprise and annoyance.

'Shall we go home, or do you want to walk?' Chandan asked the group, still smiling.

Both Mona and Lavanya nodded. 'Yes, let's go towards our school.'

'And you, Rocky? You look shaken?' Chandan continued to grin from ear to ear.

Rocky, still reeling from the intensity of the recent events, hesitated for a moment before mustering a faint smile.

'Yes, let's go.' Rocky remarked with a lingering sense of unease.

They walked straight and then took the right.

'That's the *Naher*,' Chandan remarked, pointing towards his left. It's the Sharda Canal. It was built by the British and is the longest irrigation canal in the state. It originates from Banbasa, which is in Pilibhit, from the Sharda River, also called the Mahakali River in Nepal. The canal is the longest in Uttar Pradesh and covers almost a thousand kilometres.

Mona turned towards Chandan.

'You know so much Chandu.'

Chandan smiled. 'It's good to be curious.'

They walked and reached the Central School, also known as Kendriya Vidyalaya. They stood near the school's gate. It was a Sunday, and both the building and the ground were deserted.

'After our boards, many of us will seek admission here.' Lavanya remarked.

'Yes, it's better to study here if you get admission. It's closer to home and saves a lot of time for studies and other activities. I hope our school expands into an Intermediate college, so we don't have to change schools after our 10th boards.' Chandan responded.

'Joy goes to Rishi Mission.' Rocky remarked.

'It's a good school, but it's too far. The time you spend travelling can be better utilised in more productive activities.'

'But the students are transported to various colleges by the green bus. It's comfortable and convenient.' Rocky interjected, pointing out the convenience of transportation options available to the students of Chukchuk Nagar.

'True. But time is still a factor. You lose a lot of it travelling to and fro.'

They strolled, passing by the residential blocks where many of their classmates lived with their parents.

'Shall we go to Diya's house? Diya lives in that block,' Lavanya suggested, pointing towards a residential building on her right.

'Not now, it's getting late.' Chandan responded.

They continued their stroll and were about to reach their school when a matador zoomed suddenly from the corner of a side road and raced dangerously towards Mona. Chandan immediately pulled her to one side of the road in the nick of time as the vehicle whizzed past at full speed, missing Mona by less than an inch.

'Are you okay?' Chandan asked, the concern evident on his face.

'Yes.' Mona responded with a shaky voice. They all exchanged worried glances but were relieved that no one was hurt.

They stood in front of their school for a few minutes, still gaping with a mix of shock and relief.

'It was quite a day today,' Lavanya sighed as they returned home. Everyone acknowledged her sentiments with a collective nod.

In the evening, Mona's mother rushed to Chandan's block while he was reading a book. His mother was sitting on the sofa beside him, immersed in her knitting.

'Thank you, Chandu. Thank you, beta.' Malti Mishra burst into the room and embraced Chandan. Her tight embrace conveyed the depth of a mother's relief and immense gratitude as tears welled in her eyes.

Chandan, however, couldn't quite understand the reason for the heartfelt hug, whether it was his daring to face the ferocious canine, his swift action in thwarting the reckless driver, or both.

Chandan:

Rocky was fun that day because he was always fun when he was frightened. When the canine attacked him, he stood like a statue, unable to move. Then he moved. His hands. His legs flailing around. By then, I had already given the punch to the animal. Then his eyes widened. Then, his hands and legs moved again. It was like a display of various dance forms in the middle of the street. Then he hid behind me, behind Lavanya, behind Mona. He joined in their screams. But the mongrel was only after him, even though I was showering the punch. I don't know why. Rocky was dealing with horror and confusion. His face was a terror maze. That expression was pure gold.

My second kick sent the dog rolling to one side, slightly relaxing Rocky. But then, the animal lunged again towards him, and it was the same scene all over again.

I told Rocky to learn karate. At least, that would make him more flexible. He said he would, but I knew he would not.

Joy saved us that day. No doubt about that. He felt like a nice guy. Rocky was just jealous of him.

Many years later, I heard Joy had settled in America, married, and was an investment banker there—lots of money and lots of dogs. Malini is a doctor settled somewhere in Europe. They are now separated by more than just the Atlantic. Do they engage in transatlantic small talk? I don't know. But one thing I know. It was just a crush. Let's not make a fuss about it.

After Mona told her what happened that day, Malti Aunty came to our house and hugged me in the evening. I love her. She talks a lot—she's a chatterbox like Basu Aunty—she talks more than a million times more than Maa and Papa together. But when she came that day, she didn't talk at all, and I saw tears in her eyes.

Mona:

It was winter, and I was frozen, not due to the weather but because of the ferocious black dog. It was massive, with bared teeth and fiery eyes. It first gave a low growl and then lunged towards us. I was paralysed. It was like an electric shock travelling through my entire spine. I was trembling and breathless. Chandu is learning karate at the Capital Hall. I think he used those tricks to fight the dog. But without him that day, we would all be in the hospital for sure or maybe dead.

I could still hear the screech of the tyres as the truck swerved violently, narrowly missing me by inches. As it hurtled past, the rush of wind whipped at my clothes. Chandu saved me the second time that day.

That's the first time I saw Joy Sengupta. Rocky was talking about him when he arrived. Maybe Joy has a long life. Mummy says if someone comes when we talk about them, they live long. I want to thank him from the bottom of my heart. May he live long.

While coming back, Lavanya held Chandu's hand all the way home.

Mummy had gone to Chandu's house to say thanks for saving me. She came back home weeping—tears of joy, I think.

17

The Road to Victory

The soft hues of the setting sun bathed Chukchuk Nagar in a warm, golden glow. The aromas of the evening snacks wafted from open kitchen windows while the neighbours gathered around their verandah and garden, sipping a cup of tea and eating their snacks, making a crunching sound. Children played in the nearby playground close to the water tank, their laughter echoing through the air.

Chandan came out of his house and walked into Mona's block. He peeked through the window of Mona's study. Mona was sitting on a small study desk surrounded by textbooks and notebooks, diligently working on her homework. The room was filled with the soft hum of the ceiling fan and the scratch of her pen against paper. Chandan leaned against the window.

'Working hard or hardly working?' he asked with a grin.

Mona smiled. 'That's not funny.'

'You want to come for a ride?'

'Hmm...that sounds tempting. Let me ask Mummy.'

Minutes later, she came out. 'Let's go, permission granted,' she said with a smile.

'You are with me, Mona. Your mother will never say no.' Chandan remarked with a chuckle.

'Yes, I forgot. You are the hero of Chukchuk Nagar.' She teased.

Chandan smiled but didn't say anything.

'You sit in the front.' He said, pointing at his bicycle.

Mona settled in the horizontal top tube in the front and asked, 'Where are we going?'

'Just around Chukchuk Nagar. Let's see whether they are setting up the Durga Puja pandal at Capital Hall.'

They approached the community centre and saw that the Puja pandal was beginning to take shape, rising like a majestic haven of artistry. Skilled artisans were working on bamboo structures with vibrant fabric, creating a mesmerising drapery of colours and textures. The air buzzed with the rhythmic beats of the drums to welcome the goddess and her children as the labourers worked diligently, bringing the vision of the pandal to life. Chandan saw some of his father's colleagues running in and out and shouting at the top of their voices, ordering the labour force to set up the pandal quickly.

'We are not Bengalis. It's they who celebrate Durga Puja.' Mona remarked.

'So, what if we are not? My parents have lived in Calcutta for so long that they are more than half Bengali. My father has been appointed the revenue secretary by the Puja committee this time,' Chandan said while still looking at the upcoming pandal.

They left the Capital Hall and stopped at the Mandir, the echo of the temple bells creating a serene background. They folded their hands in reverence and closed their eyes briefly, though they didn't enter the temple.

'Let's go.' Chandan uttered, and Mona again sat in front as he started to paddle.

'Where are we going now?' Mona asked as a cool breeze danced through her hair.

'Father's office.'

He took a turn towards his left and reached the auditorium. The auditorium embraced a multipurpose identity, seemingly transitioning from a cinema hall to a stage for community events. Plays would be performed on the stage, which was bathed in warm lights, and actors from the Theatre Choir and Jharna troupe brought characters to life in theatrical performances. Song and dance competitions were celebrated with applause and cheers. Poetry renditions echoed through the auditorium. The walls were adorned with posters of past and future events.

'Who is she?' Mona asked, pointing towards a poster of a middle-aged woman, her eyes sparkling with intelligence and a confident smile gracing her lips with mathematical equations in the background.

'She is Shakuntala Devi, a mathematician. Sorry, a mathmagician. She can do anything with numbers faster than a supercomputer. She is visiting Chukchuk Nagar next week, and her show is in the auditorium.'

Mona kept staring at the poster, her eyes widening in amazement, her face turning into a canvas of awe and disbelief.

'Faster than a supercomputer.' A soft sigh escaped her lips.

'Chalo, let's go, or we will be late.'

They headed towards the offices. The buildings comprised various engineering and administrative departments exuding a charm that blended modernity with tradition.

'That's my father's office.' Mona exclaimed, pointing

towards the open window of the Metallurgical & Chemical department.

'How do you know?'

'He bought me here once to show the office.'

'That's the Civil Engineering office. And that's the engine testing department where Papa works.' Chandan remarked, pointing towards the buildings.

Chandan now took a left and crossed the Central Bank and the Director General's residence. They arrived at the post office and were about to take the right turn when he stopped.

'Let's go there,' he said, pointing towards the railway crossing on the left.

'Why?' Mona asked.

'I will show you something.'

Both got down from the cycle. Chandan reached into his pocket and pulled out a shining 50-paisa coin.

'Let's walk.'

They walked towards the rail tracks. As they reached the tracks, Chandan, holding his bicycle in one hand, carefully placed the coin on the rail line with the other.

'Let's wait for some time. The train will come any moment now,' he said with a mischievous glint in his eye.

Mona was perplexed and speechless, having no clue what Chandan was up to. A few minutes later, as the train approached, the vibrations resonated through the tracks as they both watched with excitement the coin transform into a flattened, elongated metal under the immense pressure of the passing locomotive. After the train passed, Chandan retrieved the now-altered coin.

'Keep this as a memento of my daring act,' he said proudly.

Mona took the flattened coin and laughed heartily, clapping her hands at Chandan's antics. As the train rolled by, her laughter intensified, creating a shared moment of joy between them.

But the joy was short-lived. Revelling in their playful moment, they failed to realise the imminent danger of their proximity to Nakshal Khera, a notorious area inhabited by goons. The area was very close to the railway crossing.

Three menacing figures smoking cigarettes approached them as they sat on the cycle and were ready to leave.

'What are you doing in our area? And who is this beautiful girl?' one of them grinned maliciously.

'Let us go. We are getting late.' Chandan gave a nervous response.

'Your girlfriend, huh?' the other man asked, trying to get close to Mona.

Chandan turned towards Mona.

'Mona, you go and stand there. Near that lamp post.'

'But Chandu, I want you...'

'Go and stand there, Mona.' Chandan almost screamed even before she could complete her sentence.

One of them came forward and thrashed Chandan in the face.

'She is going nowhere. We will take her to where we want.' He laughed.

Chandan parked his cycle and planted the stand firmly on the ground.

'I am telling all three of you, don't do this. Let us go home.'

The men laughed. 'And what will you do if we don't allow you to meet your Mummy and Papa with your girlfriend?'

Chandan didn't utter a word. A precise, forceful kick on the man's lower abdomen did the talking. The man screeched and sprawled on the ground with his hand between his thighs. The other two lunged towards Chandan. Chandan picked up the cycle and threw it at them with a bone-rattling impact. The other man got off the ground and pulled a knife from his pocket. Chandan quickly turned around and gave a nasty blow to his face with his clenched fist, sending the knife clattering to the ground. Chandan's swift footwork evaded the lunging attack as the other two pounced at him. He kicked them hard on their face. The sudden impact resulted in blood streaming down their nose.

As the fight continued, Mona watched this intense confrontation in shock. A small crowd had already begun to gather around them. Chandan pulled one of the hooligans by his collar. 'The next time you harass any girl, I will kill you there and then. You understand?'

The men looked at each other and knew this teenager outmatched them.

'Let's get out of here,' one of them uttered.

Someone from the crowd came forward. 'You are going straight to the police station, *gunde*,' and punched him in the face.

Dusting off his shirt, Chandan picked up his bicycle. Mona ran towards him and hugged him tight.

'That was an unexpected excitement.' He grinned.

'You are the hero of the Chukchuk Nagar,' remarked Mona, still in awe.

'That's why your mother will never say no to me being with you.'

They laughed as he paddled home with Mona sitting in front.

Chandan:

To be honest, I was frightened. It was getting dark, and Mona was with me. I think we were both too adventurous that day. Maybe we should have gone home instead of that daring act on the tracks with the coin. It was just a matter of taking the right turn—the 'right' right turn, I mean. Instead, I took the left.

I knew that I could give them a fight. I had been learning karate at Capital Hall for the last three years. I was far from a black belt, but the blue belt was good enough.

But I knew it would be difficult when he took out the knife. I knew I had to be fast. Speed was of importance here. There were three. I was trying to handle this by myself.

But I think it was not due to my karate skills. I believe it was Mona. I had to protect her. I saw that belief in her eyes. I knew that I could have killed them for her.

Mona gives me strength. I am unsure how or why, but it's always been that way. Her mere presence fills me with a sense of resilience. She always had that unwavering belief in me.

I cannot explain this, but she always has been my beacon of strength.

Mona:

I knew Chandu was learning karate. I used to practice

badminton on one side of the Capital Hall, and he used to learn karate on the other side. Chakradev had also joined the karate class but left after a year as he joined a body-building class. That, too, he left after a few months.

Chandu and I would come back together from the Capital Hall in the evening after our practice session.

That day, I was quite confident that Chandu could tackle them. But when I saw the man pulling out the knife, I froze. My heart pounded. There were three of them, and Chandu was alone. Fear gripped me, and I pleaded for him to stop. I screamed with every swing and clash of fists. Chandu turned around, glanced at me, and then gave a forceful backkick, sending one of them flying towards the other side of the road.

I couldn't help but marvel at Chandu's courage. His determination. His fighting spirit. He is like a lion.

When it was over, I rushed to his side. He smiled and then asked me to sit on the cycle. A small crowd had gathered, and the goons were taken to the police station.

While returning home, we went to Dixit's shop and ate *golgappe* and *allu chaat*.

Chandu said not to share this incident with anyone, so I didn't tell anyone and never asked him why. Chandu's friends never question his advice; he thinks through it before offering suggestions. But I think he said not to share because my parents would be unnecessarily anxious. With Chandu around me, I don't need to be afraid at all.

18

Whispers of Deception

The residents of Chukchuk Nagar were settling down for their evening dinner. The streets were silent. A dog barked in the distance while a cat ran across the street. Mona was at home doing her homework, while Chandan had gone to Alambagh market to get some medicines for his father, who had been suffering from bouts of cough and slight fever for the last few days.

The residents were unaware that a sinister plot was about to unfold in the shadows of the night, right under their noses while they were having dinner.

Kamini, whose name translated to 'beautiful', was a stunningly beautiful woman. Her alluring sway and sultry gaze left people spellbound whenever she was out walking on the streets as if she had weaved some magic around them with her beauty. Her long hair and attractive eyes were the centre of attention and attraction. But it was she who became attracted to one fortunate man who won her heart—Taaraksh—and fell in love.

Taaraksh, a resident of Chukchuk Nagar, was tall, handsome, and muscular, with the physique of an athlete. But deep down, he harboured darkness and deceit beneath the façade of his charismatic exterior. He stayed a few blocks away from Kamini's house and made every effort to catch her attention. He ultimately won.

Taaraksh was quite friendly with the Nakshal Khera goons, drinking and smoking together and engaging in eve-teasing activities. He occasionally visited the *Naher* to smoke and drink with other hooligans. From the outside, he looked perfect as he masked his true intentions under the guise of being a well-behaved gentleman with always a smile on his face. Kamini was not aware that his only intention and desire was to get intimate with her.

'I want to get hold of her at least once,' he would often tell his friends when drunk.

'Let's meet at the Polyclinic tonight. Your parents are away, and we can have more time to chit-chat,' Taaraksh suggested to Kamini one day, taking advantage of her parent's absence.

'Why the Polyclinic?' she asked.

'You have seen the new building...right? Nobody goes there as the construction is still ongoing. They have got new beds. You know what I mean?' he said with a grin.

'But Taaraksh...'

'Don't worry. Do you trust me or not?'

'I do.'

'Then promise me you will come.'

Kamini hesitated for a while as she felt an extreme unease. Her instincts urged her not to listen to him, but ultimately, she succumbed to his persuasive charm, nodding in agreement.

'At what time do I need to be there?' she asked.

'Around nine would be fine,' he remarked with a smile.

That very evening, four men accompanied Taaraksh and reached the Polyclinic.

'Is she coming?' one of them asked.

'Yes.' Taaraksh affirmed with a hint of pride. 'But be quiet. She doesn't know that you all are here.'

Each of them wore a sinister grin.

'What about the watchman? Does he know?' one of them asked.

'Don't worry. I paid him a hefty amount to keep his mouth shut. Also, Maradona is on guard, just in case,' Taaraksh affirmed with a smile.

A few minutes later, Kamini entered the Polyclinic. Shamsher, nicknamed Maradona because of his football-playing prowess and a friend of Taaraksh, stood near the boundary wall of the Polyclinic below the Amaltas tree to keep watch. The watchman looked the other way as she stepped into the dimly lit corridor of the clinic. Inside, the air was heavy, with the stench of alcohol and antiseptic mingling with the faint aroma of medication.

She saw Taaraksh smiling at her with outstretched arms. She dashed towards him and enveloped him in a tight embrace filled with affection, her head resting on his chest. She raised her head slowly, their lips close, almost touching, when she suddenly saw four men emerge from the adjoining room glaring at her. She immediately broke free from the embrace.

'Who are they?' she asked, visibly shaken.

'Tonight is the night of redemption,' one of them spoke as they all laughed.

'Taaraksh, what is all this?' she exclaimed, shocked.

Taaraksh slowly moved towards her, tenderly brushing his palm against her face with a nasty grin.

'I have waited months for this Kamini, months,' he laughed.

'Stay away. I cannot believe that you are such a monster.'

The others approached, surrounding her from all sides, their faces twisted into sinister grins.

Chandan bought the medicines and paddled his way back home. He crossed the railway crossing and entered the Chukchuk Nagar colony. He reached the stadium and then took a turn towards his left. As he neared the Polyclinic, he heard a woman's sudden, desperate cry for help. Moments later, he heard it again and knew something was wrong. As he took the right turn, he saw a moustached, tall, hefty man standing near the boundary wall of the Polyclinic, staring at him as if on guard. The area was quiet. He was convinced that the woman was facing some problems. With a sense of urgency, he quickly headed straight to the Police station, breathing heavily as he cycled.

After hearing what Chandan said, the police officer asked his men to visit the Polyclinic immediately. He, too, reached the Polyclinic and entered the building with the other policemen. Chandan reached a minute later on his bicycle. They were shocked to see what they saw. They arrested all the men, including Maradona, and led them away in chains. Kamini was weeping, tears all over her eyes and face, as the Police officer threw a towel at her to dry her face

'This boy saved you. His name is Chandan. He was the one who came to us after hearing your plea,' the Police officer remarked.

'Thank you, Chandan. Thank you so much.' Kamini uttered and embraced Chandan tightly.

That day, Chandan upheld the dignity of a woman and the

honour of Chukchuk Nagar.

A few days later, news spread that Maradona had committed suicide. Though he was not directly responsible for the crime, he was complicit. He took his life out of sheer guilt and shame because of the arrest.

Chandan:

I could never understand why Kamini went where she went. Her parents had gone to their village to attend a marriage. She said she couldn't go as she had her exams. But then, why the hell did she leave her house when she should have been studying? I didn't know her well. But Mona did. They went to play badminton at Capital Hall. They were not friends but teammates, and Kamini was much older than her. Mona never spoke about her. But one day, she said that some boys and some men from the colony and outside followed her everywhere. Mona said that Kamini enjoyed the attention. I didn't delve into it. That was her opinion.

I think Kamini should have told her parents and talked about the freedom she desired after they had come back. Parents should know everything, at least the important things. Otherwise, it's a breach of trust and responsibility.

I knew Taaraksh. He was a bad guy. Evil. I saw him eve-teasing and drinking and smoking and many other things. I never told Mona about him. It was not essential. It's good that he was arrested and sent to jail.

People praised me. They said I pulled Kamini out of danger. They said she was reckless and irresponsible, immature, impulsive, and so on. Men and women both have this tendency to blame only women. Why give men the benefit of the doubt? And why does one woman always tend to blame the other? Women should be more united.

When Kamini's parents came back, they were devastated. They struggled to face the judgment of all around them. In every block and quarter, there were whispers. Every whisper reflected poorly on their honour. 'That girl's dad,' the murmur, and then the laughter. Every glance added to the shame.

The burden was too heavy for Kamini's father, and the heart attack was massive. When they wheeled him into the Polyclinic, he died at the exact spot where, a few days ago, his daughter was striving to preserve her honour and dignity.

I could help her, but not her dad.

Mother and daughter left the Chukchuk Nagar colony soon enough. And Taaraksh is still in jail.

Mona:

Kamini was beautiful, and she flaunted it as well, which attracted the gaze of those with less noble intentions. I would always see her with Taaraksh, sometimes at the Cooperative store, sometimes at the stadium, and other places. I played badminton with her at the Capital Hall, and many boys from Nakshal Khera loitered around the place whenever she practised. I would say she was too naïve and careless. She was oblivious to the lurking dangers around her.

Are men and women equal in all ways? Yes, they are. But there are differences. Violence against women is not something new. Even Draupadi's modesty was violated by a man thousands of years ago. But then God himself had to protect her. That God, Krishna, was a man too. I think both men and women should know their limits. Kamini wouldn't have faced such humiliation, and Taaraksh wouldn't have had to go to jail if they had known their boundaries.

I told Chandu that Kamini enjoys the attention. He told me to stop thinking about Kamini and focus on my badminton. Kamini is expected to mature at her age; if she has not, she will learn or face the consequences. The same principle applies to all men, he said.

19

Teatime Tattles

What a delicious challenge it was to pass one's time in those days. Women had to train their focus on the two most important aspects of their lives—family of their own and those of the neighbourhood.

These trivial absurdities had kept the essence of the colony living on one hand and, on the other, the simple pleasures of meddling in the lives of everyone around.

Each day would unfold and swing from the chaotic morning schedule to the winter afternoons or the summer evenings tittle-tattles, hoping each day would be as entertaining as ever.

These busybodies had enormous abilities, bringing oddly disparate facts together and making a mountain out of a molehill.

It was a late December afternoon. Schools were on vacation, yet most families didn't privilege themselves from travel.

The ladies sat on a mat in the front garden of Mona's house. The knitting needles, yarns of wools, peas to be peeled and some vegetables to be cut, a pair of crochet needles, and all other objects placed in conversation with their setting transformed their domestic lives into a dynamic still life.

Mona, Diksha, Anshul, Daksh, Lavanya, Nayantara, and Bholanath sat under the mango tree, waiting for Chandan to join them. It was just another lazy winter afternoon, and the gang had to plan their evening and the rest of the vacation. However, this afternoon, they could not ignore this never-ending tedium of the aunties basking in the same sun.

'The only way to get Shristi a nice match would be if her parents could arrange a large dowry,' pronounced Mrs Deshmukh, eyes still locked on the sweater she was knitting.

'Her mother came to me to buy a suit, and nothing suited her dusky complexion. She is so fat, too; her mother should do something about it,' Nupur Chatterjee added in her rather scornful tone.

Mona's mother, peeling the pea pods, absent-mindedly added, 'I was watching TV the other day, and you know Dharmendra is having an affair with Hema Malini. How interesting, isn't it?' She looked at everyone as her eyes sparkled for being so informative.

'What affair? They are already married.' Nupur Chatterjee intervened.

'Malti, you are talking of actors and actresses. You know what I heard about Kaberi, from the other block, that she is having an affair with some boy. I heard that the boy was from her college. God knows who!' Lokhi Das added, proud of her knowledge.

'I keep my daughter under my strict watch and would have never allowed this,' she continued confidently.

The gang overhearing from the other end of the garden were alert and curious.

'Now, let's leave Kaberi's troubles to her parents. I am sure they are doing their best,' Chandan's mother added very sincerely and continued knitting with her crochet needles.

The gang continued to listen to the gossip.

'I bet Rocky would have enjoyed these gossips.' Lavanya frowned at their little gang.

Mrs Titli Basu turned around and glanced at Bholanath, who was eating some chips.

'Bholanath!' Mrs Basu called out to him. 'You are getting quite chubby. How will we find a match for you?' she smirked.

Bholanath stood up.

'Aunty, you are becoming quite fat yourself,' Bholanath added instantaneously without thinking about it.

The gang giggled a bit at this unexpected blunt comment.

'Bholanath, you shouldn't talk back to your elders like this. Now, don't worry. Why don't you come to my house? I can teach you how to make an excellent fish curry. You like cooking and eating, don't you?' Mrs Basu irked intentionally, waving the piece of vegetable she was peeling with a huge grin.

'Thanks for the offer, Aunty. I am a vegetarian. And I don't have to think of marriage,' he added inattentively. 'Nor does anyone else.' He intentionally lowered his voice for his gang, rolling up his eyes.

The little gang smiled at each other and carried on with their conversation.

Nothing really mattered as Bholanath was happy and carefree, contented with himself and his skills.

As Chandan joined them, the gang headed to Dixit's shop for some *golgappe* and *dahi bade*, a far better option, to spend their time.

The ladies continued their chitchat until it was time for them to leave. It was around 6 o'clock, time for their husbands to return home. Their prime duty would shift from this important 'social cause' to tending to their husband. A perfect caring housewife with a massive grin of accomplishment, enlightened with new-found general knowledge every day.

A few days later, there was news that Kaberi had gone into some severe depression. She had finally eloped.

This incident gravely upset her parents and was shocking for them and the residents of Chukchuk Nagar. Neighbours and friends visited her parents out of concern and offered help.

Weeks later, Kaberi's parents had decided to leave Chukchuk Nagar and resettle in their hometown.

There was news that she was eventually discovered months later, married, and settled in another town.

Nevertheless, no matter what happened to the rest of the world, the Chukchuk Nagar ladies' strangeness of character would remain unaltered. All other tensions would seem to wither away like raisins in the sun, and they would gather up on those summer evenings or winter afternoons like an old habit and gossip.

They would never mean any harm, but they would gossip about some topic, old or new, and the simple delights of colony life would prevail.

Chandan:

Mona occasionally briefs me about the gossip the

neighbourhood aunties do. I told her I was not interested in listening to that nonsense. I find it nonsensical. I believe both men and women should keep busy like my Maa. She, too, is a housewife, but she knits or reads whenever she is free. Yesterday, I saw her reading Bankim Chattopadhyay's Anand Math. Papa also either reads or listens to the radio. I have never heard them gossip.

Shristi is a lovely girl who studies in a Montessori school. Yes, she is a bit chubby, but so what? She has won the zonal singing competition back-to-back for three years. The aunties will not talk about her talents. I don't know why.

I don't know Kaberi well, but I met her a few times at the Cooperative store. I don't care whether she eloped or not—that's none of my business. If she is happy, then it's all okay.

Mona:

I am not comfortable at all about the gossip. How can the aunties think that they can orchestrate everybody's lives around them?

Some boys and girls are fat or dark, short or tall; how does this concern anyone else? It is their lives, and their parents are taking responsibility.

Is this a type of conversation that happens in intelligent societies, too? Or is it a mere outcome of these idle brains?

Do they know it hurts?

Do they realise this gossip doesn't help anyone around? Do they realise what a derogatory mode of entertainment it is?

I am glad Kaberi is all right at the end. She knew there was gossip about her in the colony.

Why is it that women always tend to pull down women?

Why must marriage be a woman's ultimate goal in life? Also, why does she have to change her surname after marriage? It is one of her identities. I don't see a man doing the same.

Nevertheless, thank goodness, Bholanath remains unaffected by what others say about him being chubby.

I also know that no matter what happens or how one feels, these aunties will again gather up, ready to create their own world of distorted symphonies with their uncared chitter-chatter. And every day will go on as it is.

20

Caught Red-Handed

It was a moonless night. It was past midnight, and the streets of Chukchuk Nagar were deserted. The residents were fast asleep.

In the cover of the darkness, three young men made their way into the neighbourhood for the sole purpose of stealing. They were thieves, and apart from the monkey menace that prevailed in the colony, the residents struggled with the additional burden of frequent theft.

The group of thieves of which these three were members arrived from a village across the *Naher*. They used to keep a watch throughout the day and carefully select their targets. Empty houses while residents were away or blocks inhabited by elderly couples were their prime focus. Within a week, three thefts happened in the neighbourhood. Cash and jewellery boxes were stolen, radios, transistors, cots kept outside, scooters, motorcycles, and even food items vanished quickly. Thieves ate up a whole tin of *gulab jamun* and *rasgulla*. They used to apply oil all over their body so that they could slip away if caught. How they broke those locks without making any noise was a puzzle. The residents had reported the thefts to the local police, but no arrests had been made so far.

Mona had her Maths exam and was studying late into the night. She was alone in the house, as her mother had gone with Mihir to meet an ailing relative in Hazratganj, and her father had gone to Varanasi to visit his brother. Chandan joined her for a couple of hours in the evening, tutoring her in Maths. Then he left, promising to return after dinner and vowing to stay with her until her mother returned the following day.

She went to the kitchen to heat the meal she would have for dinner on the stove her mother had prepared before leaving. Glancing out the kitchen window, she saw movements and shadows followed by a faint rustling sound of dry leaves. Then there was silence. She didn't give it much thought, had dinner, and returned to study.

She again heard a faint scratching noise on the front door for a few minutes. Then, a thumping noise started coming from the backyard. Then it stopped—complete silence.

After a while, as the summer heat became unbearable, even though it was ten at night, she got up from her chair and walked to the closed window to open it and let a cool breeze in. As she pushed the window open, she was so shocked that it nearly caused her to faint. Three men with thick moustaches, long hair, and gleaming white teeth stood before her, gripping the window railing, staring at her with their eyes wide open.

Mona shrieked, and the men, utterly confused, looked at each other and ran away.

A few minutes later, when Chandan knocked on the door, she didn't dare to open it.

'It's me, Mona, open the door.'

'Thief, Thief...' she cried.

'What thief?'

She opened the door after a long time. She was shaking from head to toe, and it took Chandan a while to calm her down. Mona hastily briefed him about everything.

'We have to do something about this nuisance. They stole everything from Roy Uncle's house last week, even his watch, which his father had gifted him before his death. Uncle was weeping after his watch was stolen as he was emotionally attached to the watch,' Chandan remarked.

'What are you going to do?' Mona asked.

'Let me think. You practice your Maths.'

The next evening, an emergency meeting beneath the mango tree was called.

'Friends and comrades, we have a problem.' Chandan stood up and spoke. 'For the last few months, at least six houses in the neighbourhood have reported theft. Valuables from gold, jewellery, cash, and watches have been stolen. The thieves are skilled, and they must be keeping a watch on each of the households. Otherwise, how would they know which block is empty or which house has elderly people? The theft has occurred in other neighbourhoods, too. So, we need to do something about it.'

'What are you planning to do?' Lavanya asked.

Chandan didn't speak for a while. He walked from one end of the backyard to another and finally spoke.

'We need a bait. Something that the thieves will be attracted to.'

'What type of bait?' Daksh asked while the others gave a quick glance at each other.

'Any type? Do you have any idea?' Chandan asked.

Chakradev stood up.

'I have an old iron cot lying on the terrace. We don't use it anymore.'

'And?'

'I have a silver horse statue. It's small, the size of a notebook.' Anshul remarked.

'I have made mango pickles.' Bholanath said.

Chandan smiled.

'Diksha, you have a phone in your house, right?'

'Yes.' Diksha responded.

Chandan turned towards Chakradev.

'Good. You place the cot in your garden, Chakra. And Bhola, you get one bottle of the pickles. Anshul, you get the statue. The pickle bottle and the statue will be on the cot. I will go to the police station and inform them of our plan. One of the girls and Diksha will remain close to the phone.'

'I didn't get you. What are you trying to do?' Nayantara asked.

Chandan grinned.

'Let me explain. The cot, pickles, and statue would be the bait. The thieves will see them in the garden and plan to steal them. They have also stolen food items, so they will not leave the pickles. I will visit the police station and inform them of our plan so that they are ready whenever the girls call them on the phone. Am I clear?'

They nodded.

'I am not clear about one thing. How would the girls stay up all night to call the police station?' Lavanya asked.

'The girls need to take turns. There should be two of you every night in shifts from ten to one and then from one to four. Most of the thefts happened during these hours.' He paused and then spoke again. 'You need to talk to your parents. I think they will agree. We should be able to catch them within a week if everything goes as per the plan.'

'What will the boys do?' Rocky asked.

'Hide. We will hide behind the bush and the banyan tree in the backyard of Chakradev's house. Once we see them, we need to get hold of them.'

'But they apply oil. They will slip from our hands.' Anshul remarked.

'We will put a lot of baby powder on her hands. We can also use lemon juice to help cut through the oil,' Chandan said with a smile. He turned towards Diksha. 'Diksha, please let Chaitanya know about the plan. We will need him. The more, the better.'

The next day, the girls sought permission from their parents to be at Diksha's house, taking turns for the whole week at night, which was granted. Chandan's father made it clear that they could go about it if they accompanied the guard who patrolled the area and was responsible for vigilance at night. However, even though the children agreed, they knew that the guard was useless as he was drunk most of the time. Moreover, he was too old to chase thieves.

Chandan went to the Police station with Daksh; Rocky and Bholanath went to buy the baby powder, and Anshul and Chakradev strategised their hiding places. Chaitanya said he would join them at night.

The cot with the pickles and the statue were kept in the garden in broad daylight for everyone to see. The iron cot was heavy, and it took all their efforts to get it downstairs from the terrace.

On the first night, Lavanya joined Diksha as she kept a vigil from the roof. The boys hid themselves behind bushes and trees. The guard accompanied them for the first two nights, got drunk, and slept the whole time near the bush. From the third night onwards, he didn't even join the gang.

For the first four nights, nothing happened. The operation used to be called off every morning at four.

On the fifth day, something happened. A few men approached and stood in front of the garden, looking at the cot for some time. They spoke to each other in hushed tones and then left. It was around three in the morning.

Chandan went to the Police station and informed the officer of what they had seen.

'They will come early today. I believe they were estimating the number of men required to lift the cot,' the police inspector remarked confidently.

The police officer was right. Seven crooks arrived at midnight. They tiptoed into the garden and carefully put the pickle bottle and the statue in a bag. Mona, who was on her shift, dashed downstairs from the terrace as soon as she saw the men and dialled the police station's number. Diksha, who had already completed her shift, joined her.

'We will be reaching there in two minutes.' The officer responded from the other side.

As the thieves started pulling the cot, the boys emerged from hiding.

'A nice party in the middle of the night, eh?' Chandan remarked and then pounced on one of them. The others followed, their hands smeared with baby powder. The crooks were shocked. They never expected the boys to appear from nowhere in the middle of the night and confront them suddenly. One turned around to escape, only to be met with a robust blow from Chakradev, who sent him reeling in the air before he fell. When the other thieves became active, Chandan gave one of them a fantastic karate kick, sending him flying across the garden. Chaitanya took out an empty liquor bottle and smashed the head of a bandit while Daksh rolled over and hit another below his waist. The man cried out in pain. When one burglar was about to punch Bholanath in the face, he and Rocky quickly sprinkled chilli powder in his eyes. The man cried out in agony. Moments later, the piercing wail of sirens echoed through the neighbourhood. The residents woke up with a jolt.

The policemen quickly got down from the jeeps, and the thieves were handcuffed and taken into custody before they could escape.

After this incident, no thefts were reported in Chukchuk Nagar ever again.

Chandan:

Catching those crooks was one thing. Going to school was another. We remained awake the whole night and slept for only two hours in the morning before going to school. We dozed off in our classroom, and the teachers were very irritated, not knowing the reason for our sleepiness. We decided not to tell anyone as a vow to secrecy. Kaushal Ma'am, our English teacher, was furious one day when she asked me about Shylock, and I started muttering about Hamlet. Even Shakespeare would have been angry. For us, without sleep for days together, Hamlet, Macbeth, and Shylock all felt the same. Rocky got a zero in his geography exam. But then, that was normal for him, with or without sleep. Daksh received a rebuke from the biology teacher when he made an error in describing a diagram as a fish when it actually depicted a tadpole. Diksha, who remained awake even though her shift was completed, came up with some trigonometry solutions when she was to answer simple geometry questions. Lavanya started to mumble something in the class that neither she nor the teacher could understand. Nayantara kept arguing that water is a mixture of Nitrogen and Ammonia, which was shocking for both the teacher and the students, coming from a topper of the class. Chakradev and Chaitanya didn't go to school for the whole week. Bholanath and Anshul suffered from tummy ache whenever the class tests started. Mona told me that she slept in her class with her eyes wide open.

But finally, the work was done. What we set out for was achieved. I heard the crooks endured numerous beatings in the police station. They never dared to venture into Chukchuk Nagar again.

Two months later, we were all rewarded at a function held in the Chukchuk Nagar auditorium. We felt good. Ate a lot of *samosas* that day. *Samosas* and *gulab jamun* were the gifts. Sorry, I forgot. There was also a certificate.

Mona:

Only we—the gang, I mean — can do such a thing, and

only Chandu can come up with such ideas. I saw the thieves from the terrace. There were six or seven of them. I dashed down. Diksha was dosing off on the sofa. I called the police. It was thrilling. Chandu had already informed them, so they were alert. Diksha's parents also came out of their room. Her father also spoke to the police.

Catching the thieves was an incredible moment. After they were caught, the whole neighbourhood came out of their blocks, hugged, and congratulated us. Even Chauhan Uncle came out with his dogs. He said we could borrow his dogs next time. What can the dogs do? They don't even bark. Chauhan Uncle says barking dogs seldom bite. His dogs bite.

For the next few days, we all slept. Only the cats, dogs, and squirrels were awake and held meetings under the mango tree while we slept away.

21
Worlds Apart

The boys and girls of Chukchuk Nagar lived in two separate worlds. Inside the house, the boys forever quarrelled with their sisters, while outside, they were expected to treat girls as if they were invisible. The same principle applied to the girls. If, by some cosmic accident, a boy dared to exchange a word, smile, or laugh with a girl, the whole neighbourhood would erupt into a frenzy of speculation. And before you knew it, a new saga of neighbourhood gossip would be born. So, the girls stayed away, and the boys stayed away, though they never wanted to stay away and yearned for more. Chandan's gang, however, did not have to go through this ordeal. They were neighbours, and their parents knew each other; there was trust, and there was Chandan, who was like a pillar of protection.

In the school, however, the rules of engagement were somewhat relaxed. The girls and boys spoke more freely to each other, quarrelled, smiled, laughed, and even shared their lunch occasionally. But outside the school's gate, silence prevailed as they tried their best to maintain a distance as if they were all sworn to a mission of avoiding any semblance of interaction.

There were exceptions, though. Rocky, for example. Nobody had any problem, whether he was talking, fighting, or laughing with a girl. The reason was simple. No one took Rocky seriously. And everyone knew that he was harmless. He was forever having a crush on his new and young teachers rather than his classmates or the girls in his neighbourhood. His young teachers were his area of focus even though the zeroes in his answer sheet kept increasing day by day. Chaitanya was another exception. His only true love was his whisky, cigarettes, and *paan masala*; he had a huge crush on them. He was so much intoxicated with his newfound 'girlfriends' that he never bothered about real girls. At home, he was always fighting with his sister and often expressed disdain for the female gender. 'I hate girls,' he would say.

Chandan had a crush on Lavanya; she knew it and reciprocated, too. But then, he never crossed the line and was too pragmatic to make a move. Bholanath was utterly clueless when it came to girls. They were like oil and water. He never understood them, the girls never understood him, and both went their separate ways. He happily chose cooking and food over futile attempts at understanding girls.

Daksh was the passionate type. But his heart fluttered like a fickle butterfly landing on a new love interest every few months. One day, he would die for Moushumi; on other days, it would be Mishti or Maya. Even the gang got bored of his revolving door of love interests.

Chakradev was the tall, sporty type—well-built and muscular. He had long hair up to his shoulders, sending the Chukchuk Nagar girls into a frenzy. But he had a crush on Priyal, which blossomed into love, which, years later, culminated in marriage. His romantic journey was a triumph from his teenage years.

Mona was the cutest and youngest in the group. Chandan always shielded her from male attention. No boy dared come near her, as they knew she was Chandan's friend. Chandan's protective instincts for Mona were so strong that even a mere glance in her direction would earn the offender a stern look, ensuring that they never dared to try again.

Nayantara's boldness and assertiveness intimidated the boys so much that she was never the centre of their attention. Diksha was the object of numerous crushes in the colony, but she never reciprocated.

With their infinite wisdom, the parents of Chukchuk Nagar would instruct their children to regard the boys and girls as their brothers and sisters, hoping to shield them from crushes and perils of puppy love. But then the teenage years were like a hurricane, a tornado, rendering parental advice as effective as an umbrella in a violent storm.

Parents and the neighbourhood closely monitored boys' and girls' interactions. But teenage love still found a way to blossom, albeit discreetly and with its own set of challenges. Fleeting glances, passing notes, whispered confessions, and phone calls were the means of communication. Every stolen moment became precious, with a risk of discovery, disapproval, and punishment.

In an adjacent neighbourhood, Malini Bharadwaj and Joy Sengupta, who had a crush on each other, devised a code to conceal their feelings. Malini became 'cauliflower', and Joy was 'beetroot'.

'I love beetroot,' she would say to Joy even in the presence of her parents.

'And I love cauliflower.' Joy would respond with a cheeky smile. Her parents were oblivious that they were referring to each other.

'You should eat other vegetables too. Only eating beetroot and cauliflower is not good. It would help if you tried a variety of vegetables. That will keep you strong and healthy,' Malini's father would advise.

'No, Uncle, I love cauliflower so much that I can't live without it.' Joy responded while Malini giggled.

'Too much of cauliflower causes gas,' her father remarked.

'And too much beetroot, Daddy?' Malini asked with a chuckle.

'Constipation,' the father replied.

Love, gas, and constipation were uncomfortable associations, so they changed their codes to 'strawberry' for Malini and 'butterscotch' for Joy.

'No, No, No. That's dangerous. There's too much fat and sugar. You should stop eating them at once,' the father exclaimed in alarm once he discovered Joy's fondness for 'strawberries'.

So, they went back to 'cauliflower' and 'beetroot'. And their saga of teenage love continued behind the veil of playful codes.

The fear of judgment and exclusion added an extra layer of complexity for the parents. Chukchuk Nagar had a tight-knit community where everyone was acquainted with each other. With such proximity and familiarity among residents, concealing relationships was neither easy nor viable, and families faced the implications of social scrutiny.

Despite the stringent regulations, love blossomed for some and ended many promising relationships for others. Some fought against the barriers, and some couldn't. Some had regrets, and others moved on.

But, those days of teenage crush never returned, forever treasured as sweet memories that remained in the hearts of those boys and girls of Chukchuk Nagar who had once dared to fall in love.

Chandan:

The parents, first. They were traditional and conservative-no doubt about that. Being strict and not allowing their children to mingle freely with the opposite gender was customary in those days. I can understand that. They get the benefit of the doubt. But they never once sat down with their children and talked about teenage attraction. How do children learn what's good or bad? On their own? Where were those open discussions? They were overprotective. They suffered from fear and insecurity. But if children are not exposed to the world outside at a young age, it will become difficult for them to manoeuvre through life and hinder their ability to navigate life's complexities later. Low confidence, particularly among girls, was visible even though they were sharp and had higher intellectual maturity than boys. People talk about gender equality, but I talk about gender exposure. If the exposure is equal, the result will also be equal.

Teenage crush! What can I say? It was both innocence and excitement—those butterflies in the stomach, that stolen glance, that fleeting touch, fumbling attempts at conversation, and the vulnerability of youth—unforgettable magic.

I sometimes wish I could tell Lavanya how much I like her. Maybe I will tell her one day in that cool evening breeze when she is with me, under the mango tree. I had shared my liking for Lavanya with only Mona. Mona said the first crush is a chapter of life that never truly closes. That's so true.

I hope Lavanya feels the same.

Mona:

My parents were not so strict with me and my brother, partly because Chandu was always with me and so very protective. I never saw him either as a brother or a boyfriend. That day, someone inquired about my feelings towards Chandu and what I thought about him. I said our relationship is like Meera's devotion towards Krishna. I am his Meera. He is my Krishna. He is my best friend and will forever hold that place for the rest of my life.

And I know Lavanya is his Radha or Rukmini. Chandu blushes every time she is with him. It's funny seeing him blush.

I met 'cauliflower' and 'beetroot' the other day near the Cooperative store. They had shared their codes with somebody, and that somebody shared it with somebody, and then somebody shared it with Chandu, and he shared it with me. The whole of the colony knew their codes except their parents. They were having strawberry and butterscotch ice cream together. They were smiling at each other. They were totally smitten! Hehehe.

22

St William's Convent

St William's Convent School in Chukchuk Nagar was established in 1961 after approval from the Railway board. It was a co-educational school run by the sisters of the Congregation of Jesus.

Chandan used to ride his bicycle to school with Mona sitting on the front tube. When Mona learnt to cycle, they would ride together side by side. Their uniform was navy blue trousers for boys, skirts for girls with white shirts, and a blue tie with white stripes.

Chandan's class had two sections, A and B. Chandan, Lavanya, Nayantara, Anshul, and Rocky were in section A, while Diksha, Bholanath, Daksh, Chakradev, and Chaitanya were in section B. Mona was their junior by two years and studied in section A.

While entering the school's main gate, to the extreme right was the Convent, where the nuns would reside. Adjacent to the Convent stood the church. The statues of baby Jesus and his mother, Mary, stood on an altar. During exam times, students used to rush to the church to seek blessings from baby Jesus and his mother, praying for good marks. However, infant Jesus and his mother helped only those who worked hard and were sincere, though they blessed everyone.

The school's grand three-story main building dominated the landscape. St William's was not about the million bricks but a thousand hearts, which carried more dreams than the night sky had stars. Inside its walls, knowledge thrived, nurtured by teachers who created the right emotional environment as they took on a loving parent approach towards the students.

Behind the main building was the school auditorium, which hosted various events and functions. It served as a central gathering place within the school campus, equipped with a stage for performers or speakers, lighting, and sound systems. It was also the venue for the board examinations.

On one side of the auditorium was an area with many trees displaying various flora and fauna, called the 'forest'. One day, Rocky was absent from class. When the teacher questioned him about his absence, Rocky explained that he was lost in the 'forest'.

'Lost in the forest? Were you wandering around the Sunderbans?' the teacher exclaimed. Rocky couldn't explain how he got lost in such a small, confined area and was asked to stand outside the classroom as a punishment. That was his plan: to escape the class, either in the 'forest' or outside the classroom.

On the other side of the auditorium was the playground. On one side of the main ground was the basketball court, and adjacent to it was the cricket ground. During a football match, Balwinder, Chandan's classmate, took a shot close to the goal. The goalkeeper, who was none other than Anshul, managed to catch the ball, but he flew along with the ball inside the goalpost, the impact fracturing two of his rib bones in the process.

On the cricket field, one day, after the boys had finished

their practice, a girl named Supriya, who had completed her basketball practice session, wanted to play cricket and asked Chakradev to bowl to her. Supriya was a year his junior. Chakradev, a fast bowler, was initially hesitant to bowl to a girl who had never played cricket. Chandan asked him to bowl slowly to her, and Chakradev eventually agreed. He bowled a slow ball. But slow by his standards. The ball pitched and bounced and struck Supriya directly on her forehead, causing an immediate swelling that resembled a potato. The boys were terrified as they saw a teacher coming towards them. They begged Supriya not to complain. She didn't. The teacher walked around and went away. The boys took Supriya to the first aid room for treatment. Supriya expressed her willingness not to complain on the condition that she would receive *samosas* every evening for seven days. The boys fulfilled her request. There was no other option.

At one end of the main building was the cycle stand. Most boys and girls of Chukchuk Nagar and the adjoining areas would arrive by bicycle. But there was one boy who used to derive sadistic pleasure from puncturing the tyres of bicycles. Once their bicycles were punctured, the boys and the girls had to walk home. It continued for days. One day, the boy was caught in the act of puncturing one bicycle and received a severe beating from both the boys and the girls, and he had to be taken to the first aid room for treatment. When asked how he got hurt, he said he had a fall.

During lunch break, the students enjoyed their meals from their lunchboxes, which their mothers thoughtfully prepared in the early morning hours with care and affection. Then, the boys used to play *gend-tadi*, where one had to hit the other with a plastic ball. It was a nonsensical game invented by the boys.

But eagles, which came in hordes from nowhere, would often swoop down and snatch food from the students when they had lunch. The students were advised to cover the food while eating. One day, as Daksh was eating a boiled egg from his lunchbox, an eagle descended, seized the egg, nipped at his finger, and swiftly flew away. Daksh ran to the principal's office to complain about the eagles.

'How many times do I have to tell you to cover the food you eat?' the principal exclaimed exasperatedly. 'Now, go to the first aid room and treat the bruise.'

'But what about the eagles, Sister?' Daksh asked.

'I will speak with the eagles during our next assembly. Ask your friend Bholanath to teach them how to cook so they don't snatch your food again. I hear Bholanath is a good cook,' she smiled, ruffling his hair.

Daksh wasn't sure if the principal was serious but nonetheless sought help from Bholanath.

Speaking in Hindi outside the Hindi class was not encouraged at the Convent school. The class monitor was responsible for imposing a fine of 50 paise on anyone caught speaking in Hindi. When Chaitanya was caught speaking Hindi in a history class, he was immediately fined. Chaitanya quickly took a five rupee note from his pocket and handed it to the class monitor. 'Now, don't force me to speak in English for the next ten days,' he remarked.

Kavya resided in Singaar Nagar and was Chandan's

classmate. She was the only girl in class who loved cricket and the players. She thought she loved Ravi Shastri, the famous cricketer, and adorned her room with his posters. One day, she bought an autographed booklet signed by all the cricketers who were a part of the World Cup-winning team. She proudly showed the booklet to all her classmates. After the lunch break, when she returned to the classroom, she found the booklet missing and immediately complained to the teacher. Chakradev, who was good at sports and sat beside her in class, was the immediate suspect not only because he sat beside Kavya but also because he was a cricket enthusiast. The teacher searched his bag and desk and found nothing. Then she took her to the principal.

'I have not stolen it,' he said with tears. The principal instructed him to bring his father to school the next day as she wanted to speak to him. When Chakradev returned to the classroom, he was relieved that Kavya had found the booklet nestled within a book on her desk. But he was humiliated that day. The pain followed him like a shadow inside, eating him up and refusing to leave him but leaving him with invisible scars.

In the evening, he wept, sitting under the mango tree while his friends consoled him.

Discipline was not merely a rule to be followed but a way of life at St William's. From the punctuality of the bell to the respect shown to teachers, each action was a responsibility. Teamwork, sportsmanship, and adherence to rules were of paramount importance. The teachers commanded attention, and the academic pursuits were rigorous.

One day, a sudden eruption shattered the peace and discipline of the school as two boys engaged in a violent altercation. They rained blows at each other, blood staining their uniforms. The teachers rushed to intervene, but the boys continued their brutal clash. They were swiftly expelled from the school.

In another incident during a torch march at the annual PT display function, a boy mischievously threw the inflamed torch into a kerosine tub, which burst into flames. He was rusticated there and then. Bad behaviour and indiscipline were not tolerated at St William's.

The neatly arranged wooden desks and chairs faced the blackboard in the classroom, which had large windows on either side. The students used to keep their lunch boxes and water bottles on the window shelf. There were cupboards on either side of the blackboard and a small idol of Christ above it. The walls were adorned with educational charts on both sides.

Every class used to last forty-five minutes. There were four classes in the morning, followed by another four in the afternoon, with a lunch break in between. The teachers commanded respect, and their authoritative presence demanded the students' attention.

The classroom was diverse. Chandan sat beside Sukanya, a studious girl who was also extremely good at sports. Even though she was quiet by nature, she also possessed quiet confidence. She was Chandan's good friend and would chitchat with him after every class break. Sukanya was always engaged and attentive to her studies. She helped Chandan with Chemistry, and Chandan helped her with Maths. Chandan injured his finger one day while sharpening the pencil with a blade. Sukanya rushed him to the first aid room for immediate treatment. She was always a wise and compassionate girl.

Chandan gelled with his classmates. Some were extremely naughty, some were less naughty, and some were just naughty, but they were all naughty in some way or another.

Sumit was the most mischievous of the lot. He had joined St William's in the 7th standard and was a very quiet boy in the beginning. Then, suddenly, he started behaving abnormally. During breaks, he would launch a barrage of paper aeroplanes across the classroom, causing chaos. He intentionally sprinkled potassium permanganate on another boy's new white shirt in the chemistry laboratory, turning it into deep purple. The boy was so upset that he wept the whole day.

Sumit stole and ate food from the lunch boxes on the window shelves. Chandan caught him one day while trying to steal food and warned him of the consequences if repeated. Though he stopped stealing food, he started disrupting the class by banging on the desk or tapping his pen and pencil.

But then, one day, he did something unpardonable. He sat behind Lavanya in class in the same row. While she was engrossed in a class test, Sumit slowly tied her long pigtails to the chair. Lavanya sensed that Sumit was tampering with her hair and warned him a few times. As the class ended and she stood up, she cried out in pain. The teacher ran towards her to untangle her hair and dragged Sumit to the principal's office, as everyone knew the culprit. Chandan was extremely angry at Sumit that day.

Sumit's father was called and informed about his son's misdeeds.

'Sister,' his father said to the principal, 'he was always a quiet and obedient boy. But he lost his mother last year. He is not able to cope with the loss. He was very close to her. He is just 14 years old, Sister. Please forgive him. Let me see what I can do from my end.'

After considering it, the principal reassured the father that Sumit would receive the necessary support and guidance. The teachers and staff of St William's worked on a plan to provide Sumit with counselling and support. The results of these efforts were apparent when Sumit stood fifth in the class in the half-yearly examination and regained his calm composure.

From the 9th standard, students were required to attend laboratory sessions for Physics, Chemistry, and Biology. The laboratories were designed to provide practical learning opportunities related to the concepts taught in the classroom.

The Physics laboratory was equipped with various instruments, such as Vernier callipers, pendulums, lenses, mirrors, batteries, resistors, and many others. Students were expected to conduct experiments, record data, and analyse them. Bholanath always stood first in the Physics practical exams. Jaidev, the laboratory assistant, supervised the students along with the teacher.

The Chemistry laboratory was equipped with countertops where students conducted the experiments. It was furnished with Bunsen burners, gas taps for heating, beakers, test tubes, flasks, and pipettes for measuring and mixing chemicals.

Chemical reagents, solutions, and samples were stored in labelled containers for use during experiments. Sukanya and Nayantara were the Chemistry practical test toppers.

The Biology laboratory was well-equipped with microscopes and specimen jars containing octopuses, jellyfish, snakes, lizards, and different reptiles and frogs. One jar contained an unborn human foetus. But the focus was always on the human skeleton, with its empty eye sockets to the long slender bones of the fingers and toes, kept in a glass case on one side of the room. For some students, shivers ran down their spine at the sight of the skeleton, while others, like Chandan, marvelled at it.

It was Rocky who started the rumour.

'The skeleton comes out at night and roams in the corridor,' he remarked one day while sitting under the mango tree with his friends.

'Really?' Lavanya exclaimed.

'Yes, I saw it once when I had gone to Laddu's shop in the evening. It was walking in the corridor with a torch. I could see it from outside.'

'Why would it need a torch? It has no eyes.' Bholanath enquired.

'Bhola, a skeleton doesn't have brains. Don't you know?' Rocky countered the argument.

'I heard there was a murder in the nearby village many years ago. It's the dead man's skeleton seeking revenge.' Anshul uttered.

An eerie silence prevailed under the mango tree as a squirrel jumped out from the branches of the adjoining towering jackfruit tree. The sudden movement startled the gang, causing Rocky, Nayantara, and Diksha to cry out in shock. As the squirrel ran, the gang broke into splits of laughter.

'Enough of this nonsense. Let's go to Dixit's shop for some *alu chaat*.' Chandan suggested.

The gang always listened to Chandan as Bholanath led the way.

The library at St William's was equipped with almirahs filled with books. Enid Blyton was the favourite with her Famous Five and The Secret Seven. Franklin W. Dixon authored Hardy Boys, which depicted the adventures of Frank, and Joe Hardy was also a favourite amongst the boys. The girls preferred the Nancy Drew book series as Nancy solved mysteries in her hometown of River Heights.

But Chandan's favourite was always Anne Frank's 'The Diary of a Young Girl'. He read and re-read it many times. Mona was a fan of Charles Dickens.

Then there was the staff room. The teachers would grade the examination papers, eat lunch, exchange ideas, or engage in lively discussions over tea in the staff room. It was a place for the teachers to recharge and reconnect themselves. The students would stay away from the staff room, as summons in that room often meant punishment.

Finally, the room of the physical training teacher, Mr Spoke, was in the rear of the auditorium, surrounded by trees that provided ample shade. The natural cover of trees ensured that his room remained cool even in the hot summers. He occasionally smoked and read the newspaper when free. The room had storage cabinets filled with basketballs, footballs, badminton rackets, hockey sticks, cricket kits, and other sports equipment. Mr Spoke, though a PT teacher, was also great at teaching Maths. The class got a taste of his teaching when the regular Maths teacher was on leave for a few days.

Mr Spoke was responsible for conducting the annual PT display function in school. During the display, drums and trumpets filled the air, which kicked off with a grand march past. Then, there were drills, gymnastics, races, relays, and other sporting activities. The tireless efforts of Mr Spoke, supported by the rest of the staff of St William's, were responsible for the school's athletic achievements.

During one dress rehearsal for the annual PT display function, Mr Spoke noticed Rocky attempting to avoid the drills whenever he turned away. However, Rocky didn't realise that Mr Spoke was observing him closely. Approaching Rocky, Mr Spoke requested, 'Rakesh, could you please fetch my stick from my room? It's kept near the door.'

'Sure, Sir.' Rocky responded and dashed towards his PT teacher's room, more than a hundred yards from the ground. He retrieved the stick and ran back to hand it over to Mr Spoke. Mr Spoke took the stick and instructed Rocky to turn around. Rocky complied, though taken aback by this unexpected command. Mr Spoke swiftly smacked him on his bum. Rocky screeched in pain.

'If you try to deceive me again, I will get the hell out of you. Do you think you can fool me?'

'Sorry, Sir.' Rocky responded, his head bowed in shame.

Standing close to him, Chaitanya started to laugh at Rocky's plight. Mr Spoke turned around, and Chaitanya experienced the same consequence as his friend did moments earlier.

Then there was the old music teacher, Sister Anne.

Sister Anne was strict yet fascinating. When the children's knowledge about musical instruments was quite limited to the primitive-sounding harmoniums, tabla, or sitar, Sister Anne was an accomplished pianist. She would sit in the spacious school auditorium, playing her grand piano. It would genuinely sound heavenly. Even the most inharmonious singing by the children wouldn't sound as bad, for she would play the piano louder and louder to cover up the bad singing.

When Sister Anne retired, she was replaced by another, called Sister Paula.

The first day Sister Paula showcased her talent was during a usual morning assembly.

The children were lined up neatly, in their best behaviours, for their morning prayers, and the teachers, with the headteacher and the very new Sister Paula, stood on the pedestal, facing the children.

All was done well, but then Sister Paula started singing.

She was trying to sing the 'Bells of St William's ring out far and wide...' Instead, she sang, 'The bulls of St William's ring out aar and ide...'

Chakradev looked at Chandan wide-eyed and gobsmacked as if he couldn't believe his ears. He saw Lavanya, Diksha, and the others trying hard to suppress their giggles.

'Bulls of St William's? Where are the cows?' Rocky couldn't suppress his laughter.

A sudden spurt of snigger came from the adjacent line, and Chandan knew it was Mona from the junior section. He was sure she would get into trouble, so he turned around and gestured for her to stop giggling.

Sister Paula confidently sang in the strangest accent. She sang as loud as she could. Her voice was screechy and glass-shattering. She stretched and quivered each note unnecessarily as if she were electrocuted. She continued with 'the bulls of St William's...'

That was Sister Paula's first day in school and her most unexpected singing.

Only a few children could gather the perfect composure and pretend to be dignified, while the others snorted with their partially suppressed laughter.

The teachers stared at the giggling students from the corner of their eyes.

The children dared not look up at the teachers. They knew the principal would notice.

They surely knew they were in some serious trouble.

'You know, the headteacher came to our class, asking for the names of those who laughed at the assembly. I stood up amongst the others. I couldn't lie. But Sister Paula's singing was truly shocking. We had a half-hour lecture about how accomplished Sister Paula was and how it was utterly improper of everyone who made fun of her,' Mona told the gang in the evening under the mango tree.

Outside the school, across the boundary wall, was Dewalal's *samosa* shop. Students would run to the shop after school to eat delicious *samosas*. The school, however, discouraged students from eating from the shop due to their lack of nutritional value, though the *samosas* continued to be a popular choice. During the lunch break, students would scale the boundary wall and toss the money to Dewalal, who in turn would hurl the *samosas* back to them wrapped in a paper packet. If the students were caught eating *samosas* from the shop, they would face fines imposed by the school. Bholanath was fined multiple times but continued eating the *samosas*, *jalebis*, and other snacks.

Then there was Laddu's shop, a few meters away from the main gate of the school, which was a grocery cum stationery store. But the children used to crowd around the shop for *churans* and *sweet supari*. It's the *churans* from Laddu's shop, which Chandan used to buy for Mona.

St William's Convent School played a vital role in shaping the students' futures by providing them with a strong educational foundation. In addition to academics, sports, and other extracurricular activities were also encouraged. Diversity, along with inclusivity, was celebrated at St William's. The school's contribution extended far beyond academics, influencing the personal growth of students and future success.

One Sunday afternoon, the gang sat under the mango tree with only one agenda: to discuss their school and the teachers. Chaitanya joined them on one of those rare days instead of going to the *Naher*.

Chandan initiated the discussion.

'Let's first talk about our school. Are you all happy to be a student of St William's?' he asked his friends.

'Yes, we are,' Nayantara said, 'though I also feel that the teachers spoon-fed us a lot.'

'I disagree.' Chaitanya remarked. 'I think their approach is more parental, so they care for every student. It may feel like spoon-feeding, but actually, it's nurturing.'

Lavanya intervened.

'See, let's be practical. St William's is a good school. However, our parents enrolled us here as it's located in Chukchuk Nagar, close to our house, and is an English medium institution.'

'I agree,' Chakradev acknowledged. My father says one needs to be good in both language and Maths. In our country, whoever speaks English is taken more seriously.'

'Yes, that's the impact of the two hundred years of the British rule.' Diksha added.

'The school encourages sports, which I like.' Chakradev remarked. 'I think Mr Spoke is the best teacher in the world.'

While munching on potato chips, Bholanath asked, 'Who do you think is the best teacher in school?'

'To answer that, we must establish the criteria for what constitutes a good teacher.' Chandan replied.

'Someone unbiased towards the students.' Mona added.

'Do you have a favourite teacher, Mona?' Anshul asked.

'Yes, I do.' Mona answered.

'If you can have a favourite teacher, then why can't they have a favourite student?' Anshul pressed further.

'Because it's them who is imparting the knowledge, not us. We are the receiver.'

'So?'

'So, the distribution of the light of knowledge has to be equal. For that, the teacher needs to remain impartial towards their students. Otherwise, some will receive more light while others will be left in the shadows, engulfed in darkness.'

Everyone clapped at Mona's insightful words.

'Mona is a big girl now. Light, knowledge, distribution...Oh! My God! Mona should start teaching us.' Bholanath remarked while Mona laughed along with the others.

'This is just Physics, Bhola—light, shadows and darkness. You would know better. You are the best in Physics.' Mona remarked with a chuckle.

They continued to discuss their teachers.

'I think Patel Ma'am, who taught us Sanskrit and Hindi, is my favourite.' Chandan remarked.

'I agree. She is impartial in all aspects. She always maintained a balanced approach to addressing student concerns and conflicts. Do you remember how Madhav used to fail in Sanskrit and how hard she worked with him to enable him to understand the subject? Madhav scored 90% in Sanskrit in his final exam.' Daksh remarked.

'Let me tell you something,' Bholanath intervened. 'My grandfather was a professor of Mathematics at the Benaras Hindu University. He told me once that it's not Maths that defines a person's intelligence and analytical ability but language, particularly Latin and Sanskrit. It seems that to decipher, interpret, and understand Latin and Sanskrit, the brain needs to exert twice the effort compared to solving mathematical problems.'

'Really?' Chaitanya exclaimed.

'Yes, and you will observe that any teacher of Latin and Sanskrit will tend to lead a very disciplined life. They are very careful about their diet, daily routines, and exercise. They are also very selective and careful about choosing their friends. I don't know the reason, but there might be some connection between these languages and the life patterns of those who study them. My grandfather said Sanskrit is the most evolved, spiritual, and scientific language. The way the words are pronounced in Sanskrit has an impact on the mind and the body.'

Chandan's mother came out of the house and addressed the gang.

'Do you want something to eat?' she asked.

'Yes, Aunty.' Bholanath immediately responded with a smile.

'Okay, let me get some snacks for all of you. Chandu, come inside for a second.'

Even though it was summer, the jackfruit, guava, and mango trees provided ample shade. A gentle breeze whispered through the leaves, offering a soothing respite from the heat. Squirrels playfully darted among the branches while two cats lazily stretched on the cool, earthly ground beneath the trees' expansive shade.

Accompanied by his mother, Chandan emerged carrying trays laden with biscuits, *bhujia,* and glasses filled with chilled *lassi.*

'Enjoy the *lassi.*' Jaya Chandola remarked with a smile and then went back inside.

As usual, Bholanath was the first to dive into the snacks and *lassi.*

'Who is our next favourite teacher?'

'For me, it will always be Kaushal Ma'am. Because of her, I have started to love the English language,' Diksha remarked.

'Yes, though she is very strict. Many of the students have nicknamed her 'Hitler'.' Anshul added.

'Whether she is Hitler or Napoleon is not the point. What we can get from her as students is the point. She is a very good teacher, there is no doubt about it, though I know she has her favourites,' Daksh asserted.

'Diksha is one of her favourites.' Chaitanya remarked with a chuckle, glancing at his sister.

'I am not good at languages, but you are right. Kaushal ma'am has helped me get my basics right and understand the fundamentals.' Chandan admitted. 'Otherwise, I would be lying in the grave beside Shakespeare.'

'Many of us would die to be at the side of his grave.' Chaitanya quipped with a grin.

Everyone laughed.

'What about Gondhalekar Ma'am? I think she is the best Economics teacher.' Nayantara remarked, sipping on the *lassi*.

'Yes, of course. Did you know that she accepted answer sheets only from the right side of her desk and not from the left side?' Rocky, who had been on mute all the while, which was a miracle, remarked.

'What do you mean?' Chaitanya was intrigued.

'She only accepted the answer sheets from her right side, insisting they be placed on the right corner of her desk. Once, I approached her from the left, but she didn't even look at me. It wasn't until after the other students on her right submitted their answer sheets that she turned towards me and remarked, "Child, don't you have any observation?" I didn't understand at first, but then I realised that she accepts submissions only from her right side. So, I moved towards her right and submitted my answer sheet.'

'That's funny.' Lavanya giggled along with the rest.

'It's not so funny. I received a zero on the test, and Mrs Gondhalekar said I should get negative marks because of my poor observations.'

Everyone burst out in laughter.

They munched on to the snacks.

'What about our history teacher?' Mona asked the group.

'I think Miss Kapur was the most beautiful teacher I had ever seen. She should have been in the movies,' Rocky remarked, initiating a discussion, which was his domain.

'That's true. She was gorgeous and a super teacher. Miss Kapur made me fall in love with history,' Chandan added.

'You fall in love with stupid things,' Lavanya remarked. Her eyes narrowed, and a frown creased her forehead.

'What does that mean?'

'Nothing. There were more beautiful teachers than Miss Kapur.'

'Are you jealous of Miss Kapur?' Chaitanya chuckled.

'Why should I be?' Lavanya asked, looking the other way.

'Well, Chandan likes her. She has made him fall in love with history.'

They laughed, but Chandan intervened. 'Friends, we need to respect our teachers. Miss Kapur is an extremely good teacher and a very helpful one, too. Let's leave it at that.'

They munched on the snacks for a few minutes in silence.

Then Lavanya spoke,

'We are talking about the teachers who are teaching us now. But our primary school teachers were also terrific.'

'Yes, of course.' Anshul nodded in agreement. 'Take, for example, Gauria Ma'am. She was my class teacher when I was in 1st grade. She was so strict.'

'Yes, I remember. She was my class teacher, too. She would be blunt and speak straight to the parents during the parent-teacher meeting. Indiscipline was absolutely not tolerated,' Nayantara added. 'But she is one of the most lovable and finest teachers I have ever encountered.'

'Gauria Ma'am is from Nagpur.' Anshul remarked. 'My maternal grandfather lived close to her house. He had seen her as a little girl.'

'Oh! That's quite a coincidence.'

'Yeah, but that doesn't mean she was lenient with me. In fact, it was the reverse. I hear that she is still a perfectionist.'

'And Faria and Almeida Ma'am.' Chaitanya chipped in. 'What patience they had with us.'

'Especially in your case.' Diksha quipped. 'Maintaining patience with you is itself an achievement.'

'Shut up.' Chaitanya snapped at his sister.

'Yes, their patience, sense of humour, warmth and affection, encouragement...great teachers are good psychologists. One should be careful if one chooses to be a teacher. They can't go wrong, and if they do, many students' lives will be ruined.' Chandan remarked.

The gang discussed Mrs Deshpande, who taught Mathematics; Mrs Sharma, who guided Physics; Sister

Lorena, who enlightened the students in Chemistry; Mrs Vaidyanathan, who taught Biology; and Sister Gabriella, who imparted knowledge in Geography. Each one of them was renowned for their excellence and dedication to education. They brought a wealth of knowledge to the classroom. Their commitment to excellence empowered the students to reach their full potential.

St William's of Chukchuk Nagar, with its outstanding faculty and curriculum, had set the standard for educational institutions not only in Lucknow but across India.

Chandan:

St William's had a profound impact on me and shaped my life. But before talking about my school, I would like to say a few things about Chukchuk Nagar.

Chukchuk Nagar was a middle-class community where the parents held high expectations for their children's academic and career success. They wanted their children to study hard and get admission in engineering, medicine, chartered accountancy, or management. While some managed to meet these expectations, others struggled to do so. Those who didn't were often not fully appreciated. I love Maths, but I have never wanted to be an engineer. My parents never put any pressure on me. But then, I was just lucky. For many others, it was a battle. I wish parents had encouraged their children to follow their passions rather than conform to societal norms of success and failure. One of my classmates, Kartik, was an excellent poet. However, he faced constant scoldings from his parents for not getting good marks in science and economics. How can a poet be expected to crack mathematical problems when his true passion lies elsewhere? It was a challenge growing up in Chukchuk Nagar.

My friends and I were never excellent in our studies, though we were good. I was not so hardworking, but I was sincere. Nayantara was an exception in our group, always standing first in the class. She really worked hard. But then Lavanya, Diksha, and Bholanath had the sharpest minds. Mona was extraordinary. She would never study for more than an hour but still managed to be in the top three in her class across all subjects. I saw her study quite often. It felt as if she was meditating. Such was her power to concentrate. Rocky was another exception. He never studied at home except during exams, but despite all his idiosyncrasies, he was very attentive in class whenever he was not venturing out into the 'forest'.

About my school...well, I am sure about one thing. I am not going to get such outstanding teachers again in my life. They would teach us like our own mothers or sisters. They were compassionate and had a keen sense of observation. They were caring towards each student. You don't always get to see this. It's rare. The school is fully responsible for instilling a sense of integrity and discipline in me. That's for sure. I think some of us were plain lucky to study at St William's.

Mona:

I love my school. I love my teachers, I love baby Jesus and his mother, Mary, and I love playing badminton and basketball in school. The Leadership Training Service program gave me confidence and made me an empathetic girl. The emphasis on community service, like the Social Productive Work, taught me the importance of giving back to society. I will study hard and uphold the reputation of St William's.

Chandu says we will not get such great and caring teachers again, and he is right. I wish all my teachers a long and healthy life. Their presence will make a difference in this world and make it a better place to live.

Chandan and Mona cycling around Chukchuk Nagar.

Chandan with his friends. (From left to right) Daksh, Anshul, Rocky, Chandan, Bholanath, Chakradev and Chaitanya.

(From left to right) Lavanya, Diksha, Mona and Nayantara.

Mango tree meeting and the adjoining jackfruit tree laden with fruits. Chandan, with his friends, is in the centre, flanked by Lavanya on his right and Mona on his left. Bholanath is standing behind him.

Chandan with Mona on his right and Lavanya on his left.

The children playing Holi in Chukchuk Nagar.

Chandan with his friends sitting on the pipes of the water tank, flanked by Rocky on his left, Bholanath on his right and Daksh standing behind him.

Durga Puja celebration at Capital Hall

The children celebrating Diwali at Chukchuk Nagar

Mona and Mihir playing in their backyard.

(From left to right) Chaitanya, Chandan, Bholanath and Daksh at the LPG Railway Station. Chaitanya is seen smoking here.

Police officer Raj Raghuvanshi at the Chukchuk Nagar Police Station punishing hooligans.

Chandan's first birthday celebration.

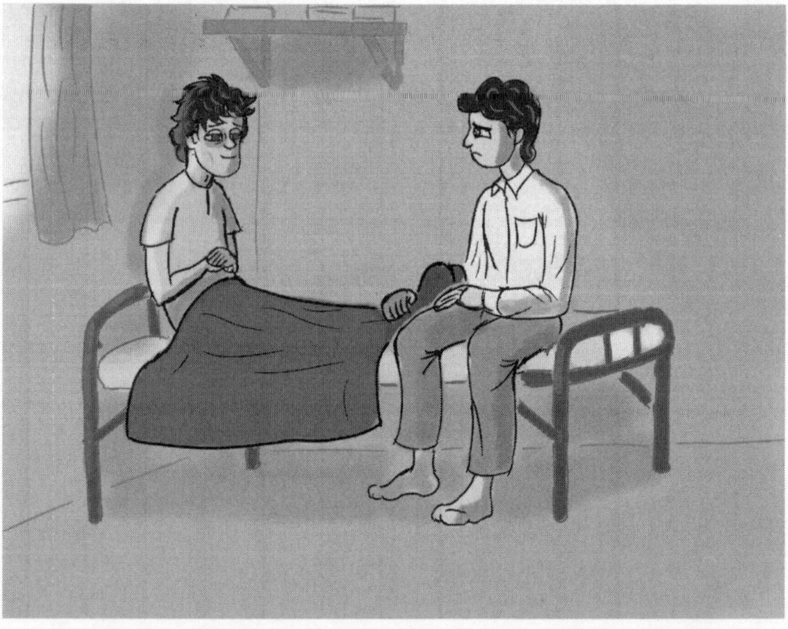

Chandan with Chaitanya, who is sick and bedridden.

23

Night outs to Results out

The time was difficult and demanding. They all woke very early in the morning, and some studied for the whole night, which they called 'night outs'. They had started preparing for their 10th board examination scheduled after three months. The days were quite restless as they got busy with their studies. Except for Mona, who was still in the eighth grade, the rest of the gang rarely came out of their rooms and met for an hour only on Saturday evenings beneath the mango tree. Their rooms had textbooks and notebooks scattered throughout, and their mothers got busy serving them endless cups of chai.

They worked on equations, formulas, historical dates, essays, and plant and human anatomy. They would go to school at eight, return at two in the afternoon, and, after a short break, continue to pore over their notes. Sometimes, there would be night outs as some of them preferred to study late into the night. The pressure mounted each day. Bholanath started to lose weight, which caused his mother to feel anxious as she attempted to ensure that he ate enough. As the examination dates drew closer, there was extreme stress and fatigue coupled with anxiety, which spread through the group. Sleepless nights became routine, and Rocky and Daksh didn't even sleep for nights at a stretch due to last-minute crunching. Anshul and Bholanath were the coolest ones, with plenty of rest and sleep compared to the others, while Nayantara, Lavanya, and Diksha burned the midnight oil. Chandan was more disciplined and preferred an early bedtime and early rising.

On their first day of the examination, they were very nervous as they entered the school auditorium, the examination hall. There were two papers daily from nine to eleven in the morning and again from one to three in the afternoon. For the next ten days, they poured their thoughts onto the answer sheets, a test of their preparation and hard work. An invigilator sat on the auditorium stage, overseeing the students while teachers moved around the room for supervision. After the second day, they felt much more comfortable, and their worries were reduced to some extent.

On the last day of the examination, when the final bell rang at 3 p.m. after the final test, the students felt a wave of relief wash over them. They felt lighter, and after days of intense turmoil, they smiled, laughed, joked, and played cricket on the school ground opposite the auditorium. Bholanath dashed to Dewalal's shop to have *samosas*. He later told Chandan that he had six *samosas* with *chutney* that day.

The general expectations in the neighbourhood were consistent. Everyone was confident that Nayantara would score the highest marks, followed by Lavanya, Chandan, and the rest, with Bholanath and Rocky at the bottom of the list.

Two months later, the results were declared. When the gang went together to check the results on the bulletin board, it stunned them. Nayantara collapsed, almost losing consciousness, followed by Bholanath, who succumbed to a similar fate, though for an entirely different reason. They checked and rechecked the result sheet with disbelief.

Name	Marks
Bholanath Sharma	92.6%
Lavanya Iyer	91.4%
Chandan Chandola	89.2%
Diksha Nair	88.1%
Nayantara Iyengar	86.1%
Daksh Chopra	83%
Anshul Deshmukh	81.3%
Chaitanya Nair	80.7%
Rakesh Sood	78.8%
Chakradev Gopalakrishnan	77.4%

Nayantara and Bholanath regained consciousness almost simultaneously and cried in unison, 'This can't be true.'

There was no celebration by the gang and no cheers as Nayantara mourned. She lay motionless on her bed for days with a blanket spread over her. She refused to eat or drink, staring blankly at the ceiling. She had always stood first in the class and faltered where it mattered the most—a shadow of failure cast over her. An uncanny silence prevailed in the room as she refused to go out and meet her friends.

Chandan walked into her room one day with Mona. Nayantara saw them, tried to avoid their gaze, and started to weep.

'What's wrong with you? Are you coming to the mango tree meeting tomorrow or not?' Chandan asked.

'No.' Nayantara curtly responded, looking the other way, wiping her tears.

'And why so?'

'My wish.'

'If you don't come tomorrow, you will cease to be my friend,' Chandan warned.

There was silence for some time, and then she spoke,

'Chandu, I have failed.'

Chandan gave a quick glance at Mona and then turned towards Nayantara.

'Failed? With 86%? Are you kidding me? None of us celebrated our success just because of you. Bholanath always felt that he would fail the exams... he didn't even celebrate with *golgappa*s or *samosas* after coming first in school. That's the sacrifice he made for a friend - for you. He has lost two kilograms and is continuously thinking about you. Thinking about you, Nayantara. But you are a selfish giant. You don't respect friends. You are self-centred. Never show me your face again if you don't attend tomorrow's meeting.' Chandan shouted and then stormed out of the room.

Nayantara started to cry while Mona tried to comfort her.

The next day, as the gang sat beneath the mango tree engaged in lively chatter, Nayantara arrived. A sudden hush fell upon the group. Chandan stood up and hugged her tight, followed by the rest. Bholanath hugged her, and she did the same. Tears flowed, Rocky shared a joke, everyone laughed, and Bholanath opened three big boxes of *jalebis, gulab jamuns,* and *samosa*s, which they indulged in like a feast fit for kings.

The gang was back with a bang.

Chandan:

Frankly, I was not too surprised that Bholanath topped in

school. I knew he was brilliant, but I also knew he was lazy. He had lost his Economics book and was completely unaware of it. Then he realised a week before the exams. That made him rush to Kumar Book Depot in Alambagh to buy a new book. Can you imagine? He was never too serious about his studies but quickly grasped things. He never studied hard but could focus his attention whenever he wanted to. He read the whole Economics book in two sittings, two consecutive nights, and was done with it. I think he scored 85% in Economics. He was very sharp with an elephantine memory and could afford to be lazy, unlike us. In Physics, he was a master.

I felt sorry for Nayantara. However, I know that her grief was more due to Bholanath and both the girls scoring higher than her. Nayantara had always been very competitive, and her grades deeply affected her. That day when she came, we all felt happy. After all, she is a friend.

I was happy with my marks. I never expected too much, but I was glad to score 98% in Maths. I could have done better in History and Geography. But somehow, I have suddenly started liking both these subjects. The other good news is that our school has introduced the intermediate board, though it's restricted to the science stream. I have chosen science so that I can continue to study at St William's. Bholanath, Nayantara, and Daksh will join me. Chaitanya, Diksha, Lavanya, and Anshul joined St John's as they took up Commerce and Economics. Rocky has taken up history and joined the prestigious Vidyasagar School of Arts along with Chakradev. Vidyasagar and St John's are morning schools and not too far from Chukchuk Nagar. So, our mango tree meetings will not be impacted.

A few days after the treat Bholanath gave us under the Mango tree, we went to Alambagh for another treat at the Pratap Chaat Corner. We ate *dahi bade, allu tikki* and *golgappe*. I am amazed at watching girls eating *golgappe*. They open their mouth wide, downing it in one swift gulp. Then, they clamour for more tamarind water. That day, Lavanya and Mona gulped ten *golgappe* each, while I could only eat four in the stipulated time.

We also went to Nath General Stores that day. Daksh and Diksha had to buy something. The shop owner, whom we called 'Uncle', was a very nice and kind gentleman. Always in a white kurta and pyjamas, he smiled at us and gave us chocolates for free. From there, we went to Shivam Sweets. Chakradev wanted to pack some *chole-bhature* and *dosas*. He was expecting guests at home, so his mother had asked him to get some.

Overall, we were all happy that we did well in our board examination. Maa and Papa were happy. But Papa said that the war had just begun. That was a surprise for me. I thought it had ended.

Mona:

I am so happy for Chandu. In fact, all of them have made me proud. But Chandu is a different kind. He is never too thrilled about anything. He said he would teach me Maths and science to prepare me for my board examination after two years. He also gave me all his notes. He told me to get serious now and not to watch too much television. He also said that he would teach me cycling and swimming. I said no to swimming immediately. I don't want to learn to swim in the dirty water of the *Naher*. He laughed. Okay, cycling then, he said.

24

In the Wake of Heartbreak

The boys and girls of Chukchuk Nagar fell into four distinct categories.

The first category consisted of ambitious students who were fully focused, dedicated, hard-working, and determined to succeed in life.

Families in Chukchuk Nagar belonged to the middle-class section of society, and this first category understood the value of education and the sacrifices of their parents. They excelled in their studies and gained a reputation for being sincere and hard-working. They maintained an impressive academic record, many securing admissions to the prestigious Indian Institute of Technology (IIT) or other top-class engineering colleges, medical colleges, and management institutes like the Indian Institute of Management (IIM). Some became Chartered Accountants, joined the Armed Forces, excelled in sports, and represented the state in hockey, badminton, tennis, and other sports.

Some also could achieve the rare distinction of qualifying for the UPSC examination and becoming a Civil servant. These boys and girls were known for their passion, focus, hard work, and unwavering discipline. They overcame every obstacle to realise their dreams.

The second category fell between the best and the mediocre. They were not ordinary, but they were not great either. They were good but not consistent in their performance either in academics or sports and hence didn't secure the highest grades, though they had an enthusiasm for learning. They also explored other interests beyond the scope of traditional academics. This category excelled in extra-curricular activities, sports, community service, and cultural pursuits. This group defined success on their terms.

Then there was the third category. This group, primarily boys, excelled neither in academics nor sports or extra-curriculars. Their grades were average, and they did nothing notable. They were not interested in anything and had a lack of interest in whatever they undertook. There was a certain dullness around them. They had a sense of contentment and never put extra effort into achieving something. They had no goal in life and were happy without aiming to contribute anything significant. They were the happiest when eating, sleeping, lying on the bed, or doing nothing. They would get irritated even if asked to perform simple household tasks.

Finally, there was the fourth category. They did nothing except daydream and fall in love. They thought they were always in love.

But it was the story of Aparna Advait and Aurobindo Bagchi that brought colour, mostly in black and white, to the mundane canvas of life in Chukchuk Nagar.

Aparna, whose beauty was as captivating as her voice, was in the second category. Though not an extraordinary student, she did well in her studies and was an extremely gifted singer. Her morning ragas echoed through the streets and narrow lanes of Chukchuk Nagar, creating a divine melody in the early morning air. She was a rare blend of musical talent and ethereal charm. Tall with beautiful sparkling eyes and long flowing hair, her appearance was charming.

Aurobindo, her neighbour, belonged to the fourth category. If the girl happens to be beautiful, a singer, and above all, one's neighbour, then it was the icing on the cake for this category of people.

Aurobindo's father, Shivoprasad Bagchi, and Amrit Lal Chandola worked in the same department. They were colleagues, and Chandan often visited their home to savour the aromatic delights of Mrs Bagchi's cooking, particularly the sweet dishes she prepared during the Durga Puja and Dusshera festivals. Many times, he had taken Mona along with him.

Aurobindo took three years to pass his tenth board examination and another three for his intermediate. By the time he joined college, where the situation was very shaky again, he was deeply in love with Aparna. Aparna, who was much younger, was already completing her master's degree in philosophy, while Aurobindo struggled in his first year of graduation.

The first thing Aurobindo did every morning was peek through her room's open window whenever she started with her ragas. Once she completed her improvisation of the first classical mode, he used to clap and shout. 'Excellent, Aparna. You are mini-Lata Mangeshkar. Keep it up.' There were other awkward attempts to impress her. He started writing love letters followed by love poems that were so cringe-worthy that the most tolerant would wince in sympathetic embarrassment after reading them. His days were spent in a world of daydreams, and at the centre of those dreams always stood Aparna, his love, his soulmate, and his future wife. Or so he thought.

'Aparna, how are you?' He used to ask whenever she came in and out of the house. He stood at his gate to welcome her. Aparna used to roll her eyes and walk away.

Slowly, Aurobindo's antics became a source of neighbourhood gossip that made Aparna and her parents uncomfortable and anxious. Aurobindo was foolish but in no way evil. There was a certain innocence in him, and he genuinely loved Aparna. Despite all his stupidity, Aparna knew it. When Aparna suffered from a bout of dehydration and had to be admitted to the hospital, Aurobindo stayed by her side throughout the day and night, even when the doctors asked him to leave. When Aparna's mother once required a blood transfusion, suffering from anaemia, it was Aurobindo who ran to the hospital to donate his blood. He cared for Aparna's pet dog, Tolly, for a month when Aparna and her family had visited their native place. It was Aurobindo who grabbed his umbrella and instinctively rushed to shield Aparna from the unexpected shower. It was Aurobindo who, armed with a cookbook, embarked on a mission to cook dinner for Aparna even though he could have asked his mother to do so. The result was spilt ingredients and burnt dishes.

And every Sunday, he would present her with a rose.

'Why, only on Sundays?' she would ask.

'Just like that. I don't have so many roses in my garden.'

Aparna and her family left for her native place the day she

completed her final exams. A month later, the Bagchis received her marriage invitation card. Aurobindo was speechless. He was shattered.

When Aparna visited Chukchuk Nagar after her marriage, accompanied by her husband, and met all her friends in the colony, Aurobindo hid in the backyard, where shadows danced and merged in the darkness. But no one, not even he, noticed the shadows in his eyes.

There were many in Chukchuk Nagar, like Aurobindo, who succumbed to the clutches of aimlessness and were trapped in the maze of daydreams that led to missed opportunities and regret in their later years. Their potential was wasted as they grappled with the bitter realisation that they let their most valuable asset, their time, slip through their fingers, wanting another chance to rewind the clock in the fading twilight of their existence. But alas! The opportunity never came again as no one can turn the hands of time.

Years later, when Chandan met Aurobindo at the LPG railway station, he was shocked to see a middle-aged man pushing boulders with others under the hot sun, his shoulders stooped, his threadbare clothes clung to his slender frame. He removed the white scarf around his neck, wiped his face, and asked, 'Chandan, is it you?'

'Yes, what are you doing here, bhaiya?'

'Can't you see? I am pushing the boulders. Then, I have to cut the overgrown weeds. They are laying another railway track.' He smiled, still wiping his face, pointing toward the tracks.

'But why are you doing this?'

'This is the only job I can do. I wasted my time. I wish I had studied hard.'

Chandan didn't know what to say.

'Where is uncle and aunty?' Chandan asked after a prolonged silence.

'Both dead. Mother passed away last year.'

'I am sorry.'

'No, it's okay. They died long ago after I turned out the way I am.'

Both were silent for a while, and then Aurobindo asked,

'Any news about Aparna?'

Chandan was taken aback by that question. He somehow tried to maintain his composure.

'Yes, her family now resides in Paris. Her husband works for the Ministry of External Affairs.'

'Good for her, good for her. I hope she still practices her ragas,' he smiled. 'Chalo, I will see you later. There are lots of stones to remove.'

'You are a good man, bhaiya.' Chandan uttered.

Aurobindo looked straight into Chandan's eyes.

'Doesn't matter. It doesn't help.'

As Chandan turned to go, he felt a tear drop fall on the white boulders surrounded by the overgrown weeds as an empty goods train rambled past.

Chandan:

I could never forget that meeting with Aurobindo. I felt a profound sadness for him. In his eyes, I saw a reflection of a good man but burdened by lost love and unfulfilled dreams.

I met him again a few years later. He was thinner, his hair a tangled mess with his dishevelled white and black beard as he was vigorously coughing. He said he had a fever, but he had to work. I touched his shoulder while he coughed to provide some comfort.

Regret is what I saw in him. Only regret. And his love for Aparna. From head to toe.

I don't know whether he was foolish, stupid, or silly. Yet, amidst it all, one undeniable truth remained- he was a good man.

He passed away a few months later on the side of the railway track. He coughed and coughed, wracked by endless fits of coughing. The doctors said it was tuberculosis. He was cremated near the *Naher*. I was there.

That marked the conclusion of Aurobindo's life chapter.

Aparna heard about his death much later while on a visit to the city. I met her and told her what Aurobindo had told me. I am sorry, she said.

Three simple words-I am sorry-a small and sweet acknowledgment for a stupid neighbour who spent his entire life doing nothing but thinking about her.

She was in a hurry. She said she had to go shopping at Hazratganj market. So, she left.

And that was the end.

Mona:

I have been to Aurobindo bhaiya's house a few times with Chandu. Bhaiya was funny, always cracking jokes and making us laugh. He showed us a 'magic stone' he had bought from someone that would bring him good luck. He said that the stone would help him pass the exams. He said that he paid five hundred rupees for the stone. I was shocked. It later turned out to be an ordinary roadside rock used for sidewalks made from recycled materials. He said he would start a business before he got married to Aparna so that he could take good care of her.

I wept the whole day when I heard about his death because of his childlike innocence and honesty. The world feels a little less bright now.

25

Colours and Chaos

It was all about fun and freedom. On that day, the whole Chukchuk Nagar colony transformed into a canvas of colour—the spectacle of the Holi festival.

But the celebrations commenced a week in advance. All the women in the neighbourhood got busy preparing the *gujiyas* (sweet fried pastries), snacks, and other dishes as the children ran around buying water guns and colours from the shops at the Cooperative store. On the day of the festival, the whole colony came together to smear and splash each other with coloured powder and water, all in good humour.

'What's the plan for Holi?' Chakradev asked when the gang was idling beneath the mango tree of Chandan's house in the afternoon a few days before the festival.

'We first need to get the dry leaves, twigs, and wood for Holika Dahan.' Mona suggested.

'When is Holi?' Chaitanya asked.

'Next week.' Chandan responded.

They all sat in silence, contemplating how to prepare for Holika Dahan and Holi. The leaves fluttered in the breeze, and a cat passed by, observing them with amusement.

Chandan stood up and addressed the gang.

'Bholanath, you get the dry branches. I saw a tree being cut, the one opposite to your block. Are the branches still there?' he asked Bholanath.

'Yes, they are available.'

'Then get them quickly before someone takes them. You can keep them in your garden or bring them here.'

Bholanath nodded.

'And Chaitanya, get those dry leaves and twigs near the *Naher*. You are a frequent visitor there, I know.' Chandan said with a smile.

'What about us?' Nayantara asked.

'You and Diksha will help the boys build and light the bonfire for Holika Dahan in the park behind the Polyclinic. Mona and Lavanya will go with Chakradev and Daksh to buy the sweets from Dixit's shop.'

Chandan drank a glass of water and continued, 'We will distribute the sweets to our neighbours during Holika Dahan. I will get the music system from Rudransh bhaiya. We can play some devotional songs. And we need to clean up the area once the festivities are over. Do you have any questions?'

Daksh stood up.

'What about Holi?'

'I am coming to that.' Chandan responded. 'We will go together to buy the *gulal* and watercolours. We need two buckets to mix the colour powder with water and some *pichkaris* (water guns) and balloons.'

'I have two little drums at home. We don't use it. I will get them.' Anshul volunteered.

Everything went as per the plan. On the night of Holika Dahan, the air was infused with electric energy that crackled like the flames soon to be ignited. Bholanath had dragged the dry branches all the way from his house while Chaitanya, as instructed by Chandan, gathered the twigs and dry leaves from the wooded area adjacent to the *Naher*.

They made a beautiful bonfire, one branch on top of the other in the shape of a pyramid scattered with twigs and dry leaves. The whole neighbourhood started to gather in the park a couple of hours after sunset with happy, smiling faces filled with anticipation and excitement. Jaswinder Singh, the eldest in the neighbourhood, was granted the privilege of lighting the flame first with the help of his wife. Devotional songs were played on the stereo, the children distributed sweets, and all prayed for prosperity, health, and happiness. Dry leaves and peanut shells, along with grains and coconut, were thrown into the fire. Effigies of Holika were burned. As the flames reached skyward, everyone in the neighbourhood danced in circles around the fire amidst joyous shouts and laughter. 'Holi Hai'

Early the next morning, the children went to the park and cleaned the area. They removed the ashes from the bonfire, which had now cooled down. Mona, with the help of a broom, swept the area around the bonfire site, supported by Anshul and Lavanya. Rocky collected the debris in a bag and kept it at the corner of the park for the garbage pickers to pick it up the following day. Chandan, Daksh, and Nayantara cleaned the surrounding area. Bholanath checked for any smouldering residues with a shovel.

They returned home hand in hand, excited about the main event. That is to throw colours and splash water balloons at strangers from rooftops. The festival provides the licence to indulge in pranks that one would not dare dream of committing on any other day. Girls could mingle freely with boys; the poor could celebrate with the rich, and even caste differences, which were predominant in the Hindi heartland, were forgotten. This license of freedom, however, was only for a day.

In the neighbourhood, Mrs Titli Basu was the first victim. She had dressed up in a yellow saree and full makeup and had already started playing Holi with her family, smearing the faces of her husband and sons with coloured powder. Then, she ventured out into the neighbourhood to play Holi. Rocky saw her and crept up from behind a bush where he was filling his water gun with coloured water. He poured a bucket of water on her head from behind.

'You rascal, I will teach you a lesson,' Mrs Basu shouted as she turned around and saw Rocky.

Rocky laughed and ran away. 'Aunty, *buraa naa maano Holi hai*.' (Aunty, don't be offended. It's Holi)

Then, the riot of colours, dance, and fun started. They all gathered at Anshul's house. Two drums were filled with water up to the brim mixed with colours, and water-filled balloons were kept ready, as were the water guns. Anshul, Daksh, Chandan, Mona, Chaitanya, Chakradev, Lavanya, Nayantara, Diksha, Rocky, and Bholanath were all part of the gang. Even Bhamsi joined the gang that day, who had come all the way from Singaar Nagar. The gang was called the 'toli', which meant the gang of celebrators.

The adults, too, came out of their homes, the children ran around with joyous shouts and laughter, and the streets of Chukchuk Nagar came alive. They were all enveloped in colourful chaos. Anshul's mother prepared a large platter of *gujiyas* and snacks for the children. Bholanath was the first one to pounce on it. Urvashi Iyengar, Nayantara's mother, prepared vada and Obbattu, a sweet filled with jaggery and coconut, while Lavanya's mother prepared *kheer*.

Chaitanya went to the terrace and aimed a water balloon at Mr Kulkarni, who resided in another neighbourhood. He was a colleague of Chaitanya's father's and had come to celebrate the festival with his other friends. Mr Kulkarni was completely bald with a shiny dome that resembled a polished cricket ball. His head was so glossy that it could blind onlookers in the sunlight. For Chaitanya, that was an ideal target for bouncing a few water balloons on the man's head. He threw it with full force aimed at Mr Kulkarni's head, but it splashed down directly on his father's head instead. In retaliation, his sister Diksha, fiercely protective of their father, delivered a tight slap to Chaitanya's cheek. Without picking up a quarrel with his sister, Chaitanya silently came downstairs, rode his bike, and left for the *Naher*.

With the *gulal* in their hands and the water balloons in their pockets, the 'toli' roamed around Chukchuk Nagar. They first visited every house in the neighbourhood. The Nayyar couple offered them a plate of *gujiyas,* and Daksh's father gave them a big pack of coloured powder. They visited every family, but Rocky stayed away from Mrs Basu's house for fear of retaliation. They strolled towards the Cooperative store, then the stadium, and then turned left from Capital Hall towards their school. Spirited shouts of 'Happy Holi' filled the air as several other 'tolis' roamed around the streets of the colony.

On their way, they met some friends and acquaintances who resided in other neighbourhoods, smearing colourful streaks on each other's faces. Cheers erupted from every corner as everyone joined the festivities with equal fervour. Young men zoomed in on their bikes, laughing and shouting, riding at full speeds, causing a deep throaty rumble as they removed the silencers of their bikes.

The boys had moved slightly ahead of the girls as they took another turn, disappearing from their view. Mona, Nayantara, Lavanya, and Diksha were chitchatting and trailing behind the boys. Just then, four youths in two motorcycles zoomed past the girls, shouting, laughing, and staring at them. '*Kya maal hai*. What a catch,' one of them commented.

Nayantara, always confident and assertive, shouted in response. 'You dogs. Stupid fools.'

The men stopped their motorcycles, turned back, and blocked their path.

'We are what?' one of them asked, the smell of alcohol lingering on his breath.

'Fools, Dogs.' Nayantara repeated as the other girls trembled.

'Let's go.' Diksha whispered.

The man dismounted from the bike, approached Nayantara, grabbed her by the head, and forcefully kissed her on the cheek. 'Next time, it will be worse. For all of you,' he warned before swiftly returning to the bike. His friends laughed and sped away, leaving the girls in shock.

Nayantara was speechless for a moment. The suddenness of the assault left her stunned, unable to find her voice amidst the chaos of emotions swirling within her. After walking some distance and not being able to locate the girls, Chandan and his friends turned around and reached back to the corner of the road. There, they saw the girls standing, all quiet and silent.

'What happened?' Chandan asked.

And the girls started to cry.

Chandan:

We returned home immediately after the incident as Mona narrated the ordeal. We all felt a raging anger and fury building in us. We sat beneath the mango tree in silence as Maa served us sweets and snacks with cold drinks, oblivious to what had just happened to the girls. I didn't share anything about the incident with her or Papa. I am not sure about Nayantara and whether she shared it with her parents. But we never brought up that topic again. It was never discussed.

But a change swept over Nayantara after that incident. Her confidence ebbed. She was a confident, bright girl, but her academic performance took a sudden downturn after this incident. She became quiet. Her energy dimmed. We tried our best to uplift her spirits, but we were unsuccessful. The men did the wrong, and she had to suffer. She bore the consequences of the men's wrongdoing. Why are girls like that? Why do they endure suffering and fear and lose their confidence because of someone else's offence? I get terribly angry just thinking about it.

But then, being a boy, I may not fully understand how a

girl experiences those emotions.

Mona:

I could never forget that Holi. We were laughing and chatting, and all of a sudden, we were all in tears. It's a festival that marks the victory of good over evil. But that day, the evil triumphed. We were so afraid. I spoke to Chandu about Nayantara. He asked me not to broach that subject again. He wanted us to give Nayantara more space. She will heal on her own, he said.

Yesterday, Rocky shared a stupid joke, and Nayantara laughed after a long time. I feel like the healing process has started.

26

Whistles and Wheels

Lau Path Gamini, or LPG, was a quaint little Railway Station next to Chukchuk Nagar. The railway lines were like a boundary between Chukchuk Nagar and the outside world.

The railway station, though small, offered some facilities: two ticket counters, one small waiting room, one food stall, and two restrooms. Behind the main building was a cigarette shop, which Chaitanya visited whenever he was bored of the *Naher*.

Due to its proximity to Nakshal Khera, the girls rarely visited the railway station unless they had to board a train. The boys would visit the station often. They used to sit on the cement benches, huddled together, watching and enjoying the thrill of the superfast trains zipping fast while Chaitanya and occasionally Daksh enjoyed their smoke.

Few trains stopped at the station. Most zoomed past, the whistle and the metal wheels clanking against the tracks echoing throughout the neighbourhood. The residents of Chukchuk Nagar could tell by looking at their watches which train was zipping past.

'It's Gomti Express,' one would say.

'No Yaar, it's Pushpak. On right time.'

'When will Mahamana Express arrive?' asked another.

'Delayed. Running late by an hour.'

'How do you know?'

'By experience,' was the prompt reply.

Bholanath used to buy piping hot *samosas* from the nearby 'Rasangan', one of the most popular sweet and snack shops near the station, while Chandan used to get *rasgullas* from the same shop. Anshul and Chakradev would get peanuts and puffed rice, known as *laiya chana.* While eating the snacks, they would walk from one end of the platform to the other and often balance themselves on the edge of the platform with their legs dangling freely, leaning forward whenever they heard the chug of an approaching train.

They knew the station master, Mr Ramesh Shandalya, quite well. They would often visit his cabin, and when not too busy, Ramesh Shandalya would tell stories about the railways and his experiences on the job for almost thirty years. He showed the boys the rail map with flashing red and blue lights, which tracked the trains on that route, and explained the railway network and how it functions in India.

A few passengers would sit in the waiting room and sip tea while others walked up and down the platform, impatiently waiting for their train to arrive.

Sitting on the bench outside, the boys sometimes witnessed an old lady scolding a younger one inside the compartment whenever a train stopped. They knew it was a never-ending squabble between the mother-in-law and her daughter-in-law. They used to see the passengers laughing, talking, or playing a game of chess or ludo. Some read a book or a newspaper while others ate their meals. Some would look out of the window; some would sleep while the ticket inspector moved through the compartments to check tickets.

Some passengers would call the vendors on the platform to buy snacks as children jumped and moved around under the watchful eye of their parents.

One incident at the LPG Railway station merits mention. Some passengers had arrived to board a passenger train to Kanpur with their families. Some sat in the waiting room, while others strolled on the platform. Little children ran up and down with outstretched arms, shouting and laughing. Chandan, Daksh, Chaitanya, and Bholanath were sitting on a bench and discussing the India-Pakistan cricket test match, which was underway. It was around six in the evening.

A boy who was about five years old was walking playfully and stood near the edge of the platform with other kids his age. His parents, who had come to board the passenger train, were sitting on a bench talking to other passengers. The signal changed from red to green, letting a superfast train pass through before the arrival of the passenger train. They could all hear the rattling on the tracks and its glaring headlights as the train approached. As the boy turned around, surprised by the sound, he lost his balance and slipped. He fell on the tracks a few meters away from the approaching train.

Frightened, the boy started to cry. Shivers ran down the waiting passengers. The boy's mother screamed in terror. There was absolute pandemonium as panic gripped the railway station.

Chandan and Chaitanya sprang out of their seats, ran, and jumped on the tracks. They pulled the boy to one side seconds before the superfast train sped past. It took time for all to regain their composure. The boy's mother cried her heart out, tears of relief filling her eyes as the boy clung tightly to his mother.

That night, Chandan shared the incident with his parents. Both were shocked. After a while, his father smiled.

'I am proud of you,' he said, giving Chandan a tight hug while his mother dashed to another room, wiping her tears.

Despite this incident and the continuous sound of the trains rattling past, the quaint little LPG Railway Station offered solitude, where time was slow and life was bliss. Like all railway stations, it provided a glimpse of the varied colours of India.

Chandan:

I used to visit the LPG railway station quite frequently. Sometimes alone and sometimes with my friends. Mona also joined me a couple of times. Some drunk hooligans would also visit the station, so I never encouraged the girls to join us.

The little station was my go-to place whenever I was sad, like on the day of my birthday, which was never celebrated. I used to feel a little low, but then the station was magic. It made me happy. I don't know why. Maybe the trains, the passengers, the chatter, or sometimes even the station master, who would offer me a cup of tea or a glass of sugarcane juice during the summers whenever he saw me. Railway stations are like the essence of life. Like the trains, we are also constantly running towards our destination.

My destination? Unlike the trains, do I know where I want to go? I have my doubts.

Mona:

Chandu told me about the boy and how he was saved. My heart had already stopped beating while he was narrating the incident. I started crying, and he asked why. I didn't have an answer. So, he embraced me tightly. Maybe I wept thinking of his safety. Lavanya came to my house the next evening. She was shocked when she heard about the incident. I saw her turning pale. Then Chandu came and sat next to Lavanya and comforted her.

I told Chandu not to go to the station again. He laughed. 'That's my sanctuary. I am a rail Putra (son of the railways), and you are a rail Putri (daughter of the railways),' he said. 'How can we stay away from a railway station?' he asked. That made me smile. Then he left smiling and humming a tune.

27

Broken Wings

Sukanya had just left home for school on a bright spring morning. She used to walk to school alone, occasionally accompanied by her neighbour, who was a year younger than her. She was in her school uniform: a navy blue neatly pleated skirt, a white shirt, a navy and white striped tie, and a navy blue cardigan. She was a student of St William's Convent.

'I love you.' The voice was quite flustered.

Sukanya turned around and saw a rugged-looking young man. He was around his early 20s, dressed in dirty baggy capris and a worn-out T-shirt. He stood beside her while his other friend waited at a distance on his bicycle.

'What! Have you lost your mind? I do not have time to listen to all this.' Sukanya replied brusquely.

Sukanya was Chandan's classmate and lived in a different neighbourhood. They encountered each other in school every day and occasionally at social events. Though she was not in Chandan's inner circle, she was quite close to him and Mona, as the girls represented the same team in the school badminton games. She was tall and athletic, with an intellect that shone brightly in her academic pursuits. During their cycle ride to school, Chandan and Mona passed by Sukanya's house almost daily, as that was the shortest route. Sukanya had been aware of two young men trailing her on her way to and from school for the past two months.

'...But... but, I have been following you, and I love you.' The young man's words were distraught at this point.

'How dare you! Leave and never bother me again.' Sukanya asserted. Though nervous, she managed to conceal her anxiety.

It was still early, and the road was relatively silent apart from a very few school children or the milkman, with cans cycling his way to deliver milk, a couple of early morning joggers, and a few scattered individuals engaged in their daily routines.

'But I love you, Sukanya,' the man persisted.

'How do you know my name?' Sukanya exclaimed in shock.

'I know everything about you, Sukanya. If you can't be mine, you cannot belong to anyone else.'

'Get lost. I will call the police,' she retorted.

'I am begging you. Just tell me that you love me. Please.'

Sukanya turned away and started to walk off.

Chandan had turned towards Sukanya's house on the way to his school. Mona, as usual, sat on the back carrier.

The man strode forward briskly, took out a small bottle from his pocket, and splashed a thick yellow liquid on Sukanya's face.

Sukanya let out a heart-piercing wail.

Chandan, a few feet away, watched everything unfold before his eyes. The man, along with his friend, swiftly rode off on their cycles and vanished before a small crowd gathered to assist Sukanya, who lay on the street writhing with pain. It was an act of vitriolage, an acid attack.

Chandan jumped from his cycle along with Mona and ran

towards Sukanya.

'Mona, you go to school and inform Sister Lucy. I will get her to the Polyclinic.' Chandan instructed.

The small crowd took a few minutes to recover from what they had just witnessed. Sukanya continued to scream in an agonising cry of pain. Chandan noticed that one side of her face was severely damaged due to the burn on the skin. Someone from the crowd swiftly transported her to the Polyclinic in his motorbike as Chandan, and the rest hurried towards the hospital.

Dr Chakraborty was at home during that early hour but rushed to the Polyclinic as soon as he received the news. He entered the emergency room, where Sukanya was lying on the bed wriggling with pain, and with the help of other doctors and nurses, started to irrigate the wounds with water. Saline boluses were administered. Eye, mouth, and ear exploration were done, and affected areas were rinsed with water. Simultaneously, the police were informed, and a case was filed against the miscreants.

However, due to the severity of the burn, Sukanya had to be relocated to another hospital since the facilities in the Polyclinic were insufficient for handling such cases.

'Doctor *saab*, please save me. I want to live,' she had pleaded.

She fought bravely like a champion till the very end and then succumbed to the injury a week later. The doctors said that they tried their best, but her windpipe was severely damaged, and the infection she had contracted due to the burns was severe.

That day, Chandan lost his classmate, Mona lost her badminton partner, and her parents lost their only child.

Chandan:

I don't want to say much. The pain is unbearable, and I would rather not dwell on it. But Sukanya was a friend, and I can't forget her. She sat right beside me in my class, and we would chitchat during breaks. She had escorted me to the first aid room when I had injured my finger with a blade.

She was extremely good in sports, particularly badminton and basketball, and demonstrated excellence in academics, too. She was not the first in the class, though—that place was already permanently taken by Nayantara—but she consistently ranked within the top five.

I think about her parents. Their world has been shattered, and they can never fill the void. The world will move on, but their hearts will ache with never-ending sorrow. Is it a fair world that robbed them of their most precious treasure?

I had never witnessed such an incident in Chukchuk Nagar before. I had often heard about such attacks elsewhere, but that day, I saw it before my eyes. I shudder to think about it. I shudder to think how Sukanya must have felt. The doctors said it was concentrated sulphuric acid. Concentrated sulphuric acid? Are you kidding? That can cause the severest burns.

I don't know whether they caught hold of the miscreants. However, I know it was the start of an era that generated intense fear among the residents of Chukchuk Nagar. Teenage girls no longer felt safe and needed to be escorted. I worry about Mona. I worry about Lavanya, Diksha and Nayantara. I worry. I only worry these days.

Mona:

I have never seen them crying. But all the boys wept, sitting beneath the mango tree. I could see only tears in our eyes and their eyes. Sukanya was their classmate. Chandu and all the boys, even Rocky, who is so talkative, didn't speak for many days. He has gone so quiet now. Nayantara and Diksha have almost stopped visiting us. Lavanya does come occasionally. I tried to talk to Chandu. He tells me not to go alone anymore. He gives the same advice to all the girls. I went to the Cooperative store alone a few days back, and he shouted at me. I had never seen him so angry. Whenever he is angry, I tell Lavanya, and she talks to him and calms him down.

Tears are swelling in my eyes again.

I will miss you, Sukanya.

28

The Unity Club

Waseem Khan was short, slender, and wiry with an ordinary appearance. But those steely eyes, which could cut through steel behind a pair of glasses, told a different story. Khan was a towering force on the football field.

He was the football coach of the Unity Club, the only football club in Chukchuk Nagar at the time. His students revered and feared him, trembling in his presence due to his ferocious intensity and unwavering discipline. He had only one demand—absolute dedication and excellence.

Guruji, as his students addressed him out of reverence, commanded immense fear and respect from the players. His strictness was legendary. Excuses and mediocrity were not tolerated.

His rulebook was uncompromising, and Guruji was unforgiving. Despite being a devout Muslim, he took the boys who belonged to the Hindu faith to the adjacent Hindu temple near the Capital Hall to take their oath within the temple premises. His students were required to take a handful of water from the hand pump, pledge their commitment, and drink it. The players were to wear a blue jersey with a stringy 'V' attached to it. 'V' stood for victory.

With one hand behind his back and holding the stick with the other, Khan addressed the boys standing on top of a podium, 'Let me be clear at the beginning. You are here to learn and play football. Apart from playing and learning about the game, you will not do anything. There is no leisure here. I will not tolerate it, and you will not be spared if I see you watching movies or television, playing with marbles, and flying kites. I will break your hands and legs if I see you gossiping or chitchatting aimlessly. Whatever I have mentioned above needs to be followed; otherwise, you will all get a taste of my stick. Do you all understand?'

The boys nodded.

'Now, go and run three rounds around the stadium to warm up.'

The consequences of breaking the rules were severe. Guruji never used to talk much. His stick did it for him. A few times, his cane broke as it struck against disobedient hands, legs, or backs. He used to get a new, thicker, and heavier stick every time that happened. There were many cases where players couldn't hold their bladder in his presence due to fear.

Guruji resided in Nakshal Khera, where even the local goons were terrified of him. He would commute to the football ground on his bicycle. On weekends, when most families relaxed at home, and the boys seized the opportunity to sneak away to watch a movie at the Chukchuk Nagar auditorium or on their newly purchased television sets, Guruji would arrive unexpectedly at their home on his bicycle, which filled his students with terror. If they were caught engaging in activities not aligned with their pledge, like watching television or playing with marbles or flying kites, the cane would come out and start 'speaking', often in the presence of the boy's family.

Chandan, Anshul, Daksh, and Chakradev joined the Unity

Club. But within two months, Guruji kicked Daksh and Anshul out. Chandan left after two years as he started to play more cricket and basketball, while Chakradev continued for some more time.

Though Guruji was strict, his method yielded results. His club had become so famous that many of his students received job offers on sports quota in state and central government positions and the private sector. Parents wanted their boys to be trained and tamed by Guruji as they were confident in his ability to nurture and develop their sons. There were students of different age groups, and batches were made accordingly.

Guruji was an interesting character. But the reason why Daksh and Anshul were kicked out of the club was far more fascinating.

Daksh and Anshul set out to watch a movie in the Chukchuk Nagar auditorium without informing their parents, the worst possible action they could have taken according to the Unity Club protocol. They bought the tickets and sat on the side seat of the last row to avoid any attention. They clapped and laughed and enjoyed every bit of the movie. They got up and sneaked out for a washroom break in the interval. As they turned a corner and approached the washroom, they saw Guruji standing with his hands on his waist, with an intense menacing glare as if he were waiting for them to come out of the hall.

'Welcome, boys,' he remarked. 'How is the movie?'

Shivers ran down their spines. In panic, they both pretended to faint, collapsing together. Water was sprayed on their faces to revive them by someone who had also come to watch the movie. They slowly opened their eyes and saw Guruji still standing in front of them. They played dumb and asked innocently.

'Where are we?' Anshul mumbled.

'How did we get here?' Daksh murmured.

Guruji leaned forward, put his hand on Daksh's pocket, and pulled out two pink-coloured cinema tickets.

'Enough boys. Now get up. This is how you got here. I not only know that you are here but also know who bought these tickets,' he said, waving the pink paper at them.

Daksh didn't give up easily. He continued to fake selective amnesia.

'Who are you?' he asked his Guruji, his eyes half closed.

'Well, you may have forgotten me. But you surely can never forget this.' Guruji remarked, brandishing his cane this time.

Both sprang up and started to run. But Guruji got hold of both of them and delivered a resounding smack on their buttocks with his cane.

'Don't ever you fools show me your face again,' is what they last heard while running.

True to their Guruji's words, they never showed their face again. But they could never figure out who tipped off Guruji about their whereabouts.

Chandan:

I had a strong suspicion about who tipped off Guruji. It was Baljeet, who resided in Nakshal Khera and was Guruji's neighbour. Baljeet had joined Unity Club a couple of years before us. My interaction with Baljeet was limited to the football field and the occasional encounters at the Cooperative store. He was a good player—nowhere near Chakradev, but good enough.

He had a few fights with Daksh and Anshul for reasons I am unaware of. But Daksh had told me that Baljeet and his brother Balwant mixed with the wrong crowd, occasionally drank and smoked, and once whistled at Diksha and Nayantara when they were returning home from school. It was then that they had picked up their first fight.

However, Guruji's primary frustration with them probably stemmed not only from their movie-watching habits but also from the ongoing pranks they persisted in playing on the field despite Guruji's repeated warnings.

Daksh once put a lifelike plastic toy snake in a player's trouser pocket, which the player had hung on a hook before heading into the field in uniform. Upon discovering the snake, the player was so terrified that he fainted. No one knew who was behind the mischief, but Guruji was sure it was Daksh as he saw him loitering around the changing room that day.

Daksh and Anshul always pretended to be injured during practice, forcing Guruji to run over and gauge the situation. As long as they were in the ground, the children were Guruji's responsibility, and their frequent pretence troubled him.

They also used to mimic Guruji's whistle blows often, which led to confusion and chaos on the field. They tampered with the equipment, shoes, and gear, greatly infuriating Guruji.

Being caught in the cinema hall was the final nail in the

coffin.

I never had any problems with Guruji. Neither did Chakradev. We both loved football and continued to thrive under his guidance until I switched to basketball and cricket. Even though he was strict, he was a good man. He genuinely cared for his students. Beneath that toughness, he was compassionate and understanding. His guidance was not limited to the field but also off the field. Even after I left football, I used to meet him often. We talked, laughed, and exchanged ideas on sports in general. Occasionally, he would extend an invitation for a spicy *chaat* at the Dixit Sweet shop.

He left a lasting impression on me. In him, I found not just a coach but a mentor and a role model as well.

Mona:

I had met Guruji quite a few times. He was so thin that I thought he was a marathon runner, as most runners are thin. Chandu told me he is very strict, though it never felt so from the outside.

I am not a football fan, though I would go to the Chukchuk Nagar stadium with Chandu to watch football matches. Unity Club won a few times. I remember Chakradev being given a prize for scoring the most goals. After he was awarded those prizes, Chakradev would take us to the Dixit shop for a plate of *tikki, dahi bada*, and sweets.

29

Durga Puja

Autumn. The month of the crisp, cool breeze. The soft rustle of the fallen leaves. The fiery orange and yellow of the *amaltas* flowers as they bloom like scattered jewels. The intoxicating scent of the night jasmine in the cool night air.

But when Chandan and Mona started to carefully pluck the jasmine flowers early in the morning, it reminded the neighbourhood that Durga Puja was nearby.

Navratri is a nine-day festival celebrated all over India, though the Bengali community starts its celebrations on the sixth day. Chandan's parents lived in Calcutta, so they were aware of all the traditions and rituals of Durga Puja.

Around two weeks before the start of Durga Puja, the Puja committee of Chukchuk Nagar started to work on the construction of a temporary pandal in front of the Capital Hall. The pandal was set up to host the cultural programmes scheduled for the evenings during the Puja days. In the daytime, however, people gathered beneath the pandal, eating, chatting, and playing cards. On one side of the pandal were numerous makeshift shops and eateries where children and adults enjoyed snacks and other mouthwatering cuisines.

Durga Puja was a momentous occasion and a vibrant affair in Chukchuk Nagar. It used to be celebrated in the Capital Hall, which bustled with activity and community spirit for five days.

The Capital Hall served as the venue for the puja ceremonies where the idol of goddess Durga and her four children, Ganesh, Lakshmi, Saraswati, and Kartikeya, was installed. For five days, the chants and prayers echoed in Capital Hall as devotees from the colony and nearby areas came to seek blessings from the goddess. The air was filled with the rhythmic beat of the drums and the resonating sound of the *sankha* (conch) infused with the aroma of *dhoop* (incense), which created a divine ambience. The puja started in the morning, followed by *pushpanjali*, the sacred offering of flowers to the goddess, amidst chanting the mantras and prayers. It was then followed by prasad distribution, which is the 'blessed' food, primarily fruits, first offered to the goddess and then distributed to devotees.

In the afternoon, *bhog,* the sacred food comprising rice, pulses, and other traditional delicacies, was distributed to all. The *bhog* used to be prepared in big utensils and large vessels right behind the Capital Hall, where one of the Puja committee members, the *bhog* secretary, used to look after the preparation and distribution.

Children ran around with toys and balloons while the men enjoyed a game of cards beneath the pandal. The womenfolk remained busy either with the puja activities or chatting. The Durga Puja was like a get-together, particularly for the Bengali community in Chukchuk Nagar, though many non-Bengalis joined in the celebration.

In the evening, the sandhya aarti was performed, followed by a *sankh* competition, in which the participants showcased their skills in blowing conch shells. Their performance was evaluated based on the clarity and duration of the blow.

Then there was the Aarti competition. Devotees waved and danced with a lighted earthen pot filled with coconut coir and camphor. Many enthusiastic participants often gripped the pot between their teeth while dancing to flaunt their boldness and stupidity.

Every evening, people gathered below the pandal to witness the dance drama and other cultural activities. Some visited the adjacent ground to watch Ramlila. The cultural activities continued well past midnight as Ravana's evil laughter echoed through the neighbourhoods of Chukchuk Nagar.

And then there was love. Love blossomed at Capital Hall for five days, and the pandal became the centre of teenage love stories. Young boys, in their best outfits, and the young girls decked out in their finest sarees turned into lovebirds. The boys, with their hearts fluttering at the sight of a beautiful girl, stared and winked at the girl, while the girl occasionally responded with a shy smile, interpreted as a silent agreement, at least from one side. Some boys and girls were reserved or pretended to be calm, though their hearts were anything but still. Keeping a straight face as if devoid of earthly desires and emotions, they sneakily glanced at each other from the corner of their eyes. These divine love stories would kick off on the sixth day and wrap up on the tenth with the immersion of the goddess in the *Naher*. With the goddess taking a plunge into the waters of the *Naher*, their brief holiday romance would also take a splashy exit.

Durga Puja was not just an auspicious occasion. It was

about the spirit of togetherness and devotion, a sense of joy and community, and, above all, the triumph of good over evil and celebrating the power of the feminine.

On the tenth day, as the idols were taken to the *Naher* for immersion, a certain sadness enveloped Capital Hall and Chukchuk Nagar. After the immersion, the stage where the idols were installed felt empty, as if a family member had been lost.

But the spirit of togetherness and devotion continued as the residents looked forward to another year of Durga Puja.

Chandan:

Even though we are not Bengalis and my parents originally belonged to the Garhwal district, they had spent all their childhood in Calcutta. They could speak the Bengali language fluently and were versed in all Bengali rituals. So, the atmosphere inside and outside the house was electric during the Navratri and Durga Puja. That's the only time my parents smiled and talked a little more than they usually did.

Mona and I, occasionally joined by Lavanya, Chaitanya, and Diksha, would gather jasmine flowers from the tree in the corner of my garden every morning from the first day of Navratri. The early morning air would be quite chilly and crisp, though the blooming jasmine flowers would fill us with warmth and anticipation for the day ahead. Daksh and Rocky, with their sleepy eyes, would sometimes join us.

After plucking the flowers, we used to keep them in the Puja room. My mother would then offer them to the various gods after her bath.

I used to visit the Capital Hall frequently during that time after returning from school. I could see a lot of people running around and working day and night to construct the pandal. Mona and I spent a lot of time observing the construction of the pandal. It was real fun. Lavanya also joined us occasionally.

On the fifth day, the idols were brought to Capital Hall in the evening in an open truck. It took a huge effort to get them on the elevated platform that served as the stage. The clay idols were heavy, and we needed to be careful to set them up on the stage to prevent damage or breakage.

On the sixth day, at the crack of dawn, we would head to the pandal to immerse ourselves in the morning mantras and the soul-stirring rendition of the Mahalaya. We were all there. Mona, Diksha, Lavanya, Nayantara, Daksh, Chaitanya, Anshul, Chakradev, and Bholanath with our parents. Being a late riser, Rocky never managed to join us, though his parents did.

And then the evenings. The bursting crowds at Capital Hall, the colourful decorations, the beating of the drums, the sound of the conch, various cultural activities, the musical chants, the food and snacks, and the endless cups of tea and coffee filled us with the vibrant energy of the divine.

The cultural programmes would start after the completion of the aarti. People would gather in and around the pandal to watch the dance and drama scheduled for the evening. There was hooting, shouting, and laughter when someone stumbled over their lines or forgot their dialogues during the drama and poetry rendition.

The famous Theatre Choir and the Jharna group organised dance and drama. During one drama, the lead actor forgot his dialogue while delivering his lines. The audience started to hoot. Panic gripped the actor. To top this, the dhoti he wore suddenly loosened and slipped. He didn't know what to do and then fled the stage, leaving us all in fits of laughter.

There were sad moments, too. On one occasion, on the morning of the tenth day or the day of Dusshera, one woman from the neighbouring area performed aarti with a lighted oil lamp standing in front of the idol. Unfortunately, the goddess's saree accidentally caught fire due to the lamp. Within minutes, the flames spread. Panic gripped as people scrambled frantically and tried to extinguish the fire by throwing buckets of water. The fire was doused, but the face and the body of the idol were damaged. As per the tradition, the artisan who had made the idol was summoned. He came even though he was not keeping well. It took him a lot of effort to patch up and restructure the idol. After the incident, a sense of sadness prevailed. As evening approached, the patched-up idol was solemnly immersed in the water of the *Naher*.

After the immersion, people gathered in the Chukchuk Nagar stadium, which was packed to witness the Ravan Dahan. The children, standing hand in hand, watched the effigy of Ravana go up in flames, marking the end of the festival.

Durga Puja is celebrated all around India, but the celebration in Chukchuk Nagar was unmatched in its vibrant energy. It is what one of my relatives who came from Calcutta told me when he stayed with us for a few days during Durga Puja.

Mona:

A week before Durga Puja, our Mango tree meetings revolved around what dress we would wear. Fashion was the main topic of discussion. We would eagerly discuss and plan our outfits, though the boys were not interested in such discussions. Durga Puja, at least for the girls, was not just a religious event; it was also a time for them to showcase their style.

A saree was a staple, but Nayantara preferred bell bottoms with crop tops. It suited her tall frame. Diksha, Lavanya, and I wore sarees for all five days. The boys wore bell bottoms, but Chandu wore regular trousers and full-sleeve shirts. Bholanath always wore a dhoti and kurta during the five days of the festival.

Capital Hall would come alive during Durga Puja. From the latest jewellery trends to embroidered handbags, there was no shortage of options to complete our looks. Lavanya would look stunning in her saree and 'gajra' worn in her hair. She would request me to click photographs with her camera while she and Chandu stood together. Then, all three of us would pose for the camera. Rocky used to be the cameraman clicking our photos.

I can still smell the scent of incense and hear the sound of the dhak drums. The elaborate decoration, the stunning idol of the goddess and her children, the crowd, the makeshift food shops, a small amusement park for children, the merry-go-round—it was just fantastic, filled with laughter and celebration.

Durga Puja at the Capital Hall in Chukchuk Nagar will always hold a special place in my heart. Those memories would last a lifetime.

30

God in Chains

It was October, and the autumn trees flaunted their last burst of colours and the last smile of the year. It was the season when all the festivals lined up, knocking one after the other. It was the season when the whole atmosphere seemed to be dressed in carnival clothes brimming with joy and ready for another change.

It was also the time of year when many Hindus celebrated Kanya Puja during the Navratri. Little girls are worshipped as they are believed to represent the nine avatars of Goddess Durga or Shakti, or feminine power.

Mrs Sneha Agarwal, who lived with her husband and son, Aakash, in an adjacent neighbourhood to Chandan and Mona in Chukchuk Nagar, traditionally performed Kanya Puja each year during the Navratri festival. Mrs Agarwal was close to Mona's mother, and they often went to the *Satsang* (religious meet) together. Her daughter, Chandrika, was married the previous year and stayed in Jhansi with her husband, an employee in the electricity department. The women in the neighbourhood assisted Mrs Agarwal with all the arrangements and preparations for the Kanya Puja.

The girls in the colony eagerly hoped for Mrs Agarwal's invitation as they knew that the food she served and the gifts she presented after the ceremony was too good to be missed.

Mona, Diksha, Lavanya, Nayantara, and a few other girls

from the neighbourhood were always invited. They used to scuttle into Mrs Agarwal's house like a pack of crabs and were welcomed with a big, broad smile.

As the girls sat on the chairs, their feet were washed by the elderly ladies with milk and water, some prayers and rituals followed, and then food was served. It was generally a fixed menu of halwa poori, black masala chana, and some roasted vegetables. After the food, the elders touched their feet, and gifts were given along with some copper utensils as a part of the ritual. The girls missed Chandrika, who was always there to welcome them with her mother and then spend the afternoon with them with chitchat and laughter. This time, however, she was not around, as, after her marriage, she was staying in a city that was 250 miles away from Lucknow.

Chandrika was just eighteen when her parents decided to arrange her marriage, even though she was extremely reluctant to do so. The man was an employee in the government sector, and they thought it would benefit her to settle down even though the man was twelve years older than her.

After the rituals and the gifts, the ladies and the girls sat down for a chitchat and a ludo game. Sneha Agarwal went to the kitchen to attend to some chores while her son talked to a friend who had come by.

The postman came and delivered a telegram. Her son received the telegram and started howling after reading the contents.

'Chandrika in hospital. Come soon.'

Sneha Agarwal rushed out of the kitchen, snatched the paper from her son's hand, and screamed. Everyone gathered around her as she fainted and then regained consciousness after a few minutes.

There was silence, and everyone was dumbfounded. They never expected such an incident on the 'Kanya Puja' day when they were all rejoicing and celebrating the feminine. The atmosphere in the room suddenly filled with panic and distress. Sneha Agarwal was almost hyperventilated by the sudden mayhem and chaos surrounding the house, which was full of guests.

It was an emergency!

Chandrika was admitted to the hospital!

There was no other information given.

Lots of questions troubled their minds, but none that could be answered.

Sneha Agarwal rushed to Mona's house and banged on the door. Mona's mother hurriedly emerged.

'Malti, could you take care of the house and everything? I don't understand what to do. Aakash will be here. Please take care of him.' Sneha Agarwal quavered after quickly explaining everything to Mona's mother. Her nervous, unsteady hands shook, and she held Malti's hand.

'Don't worry, Sneha. Chandrika is a brave girl. She will be fine. You don't have to worry about Aakash,' Malti comforted her as she wiped the tears off her cheeks.

Chandrika's parents immediately took a rickshaw and left. Little did they realise that by the time they reached the Charbagh Railway Station to board the train for Jhansi, their daughter was already dead.

A few days later, news reached Chukchuk Nagar.

'Chandrika had died of burn wounds on the same day when the entire colony was celebrating Kanya Puja, the festival of celebrating women.'

'She had fought very bravely until her last breath, but she succumbed to her wounds.'

'No arrests made yet.'

Slowly, the truth unfolded. Chandrika was tortured for dowry every day from the time she entered her in-law's house. Was it jealousy, was it just an act of cruelty, or were they so greedy that they could do anything for money?

The dowry system evolved during the Vedic period. It was for the benefit of the bride, who could not inherit property as per Hindu law at that time. The dowry was given to her for her use during times of need.

With time, everything was twisted and turned for the benefit of a few. It, unfortunately, became a social evil in society that caused unimaginable tortures and crimes against women.

The greed for money and power became unquenchable.

Chandrika, who should have been worshipped as Shakti, was set aflame on a funeral pyre that evening.

That autumn, the trees and their branches moaned, too, weighed down by the abundance of fruits during the festive season.

Chandan:

Getting Chandrika married at 18 against her wish? Are we living in the 18th century? I didn't know Chandrika too well, but I knew she topped in Hindi and Economics in her 12th board exam. She wanted to study. She wanted to be a graduate. Postgraduate maybe. That's what she had told Mona. A girl and a boy have to be prepared not only for marriage but for everything in life. If we venture out without preparation, that would be a disaster. I am outraged right now. I am feeling like setting her in-laws' house on fire. And her husband, too.

Mona:

I always knew I never wanted to get married.

My idea always revolved around the perplexity of leaving my home, my parents, my little brother, Chandu, all my friends, and everyone I knew.

Beyond everything, I can't wrap my head around how this could happen!

What happened to Chandrika was horrific... horrible... simply heinous!

Chandrika did speak to me about her plans once, but now that seems like such a long time ago. She wanted to attend college, study Hindi, and become a teacher someday.

She was just 18 when they forced her to marry a man twelve years older than her.

I had discussed with Chandu during her wedding that it was too soon. She was such a young bride, nervous and unsure of what was happening, giving credence to these life-altering decisions with a smile.

I hope those people will be punished. How could they torture her? Mentally. Physically. She is dead now.

Her death is unbelievable. How can I never see her again? Death is so permanent. I will never see her ever again.

I heard the aunties talk to Mummy the other day about all sorts of things, what could be done differently, from background checking, how to do things the right way, too young or too old to get married. All those rumbling. How does anything matter now?

Why does a woman have these endless struggles that she has to endure to please everyone, be it parents or society?

She will be judged no matter what, so why not do what she thinks is right and live by her own rules?

I might be labelled a radical one day for thinking people should only marry when they feel fit or at least when they think they are ready or never at all.

Are we truly the weaker kind?

Or is this what society believes and echoes, and we live our lives in this make-believe?

Chandu is outraged and refuses to talk about this matter. The mango tree meetings are suspended for the entire week.

31

Diwali

'You just wait and watch. Someday, our country will be seen from outer space because of so many diyas and lights,' Diksha prompted, her gaze shifting from the lights around her to the darkness in the sky.

She was always excited about all the festivals and eagerly volunteered for all the chores, though not as much attention was paid to delivering them. Unlike her brother Chaitanya, who frowned at his fantasist sister and replied, 'Ya, right! First, let us finish lighting these, and then we can think about space. We have to meet at Mona's house, remember, and then go to Capital Hall.' His interest was to finish the decorations and rush to his friends for the firecrackers.

Diwali is widely known as the festival of lights. It is the light of victory, good over evil, and a light that pierces through the darkness. The three days of festivities are celebrated in the lunisolar months between the end of October and mid-November.

Almost every household in Chukchuk Nagar celebrated these few days enthusiastically and with vigour. Home cleansing, decorating, preparation of sweets like laddoos for the prayers, buying gifts of sweets and dry fruits, and then decorating the houses with twinkly lights and diyas were a part of the practice that was very fondly followed.

The festivities would start with Dhanteras, a day auspicious for buying any metal like copper, brass, silver, or gold.

It made the women and the little girls in the colony very pleased.

'Mona, I will buy you your first gold earring,' her mother announced. That year, Mona was really pleased with the little gold trinket, not knowing that in years to come, she would be holding onto it as her most precious gift from her mother.

After Dhanteras, the main celebrations revolved around the two days of Diwali. Mostly, the people did Laksmi puja on the third day, which fell on a New Moon. Prayers were offered after sunset, and lights were lit after that. The eastern part of the country offered prayers to Goddess Kali, which would start around midnight.

Chukchuk Nagar was a mini representation of India, so they would celebrate all it could encapsulate.

Laksmi puja was a part of individual households, while Kali Puja in Chukchuk Nagar would happen in the Capital Hall and the nearby temple.

The main attraction for the kids used to be firecrackers. Chandan and the other boys in the gang would ride their bicycles to the wholesale cracker market at Aiyaganj, more than ten miles away from their homes, and buy bagful of crackers at discounted rates.

A funny incident took place in the neighbourhood a few days before Diwali. The boys had already brought a lot of crackers, which they kept on the terrace to remove any moisture. Around the same time, the monkeys came to Chukchuk Nagar, again creating havoc. They had bitten two residents who were in the hospital. A meeting under the mango tree was hurriedly called in the afternoon.

'Friends, we need to do something about these stupid monkeys. They come and destroy everything. They have started biting people. We are no longer going to allow that.' Chandan initiated the discussion.

'So, what do you suggest?' Diksha asked.

'We need to use a few of the crackers before Diwali?' Chandan responded with a smile.

'What do you mean?' Daksh asked.

'The green thread bomb, basically the hydrogen bomb, makes the loudest noise. We will use it to scare the monkeys.'

He then laid out the plan.

'We will tie two hydrogen bombs and ignite them simultaneously. Most of the monkeys take their afternoon nap on the jackfruit tree. We will attack when they are sleeping.'

'When?' Nayantara asked.

'Tomorrow, at three in the afternoon.'

The next day, precisely at three in the afternoon, as planned, two 'hydrogen' bombs were fastened together. The gang kept them beneath the towering jackfruit tree, covered them with dry leaves, and awaited the animals' return from their hunt. Moments later, groups of monkeys approached the jackfruit tree. They leapt onto the tree and started feasting on the ripe jackfruits, throwing away half-eaten fruits and destroying the leaves and the tender branches, swinging from one end of the tree to another. The gang waited for them to finish their party. Following the meal, the animals then settled down for a nap. It was all quiet.

Rocky was given the honour of igniting the bomb, which

he did. As soon as he lit the bomb, the gang ran near the mango tree, and Rocky dashed towards his mates.

The bomb started with a sparkle, a soft clattering sound followed by a deafening explosion that shattered the glass windows of many nearby blocks. The monkeys, blissfully asleep on the jackfruit tree, went into a frenzied free-fall from the tree as they dropped to the ground as though pulled down by gravity, terrorised and clueless about what was happening around them. They were so terrified that the hair on their body stood straight on end as if they were porcupines. The animals scattered in every direction, a flurry of fur and frenzy with loud shrieks amidst the rustling leaves and chirping birds.

That was the last day of the monkey menace in that Chukchuk Nagar neighbourhood.

Every alleyway of the Chukchuk Nagar would be full of kids supervised by their parents while they lighted the crackers.

The laughter and joy of the people create memories that they will reminiscence throughout their lives.

On the day of Diwali, Mona and Mihir finished arranging the diyas with their mother while their father kept himself occupied arranging the crackers. Chandan was finishing putting up twinkly lights and occasionally checking with Mona for updates while waiting for the rest of the gang to arrive.

The usual plan was to enjoy part of the celebrations in their homes, then head towards the Capital Hall to continue as a part of the bigger group.

'Look, here they come,' pointed Mihir, jumping up and

down as he knew now was the time.

The gang arrived, waving at Mona, Mihir, and Chandan.

The excitement was in full swing as the kids kept bursting the firecrackers one after the other. Every alleyway of the Chukchuk Nagar would be full of kids gathered with crackers.

It was just the beginning of the crazy night. The adventures continued as they burnt crackers one by one.

As Bholanath took the twinkler and was about to set the Anar, or the flowerpot, on fire, there was an explosion. There were a few seconds of blackout and silence after that loud, unexpected noise as Bholanath screamed. Everybody ran towards him to check. The expression on his face was one like he had seen a ghost. 'I am fine, I am fine,' he cried, trying to act brave. The burn on his right hand was nothing a cream for minor burns couldn't fix. Bholanath, with his history, experience, and expertise in cooking, managed the burn quite well, as he had faced similar minor burns; only the explosion had alarmed him and caught him off guard. Mona ran inside to get the cream, handed the tube to her father, and he applied the cream gently on Bholanath's arm.

Almost getting over the tension of Bholanath, everyone got busy bursting cracker after cracker.

However, the ordeal didn't end.

Daksh, in the meantime, adjusted the large glass bottle to light the rocket. As he set the tail on fire, the bottle toppled. The blazing rocket on fire went spiral and spurted its way whistling... fizzing..., and swished its way to Mrs Nupur Chatterjee's bedroom window. A sharp scream followed, and everyone ran towards the house to check. The rocket had set Mrs Chatterjee's bedroom curtain on fire. 'You all noisy, naughty kids. Look now what you all did.' There followed an array of curses in Bengali, and Mr Chatterjee ran for damage control. Buckets of water were grabbed from every corner and unleashed upon the fiery curtain. As the flames retreated, there was a collective sigh of relief.

The craziness of the events made the festival more and more memorable.

After an hour or so of continuous fireworks, the atmosphere was thick as pea soup with smoke, and the delightful smell of freshly pulled crackers filled the air.

The little gang had to join the bigger group in the Capital Hall, where almost all of Chukchuk Nagar gathered for a grander display of fireworks.

They left for the Capital Hall with their parents. After another hour of lighting firecrackers, the gang decided to go to the nearby temple. It was around eleven at night. The parents had already started leaving for the temple just a few metres from the Capital Hall.

Chandan suggested, 'Let's go to the corner and finish the remaining crackers before entering the temple.'

The gang agreed.

As they made their way to the corner of the street, which was quite dark and silent, they were startled when they saw an unknown lady performing some prayers and some awkward ritual on the road's junction. There was an idol of a God smeared with red *sindoor* (vermilion) and a cut lemon with flowers around it.

'She is performing black magic,' Mona whispered to the

gang. 'I had seen these on TV, and they're very dangerous.'

'Just wait and watch,' Chaitanya signalled them. Chaitanya and Rocky went quietly behind the lady and lit an 'atom' bomb at a safe distance.

A huge Boooom!!! A thunderous roar and a burst of bright light shook the air with its explosive force. The sound seemed to echo on the empty streets. Dogs barked, and the streetlights flickered by its impact. The idol, along with the lemon and flowers, turned into fragments scattered in all directions due to the impact of the blast.

The lady was completely startled. When she regained her composure, she looked around at the gang of kids and cursed them in her gibberish language.

She quickly gathered and left the place, taken aback and dishevelled.

The gang quietly entered the temple, where the prayers had started on one side. They stayed there for a while and then returned to the Capital Hall. Diwali was a night-long program. As the rituals went into the night, the ladies started preparing for the puja; there were musical performances followed by movie screenings on a makeshift screen. The men sat on one side of the building and engaged in informal card games. It continued till the early hours of the morning.

The early morning sky dazzled with fireworks as the gang returned home after spending a sleepless night at Capital Hall. Even with their sleepy eyes and tired limbs, they could feel the triumphant spirit of celebration, the victory of light over darkness, and the spirit of joy and unity across homes and their neighbourhood.

Chandan:

A month before Diwali, the boys visited Aiyaganj, which was around twelve kilometres away from our house. We used to cycle to Aiyaganj, Anshul, Bhola, Chaitanya, Chakra, Daksh, Rocky, and me.

At Aiyaganj, the crackers were sold at a discounted rate in the wholesale market. They were very cheap. A green thread hydrogen bomb, which costs eight rupees per piece in the Cooperative store, would cost only two rupees in the Aiyaganj market. After buying the crackers, we would keep them in a bag on our back carrier and visit the Prakash Kulfi shop at Aminabad. After indulging in the kulfi, we would return home.

Then we got busy cleaning the house. All junk had to be thrown out, as Maa said goddess Lakshmi visits only when the house is clean. I could never understand some parts of Hindu philosophy. Maa says that renunciation of all materialistic desires leads to moksha, which represents liberation and eternal bliss. At the same time, she wants the Goddess Lakshmi to shower us with wealth and prosperity. Why does one need wealth if they have to renounce it ultimately? I need to get more clarity on this.

After cleaning, it's shopping—new clothes, sweets, diyas, and decorations. We used to visit the Alambagh market on Dhanteras and buy silver coins and a few utensils. But the real magic starts when we burst those crackers. The girls quickly covered their ears with their fingers whenever we tried to burst a big one, the hydrogen or the atom bomb.

I have never seen such terrified monkeys. The hair on their body just stood straight after the blast. Real funny. Diksha and Lavanya were not able to control their laughter.

Bholanath panicked after the burn, and Chatterjee Aunty almost had a heart attack after Daksh's rocket entered her room. Daksh ran away and hid himself in the backyard of Dr Ramulu's house. The neighbourhood joined in and extinguished the fire with buckets of water. Daksh's escapade had a repercussion. Chatterjee Aunty complained to Daksh's mother the next day, and Daksh received a slap from his mother, not only because of his act but also because he ran and hid himself without saying sorry. The expression of regret or an apology could have somewhat diluted Chatterjee Aunty's anger.

Mona said that the lady was performing black magic. I don't believe in either black or white magic. But if the women's intention was bad, we did the right thing.

Diwali was always fun in Chukchuk Nagar. But the monkeys made it funnier that year.

Mona:

It's mid-November, Diwali is over, and all this year's festivities are already ending. I am now looking forward to Christmas. Chandu is planning to visit the Alambagh church this year. I think the rest of us will accompany him.

Nevertheless, I am so fond of Diwali, for the lights and crackers. We had many adventures this year, but I am glad all ended well.

These traditions and cultures keep our history alive.

Everybody feels so much alive, and it seems the brightness of their faces outshines the light of the diyas. Chandu gave Lavanya and me some extra crackers.

These days imprint our hearts, and like gravity, they always pull us to our roots forever.

To Chukchuk Nagar, to where we will always belong.

32

A Brief Life

Rudransh Chaturvedi was a genius. He was a prodigy. He was immensely blessed with intellect and wisdom. However, the initial indications of his sharp mind emerged when he was about ten years old.

He had not completed his homework.

'Where is your homework?' his teacher asked.

Rudransh started to weep.

'What happened?' the teacher asked again, slightly shaken.

'My grandmother is not well.'

The teacher consoled him and further enquired about the situation. He didn't know that Rudransh's grandmother had died years ago.

A couple of days later, he faced the same question.

'My grandmother is serious.' was the response this time.

A week later, the question remained unchanged, though the response varied. This time, he said, his grandmother was admitted to the hospital, and then a week later, she died. That, according to him, was the reason for not completing his homework.

The teacher scrawled a message.

'Have your father sign it,' he yelled fiercely.

The next day, the teacher enquired about the signature.

'My father signed it, but it seems to have gone missing. I placed it in my bag, and now I don't see it here,' he responded, his eyes on the floor, avoiding his teacher's gaze.

The teacher was furious.

'I want to visit your place now. I want to meet your father. You sit at the back of my scooter. Where do you live?'

'Chukchuk Nagar.' Rudransh could hardly draw the words out of his mouth.

Sitting on the scooter, Rudransh didn't know what to do. The fear of his teacher discovering his lies loomed over him, and he knew that exposure could lead to expulsion from the school. His mind raced.

The teacher rode on and then, reaching Alambagh, which was around a mile away from his house, stopped the vehicle.

'Where is your house?' the teacher asked, turning around.

Rudransh thought quickly about how to respond, knowing that the teacher was a mile away and nowhere near his house.

'I don't know.' Rudransh responded hesitantly.

'What do you mean? You don't know how to get to your own home?' the teacher was now furious. They had already travelled more than ten kilometres from the school. And now the child doesn't know where his home is.

'Sir, I am only ten years old and take the bus to school every day. I have never travelled alone, and I don't know the way.' Rudransh responded with a straight face.

The teacher banged his head in frustration. He escorted Rudransh back to the school, and the boy took the bus home.

And with his wit, he narrowly escaped severe punishment that day.

That was Rudransh Chaturvedi. Clever, intelligent, and witty.

Music was his passion. He enjoyed the stage. The stage was his life, his joy. From the very beginning, and even as a kid, he understood tunes and melodies. He had an innate talent for any art form. Nobody knew how he had learnt to play the tabla, the guitar, and various other musical instruments. He knew everything from arranging intricate dance routines, dramatics with light and sound, or even the nuances of setting up the stage. It was impossible to ignore Rudransh's magnetic presence behind the scenes.

He established the 'Jharna' troupe, a dance drama ensemble that brought classical dance and drama to life via dramatic storytelling using mythological and folkloric tales. Men, women, and children who lived in Chukchuk Nagar joined the 'Jharna' group and eagerly participated in various cultural events. It was all Rudransh's show. He directed, choreographed, and attended to every element of the performance over the long rehearsal sessions, from the details of the dancing moves to the intricacies of the facial expressions to procuring the city's best sound system. The 'Jharna' group was like a revolution on the stage of classical dance and drama in innovation and advanced choreography.

Rudransh had a keen eye for details. He created vibrant sets, exquisite costumes, and visually appealing and fascinating situations ranging from social issues to historical events to personal stories. The 'Jharna' troupe performed live on Vividh Bharti to attract a larger listenership to the well-known radio programme and some TV shows.

Even without any formal training in creative arts, Rudransh rose to prominence as the undisputed rock star of Chukchuk

Nagar in a matter of years.

Chandan had joined the 'Jharna' group with Mona, Lavanya, and Bholanath, though Chandan could never understand why Bholanath wanted to be a part of the group. Bholanath had no taste or interest in any form of art and could not even render a poem properly. Taking part in extracurricular activities was out of the question, but he still went to join the 'Jharna' group. They went to Rudransh's home one evening.

'Hi, Rudransh bhaiya. We want to join the 'Jharna' group,' Chandan inquired as Rudransh sipped tea sitting on the sofa at his home.

'Why?' Rudransh questioned while gazing intently into Chandan's eyes.

'Your group will give us a good platform to participate in the cultural programmes in Chukchuk Nagar.' Chandan responded.

'Who are they?' Rudransh asked, pointing towards the rest.

Chandan introduced Mona, Lavanya, and Bholanath.

Rudransh kept the teacup on a side table and looked straight at Chandan.

'Listen to me carefully. I don't know who has sent you here. But I want to tell you that I have little patience for half-hearted actions. My group entertains people, but entertainment itself is serious business. Do you understand?'

All nodded.

'You may have the talent, but it means nothing without discipline. Do you understand?'

Nods again.

'Are you prepared to wholly devote yourself?'

'Yes.' They all responded in unison.

'Good. In our troupe, there is no place for mediocrity. Working with me is not easy. You will sweat, you will ache, and you will doubt yourself. I don't care about mere effort. Excellence is the only standard in the 'Jharna' troupe. I will be merciless; I am a tough taskmaster and demand your absolute commitment and focus. Do you understand?'

'Yes, bhaiya.'

'Then let's not waste time. Go home and come to the rehearsals every evening. Be at the auditorium sharp at 6 pm.'

The children did as they were told. For months, they rehearsed, sweating and occasionally crying, trying to perfect their craft under Rudransh's strict vigil.

Their first show created magic on stage. Even Bholanath learned the art of rendition and a bit of classical dance. Chandan participated in the drama, Mona was part of the dance troop, and Lavanya played the violin.

A few years later, Rudransh fell ill. After many tests and running around hospitals, he was diagnosed with a brain tumour. It was earth-shattering for him and his family. But even during his illness, he never gave up. He continued to work with the 'Jharna' members, organising shows all over the city. He continued to work towards his creativity even in his dying days, providing the 'Jharna' troupe with the right guidance, support, and advice.

His glorious life ended at the age of 28. He was too young to die but left a lasting legacy of inventiveness and creativity in Chukchuk Nagar. Rudransh continued to live in the hearts of the residents of Chukchuk Nagar through the incredible performances of the 'Jharna' group even after his death.

Rudransh was a truly remarkable, creative personality. He was undoubtedly a genius, a maestro who could have contributed so much to art had he lived longer. He will stay on in the hearts and souls of those who had the privilege to work with him or watch his performances.

Chandan:

I was a member of the 'Jharna' group. Chatterjee Aunty asked me to join after speaking to my mother. Mona joined, too, followed by Lavanya and Bholanath. Aparna, Aurobindo's neighbour, was also a member.

Rudransh bhaiya was a creative genius. I knew that the first time I saw him. He was a couple of years older than me and very strict. He knew exactly what he wanted from his performers, the shades of the stage setting, and the importance of various lighting and shadows on stage. His profound understanding of melody, music, and rhythm allowed him to create stories that captivated the audience. He was a master storyteller.

He was also a master technician. His selection of music, costumes, and stage arrangement was thoughtfully chosen and organised to enhance the storytelling experience. The 'Jharna' troupe invited the audience on a beautiful journey, and the performances were celebrated with all their splendour.

I was privileged to work with Rudransh bhaiya and witness his artistry on stage. He created unforgettable artistic experiences not only for the performers but also for the audience.

I wish he had lived a little longer. Because I know even in that 'little', he would have illuminated the path for those who dared dream big.

Mona:

Rudransh bhaiya was so strict. But he was always loving towards me. He would tell me often to work harder on my dance moves. I never saw him being satisfied. He would spend hours and hours on the stage, sometimes sitting on a chair deep in his thoughts. He knew the stage like the back of his hand. He performed a miracle by getting the desired performance out of Bholanath. Can you believe it? Bholanath was rendering a difficult Tagore poem on stage! That was the skill of Rudransh bhaiya. He was blunt and outspoken, but inside, he was a compassionate young man who deeply cared for his artists.

We will all miss him for the rest of our lives.

33

Personality Panorama

There were a few characters in Chukchuk Nagar that deserve mention.

Manbir Chawla was a brilliant student who studied at Christian College. He was two years older than Chandan and lived in a different neighbourhood.

Manbir suffered from a complex. Superiority complex. As he excelled in academics, his family and the neighbourhood garnered high expectations from him. Manbir was delighted in the admiration showered upon him by all in the colony who knew him, imagining a future where he would achieve greatness. Manbir didn't interact with the 'mediocre' boys and girls as he thought it was below his dignity to network with them, as he was far superior to them intellectually. His entire family suffered from a sense of superiority and arrogance, leading them to distance themselves from those they felt were beneath their social or intellectual status. They were arrogant and egotistical from head to toe.

Getting their children into engineering, medicine, or chartered accountancy was a cherished dream of all the residents of Chukchuk Nagar in those days. And when Manbir came out with flying colours on his intermediate board examination, everyone thought he would get admission to a prestigious engineering college.

But that didn't happen. He tried once, twice, thrice but

continued to struggle to clear the entrance examination. This failure was an embarrassment for him as well as his family. The stakes were high. The expectations were higher. However, after repeated attempts, he could clear the examination. Though somehow, he managed to be an engineer, his life didn't quite meet the soaring expectations that he had set for himself. Though he attained the title of an engineer, there was always a sense of unfulfillment and dissatisfaction. Even though he was disillusioned with life, he continued to boast about himself or his achievements, which were lies or half-truths. The pretension of being successful and happy became a shield against unmet expectations. His whole life was spent thinking about how others felt about him. He was never honest with or about himself.

Manbir slowly vanished into the shadows of his arrogance, a forgotten figure who no longer commanded attention or admiration.

His younger sister met with a similar fate. The family's fixation on status was evident when they looked far and wide for their daughter to marry into wealth and fame. Her father wanted the most extravagant wedding for his daughter.

'I want my daughter to be married to the richest and the most eligible bachelor in the country, which the residents of Chukchuk Nagar have never witnessed before.'

But that didn't happen either. The family's towering expectations were shattered when most marriage proposals were rejected. The daughter finally had to marry a humble clerk after a lot of delays.

That was the story of the Chawla family—a tale of arrogance, superficiality, and false illusions.

Then there was Dhanraj Singh. Dhanraj was a rowdy and aggressive young man who used to pick fights now and then without rhyme or reason. His appearance was unkempt, with a rugged beard and brown-stained teeth duc to habitual chewing *paan masala.*

Dinesh Tripathi, Chandan's classmate who lived on the other side of Chukchuk Nagar, had gone to the Polyclinic to buy some medicines. There was a long queue, and everyone waited patiently for their turn. Suddenly, Dhanraj appeared and barged into the queue, shoving those in his path aside. With his loud and vulgar language, he challenged anyone who dared to oppose him.

Dinesh stepped out of the queue to oppose the disruption.

'What's wrong with you? Why are you disrupting the line?' Dinesh asked Dhanraj.

Dhanraj glared menacingly at Dinesh, abused him, and clenched his fist, ready for a fight. The men and women in the queue exchanged uneasy glances, unsure how to defuse the tension. With a swift and brutal attack, Dhanraj kicked Dinesh hard on his stomach. Dinesh wriggled with pain as he fell on the floor but got up and retaliated with a swift blow to Dhanraj's face. As Dhanraj again charged towards Dinesh, Dr Chakraborty intervened with a few security men. Dhanraj spewed a barrage of abuses at Dinesh and stormed out of the Polyclinic.

But after many years, the tables turned when Dhanraj found himself as a watchman at a bank, where Dinesh was the branch manager. Each time Dinesh emerged from his office or entered, Dhanraj stood up to offer a salute.

Dhanraj was forced to suffer the consequences of his past actions, which reminded him of the unpredictability of fate and the importance of good karma.

Vikram Joshi was a quiet kid but extremely mischievous. Though he was underestimated by those who didn't know him well due to his reserved nature, his unpredictable actions shocked people, keeping all around him on their toes.

He used to travel to his school, far from Chukchuk Nagar, on a green-coloured minibus that picked up and dropped students from the colony to their schools and colleges twice a day. The bus would pick up students at around seven in the morning, drop them off at their respective schools, return, and then ferry the college-going students on the next trip around nine in the morning. The students, both boys and girls, chitchatted their way on the bus while going and returning from their school or college. On their way, they used to gossip about who was dating whom in the colony, have furious debates on something silly, such as whether eating apples was better than pomegranates, and pick up occasional fights.

Vikram quietly occupied the last window seat, his preferred spot. He never spoke to anyone except for occasional smiles, which were rare. He was always silent, looking out of the bus window. No one could have ever thought a dangerous idea was brewing in his mind beneath that calm exterior.

One day, he reached the bus stand a few minutes earlier than the rest. The empty bus awaited the students' arrival, who would come at any moment.

'You came early today?' the driver asked.

'Yes,' was Vikram's curt response.

He entered the bus, pulled out a vial from his school bag, opened it, and sprinkled a greenish powder on every seat except his own. He then closed the empty vial, kept it back in his bag, and sat on his spot, looking innocently out of the window.

The students started to arrive one by one and took their seats. At the exact time of departure, the driver started the vehicle.

But chaos ensued after a few minutes while the students chatted and laughed. They began furiously scratching their heads, faces, hands, and legs. Arms flailed, and legs kicked as they started rubbing all over their bodies. Their cheeks puffed up in minutes like a red balloon. The bus turned into a circus as the itch spread like wildfire. Vikram observed the spectacle with a calm and innocent expression and smiled.

But then someone saw that he was the only one not itching. The student snatched his bag, opened it, and saw the vial.

'He is the one. See, see, this is the itching powder.' The boy shouted, scratching his back and displaying the empty vial to everyone. 'He is the only one not affected. It must be him.'

After a few slaps, Vikram confessed. The bus was stopped midway, and Vikram was dragged out and beaten black and blue so much that his face puffed up like a balloon, like his fellow students—albeit for an entirely different reason. That was the last time anyone saw Vikram on the green bus.

Another episode unfolded in the same green minibus. Mohan Kalra had a crush on a girl who studied at Loreto Convent. They studied together in St William's, and after their tenth grade, he joined another school for his intermediate.

They used to travel on the bus together. Whenever he got the opportunity, he sat beside his crush. The girl used to get off the bus before him.

But then he thought about an idea. He spoke to the driver.

'I will give you ten rupees every month if you promise to slam on the brakes suddenly. Before I board the bus, I will let you know the exact location where you need to crash the brakes. The location must change every day.'

'But why?' perplexed the driver inquired.

'None of your business. You need to pull the brake. I am paying you for that.'

Every day, the driver abruptly applied the brakes at the spot decided by Mohan. Mohan toppled over onto his crush, which was his sole opportunity to make physical contact with her.

'Are you okay?' she would inquire with genuine concern.

'I am fine as long as you are with me,' he would flirt back.

His plan was successful. Every day, he would tumble into her and relish the proximity.

But then, one day, the girl didn't board the bus. It continued for a few more days, leaving Mohan anxious. Unable to cope with her absence, Mohan asked a fellow student. 'Where is she?'

'You don't know? Her father got transferred to Delhi.'

Mohan was devastated. That was the end of his joy ride.

And then there was Ashok Dhuma, a bank watchman in Chukchuk Nagar. He would have been in his early twenties, and the job was temporary and contractual. He used to stand all day outside the bank in the sweltering heat of the summers, the relentless downpours of the monsoon season, and grappling with the biting cold of Lucknow in the winters. He greeted customers with a warm smile as they entered or exited the bank. Chandan often found him engrossed in a book during lunch and tea breaks whenever he visited the bank.

For most, Ashok was invisible. He was largely ignored. No one even glanced at him. He was not important to anybody. He was just a temporary watchman. Chandan was the only one who spoke to him and occasionally shared jokes and laughter.

But then, one day, Chandan saw a small crowd gathered in front of the bank, including the bank manager and other staff members. Then he saw Ashok adorned with a garland of flowers, and everyone in the crowd shook hands with him with a smile.

Chandan went inside through the main gate and asked a man exiting the bank in a hurry.

'What's this commotion about?'

'Oh! That watchman. He passed the Civil Service examination. The results were out yesterday. He is now an officer of the Indian Police Service. Poor fellow. He struggled so much. He is an orphan. But now he is an IPS officer. His hard work has paid off.'

As Chandan approached him, Ashok broke away from the crowd and embraced him tightly.

Finally, there were Pramod Dhawan and Champak Jagga, two residents of Chukchuk Nagar who worked in the same department.

Pramod lost his wife at a young age. He never remarried and, as a widower, chose to wear only white attire. His entire house was adorned with white. Carpets, curtains, bedsheets, and even the television were all white. He used to paint in his free time, and there, too, it was always in black and white, the only instance when he allowed another colour to enter his life. He was one of the earliest car owners in the neighbourhood and kept his white-coloured vehicle spic and span. He maintained a meticulous appearance and cleanliness throughout his life. His love for his late wife never faded. He could never stop loving his beloved until his last day.

In contrast, Champak Jagga's wife passed away in suspicious circumstances. She had a fever and died within a day. When his wife's body was taken to the crematorium, Champak started discussing his plans for a remarriage with a close friend. Within three months of her death, Champak remarried someone from Chukchuk Nagar. It was rumoured that he was having an affair long before his wife died. The remarriage led to doubts and speculation on the circumstances surrounding his previous wife's death.

Chandan:

Different stories and different characters of Chukchuk Nagar. A goon transforms into a watchman, and a watchman ascends to the rank of a Police officer. A boy destined for greatness faltered under pride and arrogance, and his sister, who was supposed to marry rich and famous, faced her setbacks. A joy ride that ended abruptly for a teenager and a seemingly innocent boy did something unimaginable and unexpected. A man who did nothing except love his wife and the other who was suspected of killing her.

Chukchuk Nagar was a canvas of colours, with good and evil, virtue and vice, success and failure, triumph to despair, and from achievement to wasted potential. It's here that I first witnessed the intricate workings of Karma. Is it, not Karma that Champak Jagga and his new wife met with an accident a year after their marriage where his wife died, and he was left paralysed from head to toe? Is it, not Karma that a goon known for instigating conflicts had to salute the branch manager with whom he had previously clashed merely to assert his dominance? And is it not Karma where arrogance and pride lead to downfall?

For me, Chukchuk Nagar painted a vivid picture of Karma in action.

Or is it Newton's third law, 'For every action, there is an equal and opposite reaction,' always playing around?

Mona:

Chandu talks a lot about karma these days. I don't understand this karma stuff. He also gets too intense nowadays; he is not that funny anymore. I saw him meditating beneath the jackfruit tree yesterday. A dog was sitting beside him, gazing at him in awe.

I saw Ashok whenever I visited the bank with Chandu. He used to salute and smile at me as I entered the bank. If the queue were long, Chandu would come out and chitchat with him. I asked Ashok why he saluted me, and he said all girls and women need to be saluted. I am happy for Ashok. Chandu says he is a very big man now. I am so glad for him.

I knew Vikram. He was shy and reserved, never speaking

a word. How could he do such a thing? Basu Aunty shared the news of the itch powder with my mother. She came to our house in the evening. She said that her sons told her. One of them goes to college on the green bus, I think. Chandu laughed it off. He says Vikram is just a kid. Chandu is always so forgiving.

I never met Manbir or his sister. Even if I had, I would have forgotten. Chandu used to talk about him. They played football together in the Unity Club.

Dhanraj was a rowdy, noisy man. I saw him idling near the Dixit shop daily, smoking cigarettes and chewing *paan masala*. I wanted to kick him on his ugly face, but then I controlled myself. Chandu said not to go near him. He was both bad and evil.

I didn't know Pramod Dhawan or Champak Jagga, but I had heard about the accident. It's so sad!

34

Some other Characters of Chukchuk Nagar -Chandan's Perspective.

Apart from my neighbourhood, there were other neighbourhoods in Chukchuk Nagar with some interesting characters. I didn't know them well but often met them at the Cooperative store or other social functions. Though they were always a part of the colony 'news'.

Saachi Goyal studied at the City Montessori school, which was closer to my home than my school. She was a beautiful girl with always a smile on her face. The boys of the colony were after her, but Rocky told me that she had a crush on someone. However, Rocky was not sure who he was. Saachi had beautiful eyes, and Rocky kept staring at them. I told him that it's impolite to stare at someone like that. But then Rocky said he was experiencing '*nayan sukh*', which meant joy through his eyes while looking at her.

Saachi was quite close to Diksha. Their parents often visited each other's homes, as their fathers worked in the same department. From what I heard from Diksha, Saachi was a very wise, kind, and compassionate girl. Her smile brightened the darkest days.

Saachi's parents arranged her marriage. Diksha told me that she wanted to marry someone else, maybe her crush, which Rocky talked about. In those days, disobeying one's parents was out of the question, especially regarding marriage. However, I think that if she really liked someone, she should have fought for him.

She married a man older than her by over ten years. I saw her husband, but I was told by Diksha that the union was a mismatch based on her discussions with Saachi. She had that bit of regret, though Saachi remained kind and sweet irrespective of the circumstances.

I knew Aditi Mehra quite well. She was a year senior to me in school and was always an extremely ambitious girl. Her elder brother, who was very good at his studies, was her biggest rival as she always competed with him to excel and do better than him. She had differences with her parents, always accusing them of being biased towards her brother. It was not a simple sibling rivalry. It was deeper than that.

Aditi was intelligent and very clear about what she wanted from life. She had clarity on her short-term and long-term goals. She was quite calculative. Even her choice to marry was a calculated one. She knew the man was an assistant professor at a leading management institute in the country, which aligned perfectly with her aspirations to pursue her postgraduate studies in business management. She married him and admitted herself to the same college where her husband was a professor. Aditi had always wanted to be rich and famous. She achieved her goals with high grades in her postgraduate studies with more than a little help from her husband. But then, that was the whole plan. However, like Saachi, she was also kind and considerate.

Mansi Maheshwari was all about beauty and brains. However, there was a problem. She knew how to 'use' anyone and 'throw' them whenever required. In other words, she knew well how to 'use' and 'throw'.She would flirt with boys if she needed to get something done with their help. Her needs and desires were above all, and she was quite vocal about it. Her whole purpose was to benefit herself, even if that meant suffering for others. She could easily manipulate situations to her advantage and knew how to 'play' with people to get what she wanted. Mansi was difficult to understand, but once people understood her character, they stayed away from her. She decided not to marry, and she never did.

Unfortunately, Mansi didn't receive many blessings from those around her. Her parents distanced themselves, and her younger sister maintained no connections with her.

Kumkum Patra was a quiet girl. She spoke little. She studied in Kendriya Vidyalaya and suffered from low self-esteem and an inferiority complex for reasons best known to her. I was told that she was abused in her childhood, and that could be the reason. However, I am not sure about the accuracy of that information. She was extremely good at her studies, but even after she completed her doctorate in Sociology and was in the top three at the university, she felt she was not good enough for anything. There was always that fear of uncertainty, a certain disillusionment towards life. Her parents married her to a lovely man, and she was blessed with a boy and a girl, but she was not a happy soul. She was contented just being someone's wife or someone's mother. That, of course, was good as long as she was happy.

Muskaan Trivedi was also a quiet girl but just the opposite of Kumkum. She was my classmate and the most underrated.

With whatever interactions I had with her, I knew she was the epitome of wisdom and possessed a high level of self-confidence. She was full of positive energy and would always be at your side whenever you needed help. After passing out from our school, she completed her graduation and then her postgraduate studies and became a teacher in a science college teaching Botany to students. She had a strong sense of humour; though she spoke little, she would share jokes, those one-liners that would make us laugh. Rocky liked her, not that 'staring' way, but as a good friend. People who knew her at Chukchuk Nagar always praised her. Lavanya was familiar with and quite close to her as they both learned violin from a music teacher in the colony. She is now a happy mother of two kids and a happy wife. I found her husband quite funny and a witty man.

Finally, there was Adrika Raman. She was two years my senior in school. She was all in one. She excelled in academics right from school and joined the prestigious Indian Institute of Technology in Bombay after her 12th board. She was a terrific basketball player and a judo expert. She captained the school basketball team and won many awards. She was also an expert Kathak dancer and a brilliant debater. She married a senior manager in a multinational company, went scuba-diving with her husband, and climbed mountains in various parts of the world whenever they went on vacation. Together, they had travelled to fifty-four countries. As for independence and self-sufficiency, she was the vice president of one of the world's top IT companies. Her son was studying at the Massachusetts Institute of Technology.

Among the boys, Dev Pattanaik was a unique character. Dev studied at the Chukchuk Nagar Railway School and was a member of the Unity Club. I met him at the club. Initially, I didn't understand him well. For me, he was just another player. Later, I learned he had the habit of creating conflicts within his groups. He thought he was the best but was always insecure and needed validation. To me, he felt quite weird. He had fights with Chakradev, and in one instance, Chakradev picked him up and threw him on the ground. Dev didn't complain to Guruji as he knew it was his fault.

I felt that Dev had a strong desire to be the centre of attention. He was never happy when someone in the group received praise. He had a tendency to belittle the ideas of others. He would argue and intervene in situations that didn't require his involvement. I didn't mix with him much, and most of his friends moved away, tired of his habit of arguing and creating conflicts. I didn't like Dev, so I stayed away even though he tried to befriend me.

Brijesh Das was another character that deserves mention. His only job was to compare himself with others. Personally, I have a strong dislike for such people. He constantly compared himself with his peers, particularly regarding achievements, popularity, and material possessions. He measured his self-worth based on how he stacked up against his friends, which, to me, was a stupid thing to do. He also used to meddle in other people's affairs when it was not required. Though he tried to show the world he was happy, Brijesh Das suffered persistent dissatisfaction with himself and his life. I didn't enjoy his company at all.

Raghav Shukla was the most timid and spineless human I have ever seen. He always avoided situations where he had to assert himself or defend his beliefs. He always wanted to please people and had difficulty saying no or setting boundaries, fearing rejection and disapproval. I hate spineless men and women. I don't remember ever speaking to him much; only those occasional nods and smiles were enough for me.

Jatin Mahajan was my classmate and very outspoken. He spoke little, but whenever he spoke, he spoke the truth. Sometimes, the truth can make others uncomfortable. So, even though Jatin was right on most occasions, he was not liked. He would get angry whenever he saw something unfair or false, and his temper sometimes led to saying things in the heat of the moment, which he regretted later. This had happened quite a few times in the class as well. Jatin was a simple, sincere, and straightforward boy, but his honesty came across as brutal and insensitive, which caused him to lose many friends. Despite his flaws, Jatin was a gem of a person, kind at heart, and loved by many of his close friends. His presence was refreshing in a world where many people sugarcoat their words to avoid difficult conversations.

Jatin was an excellent footballer, and he, too, joined the Unity Club. He also played cricket well, and we have had some memorable partnerships. We were both quite close.

And then there was Harsh Agarwal, who was a year senior to me. He was the all-in-one as far as boys were concerned. He was handsome and sporty, and he excelled in academics, too. Like Chakradev, the girls of Chukchuk Nagar were ga-ga over him. He topped in school and college and represented his team in interstate cricket tournaments as the captain of the team. He was a natural leader, a very humble and kind guy. Every parent would want a son like Harsh. He was loved and respected by all in the colony. He graduated from the Indian Institute of Science and worked at the Bhabha Atomic Research Centre.

The diversity within Chukchuk Nagar helped me understand the importance of differences at a very young age. Where else could I have found Tamil, Malayali, Sikh, Telugu, Maharashtrian, Punjabi, Bengali, Kannada, and Rajasthani neighbours residing within 300 meters from each other? Different rituals, different festivals, different perspectives, different ways of life. These distinctions and the variety added depth to the colony's life. Different personalities and influences created a vibrant community, which had a big impact on me. I saw the best and the worst in men and women in Chukchuk Nagar. These varied experiences of people's thoughts and behaviours in my formative years shaped my identity and helped me understand the true meaning of 'Unity in Diversity'. It helped me to understand human nature, psychology, beliefs, thoughts, and habits. They played an important role in shaping my views and opinions and enriching my teenage experience along with my friends.

35

Man of Steel

Chukchuk Nagar Colony was a safe place compared to other parts of Lucknow in those days. Even though it was a conservative place, boys and girls could mix freely, albeit occasionally. However, some notorious gang members were either residents of Chukchuk Nagar or regularly visited the colony from outside. The hooligans sprawled the streets, staring at girls and making abusive passes with lustful intent. After sunset, the girls used to prefer venturing out with their male relatives rather than alone. Though extreme crimes like acid attacks were uncommon, regular blank calls at home, eve teasing, or stopping a girl midway to harass her while she was going to or coming back from school or college reminded the young girls and their families of the constant threat.

The threat extended even to a sports ground, where during an inter-zonal basketball tournament, a drunk man threw an empty bottle of whisky on the basketball court while the match was on, shattering the euphoria and excitement of the game. Another man was shot dead while he was strolling with his wife after dinner near the Chukchuk Nagar stadium when he tried to stop the goon trying to snatch his wife's necklace. The goons, who were essentially spoiled brats, frittered away their time in pursuit of girls, and the safety and security of the girls and their families seemed a distant dream.

In the face of such relentless harassment, parents were

forced to either seek transfer to some other place or hastily marry off their terrified daughters to protect them from the clutches of the hooligans. Some girls even went through psychological trauma with fear.

But then things changed. Raj Raghuvanshi, a police officer, was transferred to the local police station of Chukchuk Nagar, where he started his act right away.

Physically, he looked like a bandit with his rugged appearance and scars all over his face. He was tall with broad shoulders and a deep voice, though he rarely used his vocal cords. He had a revolver hanging on one side of his waist all the time. Even though he didn't use it often, he would pull it out during a confession. As soon as he did that, the crooks started telling the truth as the revolver in his hand and his piercing eyes penetrated the very soul of those who dared to look into his eyes.

The thugs were flipped upside down with their legs up, hanging on a rope, and beaten black and blue, so much so that they often lost consciousness. In some cases, they forgot the names of their fathers or mothers and, sometimes, their own. Such were the beatings that the crooks were bruised and battered beyond recognition. Raj Raghuvanshi was ruthless while dealing with criminals. He quickly became a terror for the crime world of terror.

One day, he sat astride on his parked motorcycle, in plain clothes, smoking a cigarette, wearing a pair of dark sunglasses in front of the Cooperative store, and talking to a shopkeeper. A few feet away from him, he saw a group of young men sitting on the boundary wall of the Polyclinic hurling verbal assaults, laughing and making peculiar sounds at a girl while she was returning home from her college, her head down trying to look the other way in an attempt to ignore the harassment. Raghuvanshi dismounted from his bike and strode towards this unruly group. The boys didn't recognise him as he was wearing plain clothes and sunglasses. He quickly approached the girl and requested her to accompany him towards the group of hooligans. The girl, initially hesitant, eventually agreed.

The men were laughing and sending vulgar signals to the girl.

'So...,' Raghuvanshi initiated the conversation with the boys, 'I don't speak much. Talking is not my forte. So please don't force me to do that.' He threw down the burning cigarette and extinguished it with a swift motion with his foot.

'One by one, each one of you will now get down from where you are sitting like a monkey, say sorry to this girl, and then bend down and lick her shoe. Now, quickly do what I just told you. I don't have the time to waste like you.'

The girl was shocked and extremely uncomfortable with the idea of someone licking her shoes.

'It's okay, Sir. I am fine. Let them go. It's fine,' she repeatedly pleaded.

'No, today they are doing this to you. Tomorrow, they will do it to someone else. This must stop.' Raghuvanshi was unmoved.

One man jumped from the wall, stood in front of Raghuvanshi, and asked,

'Who are you to meddle in our affairs?'

'Your affairs?' Raghuvanshi burst out laughing.

Raghuvanshi gave him a stealthy look from behind his sunglasses and whacked his face so hard that he almost flew to the other end of the boundary wall of the Polyclinic. The others swiftly descended from the perch, sensing danger. The next challenger received such a forceful kick to his groin that he tumbled towards his writhing companion, wriggling in pain. In less than a minute, they all bent over and licked the girl's shoe, one by one. A small crowd had gathered to witness this spectacle. Chandan was one of them.

'The next time I see you harassing a girl, you will be all dead. I promise that,' he said, lighting another cigarette. 'Now go to hell,' he roared.

The men ran in different directions without wasting a second while the girl smiled, thanked the cop, and went her way.

And then, on another day, the boys in the gang were sitting at the Chukchuk Nagar stadium, engrossed in idle chatter. Chaitanya, as usual, was smoking along with Daksh. Bholanath was eating a packet of *samosas*, which he had brought from Dixit's shop, while Chandan, Chakradev, and Rocky were practising basketball. They heard the sound of a motorcycle and then saw Raghuvanshi. He approached the boys, parked his bike, and then went up the stadium's stairs where Chaitanya and Daksh were smoking. Sensing trouble, Chandan and his friends joined them.

'Why are you smoking here?' Raghuvanshi asked.

No one answered. There was pin-drop silence.

'Why are you smoking here?' Raghuvanshi repeated.

Chakradev came to their defence.

'Where would they smoke, Sir? In front of their parents?'

Raghuvanshi turned around and stared at Chakradev.

'You are the smart one?' he asked.

'No, Sir, It's Chandan.' Bholanath spoke with his mouth full of *samosa*, pointing towards Chandan.

Raghuvanshi put his hand on Chakradev's shoulder and said,

'You are right. Smoking in front of elders is disrespectful. I agree. Smoking itself is bad for your health. But smoking here in this stadium, which is a public place, will also not be allowed. The next time I see any of you smoking here, I will break your legs. You understand?'

The boys nodded.

'Now go home and study. Try to do something in life instead of wasting time. Now go,' he shouted. The boys jumped down the stairs and raced home, with Bholanath quickly picking up the packet of *samosas* and hurrying after them, his protruding tummy bouncing as he ran.

Raj Raghuvanshi continued his duties at the Chukchuk Nagar colony for five years before he was transferred to another location. But during his tenure, normalcy returned to the colony in terms of peace and order, as the thugs quickly fled or reformed themselves.

Chandan:

Raghuvanshi Sir was terrifying. But he was never cruel. In fact, he rewarded criminals who had reformed. He motivated people to live crime-free lives. He never used to touch anyone who spoke the truth and confessed to their crimes. He was a disciplinarian whose sole objective was to bring law and order to Chukchuk Nagar. Abusing the girls, theft, and dacoity were not tolerated at all. I had been to his home a few times to collect donations for the Diwali festival, and he was so hospitable and generous. He introduced me to his wife and children and offered me sweets. He asked me about my school and studies. His children were studying in Kendriya Vidyalaya, he said. I asked him how he feels when he beats the goons. Very bad, he said. But then, despite repeated warnings, some people harbour malicious intentions. Those guys always need to be taught a lesson.

Raghuvanshi Sir was a true Policeman. Right and Straight. Chukchuk Nagar thrived under his watchful eyes.

Mona:

I had met Raghuvanshi Sir when I visited his house with Chandu. I was frightened looking at him with so many scars on his face. But he smiled at me and gave me chocolates. His wife offered me my favourite sweet, *rasmalai*. His daughter took me to her room and showed me her paintings. Though she studied in a different school, we became friends. While he was in the colony, the girls could venture out any time of the day and night. Once, I went alone to the temple at night. Nothing happened. On my way back, Raghuvanshi Sir saw me while riding his bike, asked me to sit on the back, and dropped me off at my home.

Raghuvanshi Sir was strict and a man of honour.

36

Beyond the Question

Significant global events occurred in 1988. The Soviet Union announced the withdrawal of its troops from Afghanistan, the Iran-Iraq war ended, and the World Health Organization officially declared that smallpox had been eradicated.

A significant event occurred in Chukchuk Nagar as well. The gang members passed their 12th board examination with flying colours. Mona stood second in her 10th board examination, scoring 91% marks.

To everyone's surprise, Rocky was the standout performer. He preferred the arts, as science or commerce was not his cup of tea. He joined the Vidyasagar School of Arts after his 10th and topped his examination with 88%, breaking all previous records. He chose history, geography, and Hindi as his main subjects and economics as an optional subject. Chakradev scored 68% but excelled in sports, and for the first time, Vidyasagar School of Arts won the inter-school basketball championship under his captaincy.

'How did you score so much?' A surprised Chakradev asked Rocky a day after the results were out as they all sat beneath the mango tree.

'Attitude, Aptitude and Altitude.' Rocky responded, focused on a *samosa* that Bholanath had brought.

'Altitude? What does that mean?'

'Well, if you are lucky and your examination room has seating arrangements that include platforms, with each row of benches slightly higher than the previous one, and you get to sit in the rearmost row, then it helps.'

'How?'

'Visibility, friend. Visibility. If in doubt, you can look around from the top and see many things.'

'You mean cheating?'

'No, friend. Better visibility. You can't score 88% by only cheating. Now let's change the topic.'

So, they changed the topic.

Chandan scored 99% in Mathematics, though Bholanath reclaimed the top spot in the science stream at St William's. Nayantara readily accepted the result this time, trailing Bholanath by just one mark. Daksh scored 81% and was happy with his grades.

'I don't know how I scored 99% in Maths. There were twenty questions. Ten questions were worth five marks each, and two were for each of the remaining ten. So, the total paper was 70 marks, and for 99%, I had to score 69.3 out of 70. So, 69.3/5 equals 13.86 questions; rounding up, it's 14...But then 69.3-70 is -0.7, which is...'

'Shut up, Chandu. Enough is enough. Be happy with your 99%. *Dimaag ka dahi mat bana*. (Don't complicate the situation and confuse me.)' Rocky almost screamed.

Everyone laughed, but Rocky maintained a straight face.

'Maybe you scored 100%, but the examiner cut a percent for your poor handwriting,' Daksh playfully suggested.

'Handwriting in Maths? I have never heard of such a thing

before.' Lavanya remarked.

'1% of 70 is 0.7. How can they cut 0.7?' Bholanath chipped in, munching on the *samosa*.

Rocky, whose extreme frustration was visible on his face, stood up. 'I will now leave if this nonsense continues.'

Nayantara could not control her laughter, lost her balance, and fell over Chakradev. Chakradev helped her back to her seat, but he could not control his laughter. Nayantara's laugh was infectious, and the others, including Rocky, started to laugh.

However, to make Rocky happy, they changed the topic and started to talk about the current 'affairs' in Chukchuk Nagar. Rocky, now extremely pleased, sat down and enthusiastically participated in the discussion.

At St John's, Lavanya scored 85.3%, followed by Diksha and Anshul. But Chaitanya, who scored more than 80% in his 10th board examination, managed just 49% in his 12th board. In fact, he was suspended for a week after he came to school drunk early in the morning. Only when his father pleaded with the principal could he stay and complete his board examination.

'Where is Chaitanya?' Anshul asked.

'To the *Naher* as usual,' his sister Diksha responded.

'Have you talked to him? I mean, he is sliding down fast.' Chakradev inquired, expressing his concern.

'My parents and I have given up. He is such a dolt. He doesn't listen to us anymore,' Diksha remarked angrily. 'Chandu, could you have a word with him? He seems to listen to you, at the very least.'

'I will.' Chandan responded.

Chandan's mother came out with plates full of sweets and snacks, offering them to everyone.

'For your success.' She smiled. Bholanath, as usual, pounced on the plates.

Mihir came and joined them for a few minutes.

Chandan ruffled his hair.

'Which class are you in now, Mihir?' Rocky asked.

'5th class.'

'Your sister has scored 91%. Do you know?'

'Yes, and I will score 95.'

Everyone laughed, and Mihir dashed out to play with his friends.

For Mona's 10th board examination, the gang had a plan. She never took tuition, but the entire gang rallied to tutor her even though they had their 12th board examination to prepare for. Chandan used to teach her Mathematics from six to seven in the morning every day. In the afternoon, after she was back from school, Bholanath would come strolling over from his house with a packet of chips and teach her Physics. Nayantara took charge of Chemistry and Biology, while Lavanya covered Economics and Geography. Rocky used to come every alternate day to teach her History and Hindi, and Diksha, with her expertise, tackled English. Daksh would visit her and quiz her on science and maths.

The gang put in a lot of effort for Mona. This, coupled with her hard work and sincerity, resulted in her emerging with flying colours.

After clearing the entrance test, the gang joined Lucknow

University for their graduation, while Mona continued at St William's, pursuing the science stream for her 12th boards.

Chandan:

To be honest, I was never a dreamer. I never thought of achieving something great. But I was sure of one thing. I would stay as close to Mathematics as I could. Mathematics gave me a certain peace and tranquillity. Whenever I was bored, I practised sums. Calculus has always been my favourite, followed by trigonometry and vectors. I was sure I would not do a job without little or no Maths—or, to put it more correctly, advanced Maths.

I chose Mathematics, Statistics, and Physics for my graduation. I was clear about selecting Mathematics as my subject for my post-graduation studies.

Mona did well, and I am happy for her. She made some silly mistakes in her Maths and Physics papers. Otherwise, she would have crossed 93%. Nevertheless, she has done well. She is more interested in Chemistry. For me, Chemistry was always the tough one, particularly Organic chemistry. Daksh and Nayantara both did very well in Chemistry.

I am worried about Chaitanya. I need to speak to him, but getting hold of him is challenging. He is always busy with his Nakshal Khera group around the *Naher*.

Yesterday was Rocky's birthday. He celebrated it twice, once at home and once beneath the mango tree. Someone gave him a history book as a gift. Rocky threw it away.

I attended the birthday parties of every gang member,

but my birthday was never celebrated, which saddened me. Mona's birthday was always about laughter, cheer, balloons, toys, and two cakes, as Mihir also wanted to cut one along with his sister.

Mona:

91% and Chandu still shouted at me because of my mistakes in the Maths and Physics papers. I said sorry a thousand times. But he wouldn't listen. He was grumbling all day long. Finally, Bholanath and Lavanya came to my rescue. Chakradev asked him to shut up; enough is enough. So, he kept quiet for a few minutes and again started his lectures. Mihir, my younger brother who follows Chandu in whatever he does, also lectured me.

I have chosen Maths and Science for my 12th boards. Chandu is such an amazing teacher. I wish I had a teacher like him in my school. Bholanath teaches Physics very well, though he is busy eating his chips half the time.

37

From Cradle to Cake

It was a hot summer afternoon, and after returning from college and completing lunch, Chandan was preparing for a siesta when his mother entered the room.

'Chandu.'

'Yes, Maa.'

'Mona, Mihir, and their father are going sightseeing tomorrow as it's a Sunday. Malti was enquiring if you would like to join them.'

'Yes.' Chandan replied enthusiastically.

'Okay, I will inform her. You need to be ready by ten in the morning.'

'Where are they planning to go?' Chandan asked, not able to control his excitement.

'She said it's the Bada Imambara, the Zoo, and some shopping in Hazratganj,' his mother's voice trailed off as she left the room.

Chandan met Mona in the evening and shared the news,

'I already know that you are coming with us,' she chuckled.

The following day, Jitendra Mishra, his children, and Chandan set out for a sightseeing tour of Lucknow. They hired two cycle rickshaws: Mihir and his father occupied one, while Mona and Chandan rode the other.

They reached Alambagh, got down, and hired an auto rickshaw for the full day.

'Sir, where do you want to go?' The driver asked.

'The Bada Imambara, Zoo, and then a bit of shopping at Hazratganj.' Jitendra Mishra responded.

'Okay, Sir.'

They reached Charbagh in fifteen minutes, and due to the heavy traffic, even though it was a Sunday, it took another forty minutes to get to the Bada Imambara. Mihir was very excited, as were Mona and Chandan. They were impressed to see this striking building of an unprecedented scale like that of the Bada Imambara. Mona's father hired a guide.

'What is your name?' he asked the guide.

'My name is Iqbal, janaab. I have been a guide for the past fifteen years.'

They stood in front of the Bada Imambara, awestruck by its architecture.

Iqbal turned towards the visitors. Mihir jumped up and down the stairs while Chandan and Mona listened intently to the guide's explanations.

'Janaab, the province of Awadh, was struck by a famine, and people had nothing to eat,' Iqbal spoke. 'To generate employment during those hard times, the Nawab ordered a grand prayer hall to be built. Citizens worked all day to bring up the building, but whatever was built was brought down at night. It was the Nawab's way of ensuring that no one was out of work until the famine lasted. This is how the Bada Imambara was built.'

Iqbal then took them to the most fascinating part of the building – the Bhool Bhulaiya.

'Janaab, *diwaron ke bhi kaan hote hai*. Even the walls have ears.' Iqbal asked them to go to one end of the balcony, and he went to the other. He then whispered, 'How are you, Janaab?' The children were thrilled to hear the whisper from such a long distance. Standing at one end more than 25 meters from where the visitors stood, he tore a piece of paper and lighted a matchstick. Both sounds were audible.

Apart from carrying sound through its walls, there was a maze of intricately interwoven corridors, and it was impossible to find the way out without the help of a guide. The guide also showed them a few tunnels built by the Nawab that led to Delhi, Faizabad, and some other cities. The tunnels had now been sealed. Iqbal then took them to the terrace. They could see the Asafi Mosque with minarets and curvaceous domes from there.

After more than a couple of hours, sensing that Mihir was no longer enjoying the historical exploration, Jitendra Mishra handed Iqbal some money, which was more than he expected. 'You keep the change,' he said to the beaming guide and hurriedly left the place with the children trailing behind him.

'Papa, it's very hot. I want an ice cream,' Mihir demanded. That demand was fulfilled. Everyone, including the auto driver, indulged in ice cream before leaving the place. The ice cream helped to cool down his son a bit. The summer heat was taking a toll on each one of them.

'Uncle, why did you plan sightseeing in such hot weather?' Chandan asked.

Mona's father didn't respond but only smiled. Mona giggled while Mihir started to laugh. Chandan was confused. He couldn't understand why the Mishra family, including

Mona, was behaving in a peculiar way, smiling and laughing at him when he had asked a simple question.

From Bada Imambara, they went to see the Chota Imambara, Rumi Darwaza, Tille Wali Masjid, and the Clock Tower, symbols of portraits of Nawabi splendour – decaying yet beautiful. Mona's father looked at his watch. It was already two in the afternoon.

'Oh, we need to have lunch. It's already two.'

They rode to Hazratganj and indulged in a sumptuous lunch at Moti Mahal. They ordered *matar paneer, paratha, daal makhani, haryali kabab*, and *pulao*. For dessert, they ordered *rasmalai* and two rounds of ice cream.

'I am full, uncle.' Chandan said, pointing at his stomach.

'Me too.' Mona remarked, nodding in agreement.

Jitendra Mishra smiled.

'Then what are you planning to do? Do you want to go to the zoo?'

Chandan and Mona exchanged glances.

'Not really.' Mona replied. 'It's too hot outside.'

'Yes, uncle. It's already four. Let's go home.' Chandan suggested.

Mona's father ruffled his hair and said, 'Okay, as you wish.'

'What about me? You didn't ask me.' Mihir complained.

'Okay, so what do you suggest?' his father asked.

'Let's go home.'

And they all laughed.

They came out of the restaurant and sat in the autorickshaw.

'Arif Sports.' Mona's father instructed the driver.

Chandan was again confused. He glanced at Mona and

received a smile and a wink. Mihir did the same and again laughed.

'Uncle, why are we going to a sports shop?'

'I will tell you once we reach there.'

Once they reached the sports shop, Jitendra Mishra requested a cricket bat, ball, and a set of gloves and pads.

'Give this a try,' he instructed, handing the bat to Chandan.

Chandan was now perplexed.

'But, why, uncle? I don't need a bat.'

'You do as I say,' Jitendra Mishra replied.

Reluctantly, Chandan examined a few bats and then selected one. 'This one feels right, uncle.'

The bat, ball, gloves, and pad were packed. Mona's father settled the bill and left the shop with the children. He asked the driver to keep the purchase on the back of the autorickshaw.

On their way back, no one spoke. They were all tired. Mihir fell asleep on his father's lap while Mona dozed off, resting her head on Chandan's shoulder. Once they reached Alambagh, Mona's father requested the driver to drop them at Chukchuk Nagar.

'For Chukchuk Nagar, you must pay me twenty rupees extra.'

'Okay.'

Chandan had dozed off and woke up with a jolt as the autorickshaw stopped in front of his block. Mona and Mihir were also roused from their sleep.

As he stepped out of the autorickshaw, he saw the crowd in front of his house, which comprised the whole neighbourhood.

Everyone was there. Daksh, Chakradev, Chaitanya,

Bholanath, Diksha, Nayantara, Anshul, Rocky, and Lavanya. All with their parents. All were smiling at him. Mrs Titli Basu, with her husband and two sons, was there. Mr Chauhan also arrived with his two dogs.

Chandan saw his garden adorned with balloons and colourful ribbons. Then he saw his Maa and Papa standing by the door smiling. Then he saw Mona's mother running up to him. Then Mona hugged him. Then Mihir embraced him tightly. Then they all started singing, 'Happy birthday to you...' Time seemed to slow down. He could hear them in bits and pieces. They all seemed to move in slow motion—a joyous slow motion of his birthday celebration.

And for the very first time in his life, he experienced the joy of timelessness.

Chandan:

My nineteenth birthday!

I had dozed off in the autorickshaw. When I opened my eyes, I saw the crowd—our own crowd, our own people. I was shocked. I was stunned.

It was all planned by my parents. Everyone in the neighbourhood knew about it except me. Even Rocky, who cannot keep anything secret, didn't share the plan with me. Going sightseeing in that scorching summer with Mona's father was also a part of the plan. They wanted me to be away while they made the arrangements to give me this surprise. Decorations, cake, sweets, snacks and all. I had some doubts when I received the cricket kit. Mona and Mihir were smiling all the way. Something was amiss, but I couldn't pinpoint it.

When I walked inside the house, I saw the colourful streamers hanging from every corner dancing gently in the breeze from the open windows. Balloons adorned the walls, and a table in the centre of the room was laden with sweets, snacks, and a huge cake topped with flickering candles. Bholanath was the first to rush towards the table; his eyes focused on the cake and the sweets. Everyone was laughing and smiling and hugging me. Even Chauhan Uncle's dogs, I thought, were chuckling. My friends surrounded me, cheering and clapping. There were lots of gifts wrapped in colourful glossy papers and shiny ribbons.

And then I cut the cake.

That day, I was being celebrated. It was overwhelming.

After they left, I asked my mother, 'Why? Why was my birthday never celebrated before?' She said the family astrologer told her not to before I was nineteen. He had said the same thing for Phuchki. My parents didn't listen to him then.

Maa and I both wept. I am not sure why. Maybe we thought about Phuchki, maybe because it was my first birthday celebration, or perhaps because I was safe and alive. Maybe all. Sadness, joy, jubilation all.

I don't believe in astrology. But I will follow what the family astrologer says. Maa said he was dead, and his son had taken over the reign. So, I will follow the advice of his son only for birthdays. Nothing else.

Mona:

I could see the shock in Chandu's eyes when he saw

everyone in front of his house. And the decorations around. He was looking so funny. He mumbled something which I didn't understand. Basu Aunty and my mother hugged him straightaway as he stepped out of the vehicle. Rocky came from behind and jumped over him. The girls giggled, looking at his face. Amusing and comical. I had never seen Chandu like that before.

The autorickshaw driver was also invited. He was hesitant at first, but then he devoured the cake and the snacks. When my father tried to give him the money, he took only a hundred rupees instead of three hundred.

Chandu was very happy that day. He was excited, and his smile stretched from ear to ear. Usually, he is so calm and composed, but that day, he laughed and laughed, filling the air like music. We were all so happy for him. After his parents, he offered Lavanya a slice of cake, the first among his friends to receive the offering. We all teased him and laughed, and Chandu blushed the whole time.

Bholanath ate half of the cake and received a rebuke from his mother. Silly boy!

The next evening, I sat with Chandu beneath the mango tree—only the two of us. He told me why his birthday was never celebrated before. I saw tears in his eyes. But then he saw Rocky coming, wiped his tears, and smiled at him. Then, one by one, the others came. Lavanya sat next to Chandu and whispered something in his ear. He blushed and then smiled.

38

The Mandal Momentum

1990 was the year of rebellion.

The Mandal Commission, headed by BP Mandal, was formed in 1979 to identify socially and educationally backward classes of citizens in India. The Commission submitted its report in 1980. The findings of the Commission revealed that more than half of India's population comprised of Other Backward Classes or OBCs, recommending 27% reservation for OBCs in government employment and higher education. The findings were left untouched by almost all the political leaders as they didn't want to disrupt the country's political narrative.

However, a decade later, in 1990, Prime Minister VP Singh, who led the coalition National Front government after defeating his arch-rival Rajiv Gandhi and his Congress Party, implemented the recommendations of the Mandal Commission. This decision sparked widespread, intense debates and student unrest across the country. The students, mostly from upper-caste communities, feared that implementing the Commission's report would limit their opportunities for education and government jobs. They also argued that it would dilute the quality of education and be a disadvantage to those who were from the general category. They protested with marches and hunger strikes.

Some resorted to self-immolation. Violent clashes ensued between the protesters and the police. Public property was damaged. Government buildings and vehicles were burned. Students from medical, engineering, and other colleges participated in the protests. Various student organisations, political parties, social groups, and even those who were no longer students but seeking jobs in the public sector joined hands to oppose the Mandal Commission's report and its implementation.

The Commission's recommendations did not leave Chukchuk Nagar unimpacted. One day, the gang sat under the mango tree and pondered their next steps.

'We need to do something about it. VP Singh has made a huge mistake. Why do we need to suffer just because we are not from the backward class?' Chakradev was the first to voice his opinion.

Chandan stood up and addressed the gang.

'Friends, we have to do something. Students are dying every day. We need to protest. The Prime Minister must go. He has made the lives of students and job seekers miserable. Yesterday, the students at the medical college sat with a begging bowl. It may be symbolic now, but that's going to happen soon. We all will have to beg without an education or job if the Prime Minister doesn't take back his decision.'

They were all silent for a few minutes. Then, Nayantara spoke.

'Let's do something about it. Let's be a part of this movement.'

'What about our parents? They will never agree to our participation.' Diksha remarked.

'There is no need to tell them. I mean, we will not inform them about what we are going to do,' Daksh intervened.

Chandan spoke again.

'Listen to me carefully. We will participate in the protests but will not do anything risky. That's not the purpose. As a first step, let us try to raise funds. Many in the colony will donate. I am sure about that. No one wants their children to suffer due to a lack of opportunities. 27% reservation for a separate group is not a small thing. It's the epitome of bias.'

He paused and then continued,

'The contributions will fund the protest activities. We cannot protest with an empty stomach. We will go house to house and request donations. The money collected will be entirely shared with the protesting groups. I know two student groups, and they will be interested. Secondly, we need to create posters. Rocky and Chakradev will take care of that. Rocky, your uncle runs a printing press, right? Talk to him. We will also require small pamphlets. Third, we need to arrange food and drinks for the protesters. Bholanath will take care of that. But I need someone to take care of him. I don't want Bholanath to eat the food himself.'

Bholanath chuckled while the others smiled.

'The girls have an important role. They need to mobilise the female students. The colony is too protective of its girls. They need to be out of their homes and fight now. Enough of timidity.'

They discussed for almost two hours and then dispersed.

They carried on their activities as per the plan. They went house to house to seek donations. The residents of Chukchuk Nagar contributed generously. Posters and pamphlets were made with slogans like, 'I voted VP. I made a mistake'. Or 'I voted VP. I am sorry'. There were some that were more explicit, such as 'Say no to Reservation' or 'Fight for Merit'. Some posters employed humour, using caricatures of VP Singh and the other leaders of his party, as well as satirical slogans to mock the decision. The gang participated in the protest through silent marches from Alambagh to Hazratganj, ending in Begum Hazrat Mahal Park, where they walked for more than ten miles and listened to speeches of student leaders and parents, including senior government officials who had lost their children during the protests.

The girls in the gang got active in getting many female students from Chukchuk Nagar to participate in the march. The boys were busy planning the protests, arranging food and drinks for the protesters, distributing pamphlets, and displaying posters at public spaces and colleges, sticking them on the walls of government buildings and bus stands. Lavanya, after a lengthy march one day, fainted and required liquids to regain consciousness.

The VP Singh government, however, stood firm on its decision to implement the Mandal Commission report. The unrest and the protest continued for a long time, though implementing the Commission's report marked a significant milestone in India's democratic history.

Less than a year later, another disaster struck the

country. On 21st May 1991, a few minutes past ten at night, the former Prime Minister of India, Rajiv Gandhi, was assassinated during an election rally in Sriperumbudur in Tamil Nadu. Dark clouds continued to loom over India and its political landscape as VP Singh lost the elections and PV Narasimha Rao took over as the 9th Prime Minister of India.

Chandan:

I don't think implementing the recommendation of the Mandal Commission was the right decision. I understand well that the backward communities in India have suffered for years. However, making the general categories suffer for the wrongs done to the backward community in the past is not the correct decision. If the political leaders really want to do something for the underprivileged, they should provide the right environment instead of reservation, particularly concerning health and education. Reservation of any kind, whether it's based on caste, creed, or gender, is not sustainable. It weakens our society. It's just a political gimmick, I think. Though, I agree that we need to pay for the sins of our ancestors.

Printing the posters and pamphlets was fun. Rocky's uncle helped us, and the boys would visit his shop when the posters were printed in the dead of the night. Chaitanya got busy arranging the posters instead of going to the *Naher,* albeit briefly. I had quietly sneaked out of the house without informing my parents on several occasions. So did the other boys. Bholanath was caught one day by his father while going out. He said he was going for a stroll as he was suffering from gas and tummy ache. His father was not convinced. Who goes out for a walk at 11 at night due to tummy ache?

But those nights were thrilling. I felt like a patriot of those pre-independence days, sneaking out of the house in the middle of the night and then discreetly overlooking the printing, with all lights switched off to prevent detection and only a candle burning in the printing room. All of us would be there with Chaitanya, smoking non-stop for the whole night. I told him to stop. He claimed that would make him fall asleep, which he could not afford on such a momentous occasion. What an excuse!

I had seen Rajiv Gandhi in flesh and blood a few days before his death. I had gone to Alambagh market to get some groceries and cold drinks as it was extremely hot. I saw a crowd near the crossroad and asked for the reason. Rajiv Gandhi is in the city, someone said—time of elections. So, I stood there and then saw his cavalcade. I saw him waving at everyone in an open jeep. He was wearing a white kurta and pyjama with a white handkerchief on his head to shield him from the heat. He was laughing and throwing flowers at the crowd. He was such a handsome young man who was always smiling.

Early in the morning of 22nd May, I heard the news of the assassination. I was shocked, dumbfounded.

Mona:

I don't understand politics, but Chandu regularly reads the newspaper. The other day, he was discussing the

Vietnam War. I don't have much interest in History. But, I gathered quite a bit of knowledge from Chandu.

Chandu said again and again that VP Singh was not right. I don't know. Maybe he is right. I mean, both are right. VP Singh was the Prime Minister. He must have thought before deciding. Chandu may be right, too. He says reservation disrupts society. Anyway, I enjoyed the silent marches, the cold drinks, and those burgers. Lavanya fainted, and Chandu ran around to get the glucose powder. Then, he arranged lemon water and sugarcane juice for her. After a while, she opened her eyes. Chandu hired an auto and took her back home. He told us to continue with our march. By evening, Lavanya was fine. Thank God!

I wept after hearing about the assassination of Rajiv Gandhi. A few days ago, Chandu mentioned seeing him at Alambagh. I watched him deliver his speeches on television. He was so young and handsome.

Life and death are both so unfair.

39

Lost in the Haze

Chukchuk Nagar had many stories to tell. However, the story of Chaitanya Nair's uncontrolled addiction was a sad reminder of the dangers of smoking and alcoholism.

Chaitanya, who performed well in his 10th Board examination along with his sister Diksha, had secured admission to the prestigious St John's Convent. The college was away from Chukchuk Nagar, though not too far.

Though he had started smoking even while in school at Chukchuk Nagar, now being away from the colony, unlike his previous school, where his activities were more controlled and monitored by his parents and the close-knit neighbourhood, the intoxicating allure of his newfound freedom allowed him to frequently skip his class and spend time with people with questionable character.

Nobody knows the exact moment of how and when it started. But when the pristine pages of his academic journey bore the strains of *paan masala* and cigarettes and the echoes of clinking glasses, Chandan became worried for his friend. They had spent beautiful times together, and he would not let his friend succumb to such habits.

Chaitanya started borrowing cigarettes from Surinder, who sold cigarettes, *paan,* and *paan masala* near the Cooperative store. He began with two cigarettes and two *paan masala* pouches a day and soon went on to twenty cigarettes and as many *paan masala* pouches. For alcohol, he used to visit the nearby Alambagh market, as there was no liquor shop in Chukchuk Nagar.

'When are you paying me for the stuff you buy?' Surinder asked him one day.

'A few more days, Surinder bhai. Don't worry, I will pay back every paise,' he said, lighting up a stick.

'You have been saying that for the last six months,' the shopkeeper sighed.

Days turned into months. The rising debt cast a suffocating shadow on Chaitanya. He could not stop the habit or pay back the debt. Surinder, a patient creditor, had given countless reminders, but empty promises of settling the dues had become the only currency of their exchanges.

As months rolled into a year, the pressure intensified. The shopkeeper, torn between compassion and necessity, decided to take matters into his own hands. One evening, as Chaitanya's parents were chatting and sipping tea in the garden, Surinder visited Chaitanya's home. He knew that Chaitanya had gone to the *Naher* to smoke with his friends, and that was the best time to meet his parents.

'Namaste, Sir. Namaste, Madam.' He folded his hands and bowed to the couple.

'Arre, Surinder, what brings you here?' asked Ravindra Nair, Chaitanya's father.

Surinder first hesitated for a while and then spoke. 'I need two thousand rupees, Sir.'

'Two thousand rupees! For what?' Ravindra Nair was shocked.

Surinder shilly-shallied for some time. He wanted to shield Chaitanya's reputation and concocted a different excuse to explain the unpaid debt to his father.

'Sir, Chaitanya has been buying peanuts for many months but has not paid. I thought of asking you as the amount is high.'

'He ate peanuts for two thousand rupees? This is unbelievable. Even a monkey would not eat so much.' Ravindra Nair exclaimed.

'It's been a year, Sir.'

'But you don't sell peanuts. As far as I know, you sell only cigarettes *and paan masala.* You guys are spoiling the kids in the colony,' the father roared.

The shopkeeper didn't know what to say. He mumbled.

'Speak loud and clear.'

'Sir, he bought the peanuts from Chacha, but I paid on his behalf.'

'Why?'

'Out of empathy, Sir. He is like my brother, and he wanted the peanuts badly.'

There was a prolonged silence amid an unspoken truth which hung heavy in the air.

'Okay, let him come back home. First, let me ask him—stupid monkey. I will give your money back. Let me also listen to that donkey's side of the story. His mom and I have never eaten peanuts worth two thousand rupees in our entire life.'

Surinder didn't say anything and left without the money.

An hour later, he narrated the episode to Chaitanya, who had come to his shop for another stick.

Chaitanya was shocked to hear what Surinder had just

told him.

'Why the hell did you go to my place?'

'Chaintu, I cannot afford any delay in the payment. You can return the money by tomorrow, or I will tell your dad. I saved you this time by lying about the peanuts. Tomorrow, I will speak the truth,' Surinder said sternly.

Now feeling the tightening grip of the shopkeeper's demand, Chaitanya wracked his brain for a way out. Anxiety fuelled a desperate idea.

When he returned home, he went straight to his father, who was sitting on a chair reading a newspaper. But it was his father who spoke first.

'You ate two thousand rupees worth of peanuts?'

'No, Papa, it's a miscalculation. I will settle that with Surinder. He made a mistake. You don't have to pay him anything.'

The father stared at his son for a long time.

'I need some money for books.' Chaitanya uttered after a long time, evading eye contact with his father.

'How much do you need?'

'Around three thousand, Papa.'

Ravindra Nair sprang out of his chair, his eyes widening in shock as Chaitanya mentioned the exorbitant cost of the books.

'Three thousand? What books are these?' the father almost cried out in surprise.

'Economics, Statistics, and Mathematics books, Papa. These are by foreign authors. Economics by Samuelson, Statistics by...'

'Okay, Okay,' his father cut in. 'Take the money from your mother. I will give it to her tomorrow.'

The next day, with the cash in hand, Chaitanya hastened to Surinder's shop, hoping to silence the shopkeeper for at least some time.

He handed the two thousand rupees to Surinder and kept the remaining thousand in his back pocket.

'But how did you get the money?' Surinder asked.

Chaitanya narrated his tactical moves and laughed.

'But then, how will you buy the books now?'

Chaitanya smiled.

'I already have the books, so I need not buy them. Papa doesn't know. I will show him the books tomorrow. I will tell him that I have brought them second-hand from the *raddi* market.'

The shopkeeper was stunned. He didn't know what to say.

But his sister knew that something was amiss. Diksha had seen her brother loitering around Surinder's shop and had once seen him smoking behind the Capital Hall while she had gone to play badminton with Mona. She didn't complain to her parents then but was sure Chaitanya was hiding the truth.

'You smoke, don't you?' Diksha asked.

'Shut up and mind your own business.' Chaitanya retorted.

'I am going to tell Papa.'

'Go to hell.'

Diksha didn't want to continue the conversation with her dumbass brother. She chose to let the matter rest. But she paid the price for daring to complain. A few days later, Chaitanya heated the key to his bike on the stove and kept it near the kitchen shelf using a pair of tongs once it was red hot.

'Diksha, I have to go out. Please bring in the bike key. I think I have kept it in the kitchen in a hurry.'

Diksha went to the kitchen and saw the key. A piercing scream reverberated through the house as soon as she touched the metal.

'Now go and complain to Papa,' Chaitanya sneered at his sister standing at the kitchen door.

Tears streamed down Diksha's face as she cradled the burnt finger in pain as her brother, swirling the key in his fingers, laughed and left the room.

Diksha complained this time. And Chaitanya that day received a real sound thrashing from his father.

But a month later, when his father, along with Mr Basu, had gone towards the *Naher* to watch Mr Basu catch fish, he saw his son, who was unaware of his father's presence, exhaling twirls of smoke, popping *paan masala,* laughing and enjoying himself with a group from Nakshal Khera. Ravindra Nair was so fuelled by anger that he impulsively removed his shoe and hurled it towards his son with full force. As the shoe wracked Chaitanya's head, the terrified son, seeing his father, leapt into the canal, swimming desperately towards the other side.

But when he returned home, his father, ready with a cane, beat him so hard that each blow left an imprint on the air. When his father kicked him out of the room, both his mother and sister couldn't recognise him with his now distorted and swollen face with bruises all over.

Chandan couldn't bear to see his friend fall into the abyss. He pleaded with Chaitanya, trying to make him understand that this destructive path his friend had chosen would only lead to ruin.

'What's the problem, Chaitanya?' Chandan asked one evening while they were together in the Chukchuk Nagar stadium with Chaitanya puffing away.

'What problem?'

'This is your third cigarette since we have been sitting here.' Chandan looked at his watch. 'It's not even thirty minutes.'

'So?'

Chandan looked him straight in the eye.

'Have you gone mad or what? You used to be amongst the top of your class.'

'What's that has to do with my smoking and drinking?'

'Your grades are slipping. Your health is deteriorating. Look at your teeth. They are stained yellow and brown. You also lied to your father. I know everything, Surinder told me.'

Chaitanya exhaled a plume of smoke and started to cough, the harsh sound echoing in the stadium. Grasping for breath, he flicked the half-smoked cigarette to the ground. Chandan tried to massage his back to ease the cough. A few minutes later, he was back to normal.

After a prolonged silence, Chandan spoke.

'You are drowning, Chaitanya, and the sad part is that I have to just stand and watch. It's up to you to change, to get back to where you were before.'

'I know what I am doing.'

'You are meant for greatness, Chaitanya.'

'Ha ha ha. Stop joking. I have drowned already.'

'It's never too late. But you have to make the choice.' Chandan continued to try.

Chaitanya stood up, looked up at the sky, and then raised his arms, waving them in different directions as if trying to swim in the air.

'You know Chandan, it's such a surreal feeling when the darkness consumes you completely.'

Chandan tried and tried and tried and finally gave up. Actually, it was Chaitanya who gave up on himself. Each puff and sip dragged him deeper into a pit of self-destruction. Coughs replaced laughter as the noose of his addiction tightened its grip. Excessive alcohol abuse led to liver failure, where his skin and the whites of his eyes turned yellow. He lay on the bed all day long due to fatigue and weakness. Friends became distant memories as his parents and sister watched helplessly as he gasped for air lying on his bed at home or in the hospital.

In the end, it was not a grand tragedy but a quiet surrender. The darkness that consumed him completely had claimed its final victory. Chaitanya was only 23.

As Chandan and his friends stood in the crematorium watching the funeral pyre rise to the heavens with tears in their eyes, another tragedy unfolded more than a thousand kilometres away from Lucknow. A series of bomb explosions shattered the tranquillity of Bombay on 12th March 1993, marking one of the most devastating terrorist attacks in Indian history.

Chandan:

I find myself replaying our conservations, time and again, searching for signs that I missed, wondering if there was more I could have done. But deep down, I knew this was his battle, and I couldn't have done much about it. But the fact that I couldn't save him will haunt me for the rest of my life.

Chaitanya was a sharp and witty boy. His jokes, keeping a straight face, used to be funny, and it took some time for us to understand, which then made us burst with laughter. We shared countless moments of joy together. Despite his addiction and even when drunk, he was always respectful towards all men and women. Though he fought every day with his sister, Diksha, it was he who carried her on his shoulders and ran to the Polyclinic when she slipped and dislocated her upper arm. He was always caring.

I remember the countless times I pleaded with him, begged him to stop smoking and chewing *paan masala* and stay away from the bottle. But then, one spirit slowly consumed the other as he continued down that dangerous path.

I don't go to a temple regularly, but I now make sure to visit twice a year, on his birthday and on 12th March, to pray for him wherever he may be. It's the least I can do for him.

The ordeal didn't end. So many families mourned the loss of their loved ones by senseless violence and acts of terror. Oh! Grief! How do you consume the soul?

Mona:

After Chaitanya's demise, we all changed. A bit of our soul was lost forever. Whenever I think about him, I am overcome by a flood of emotions: sadness, anger, and an overwhelming longing for him.

Chandu has become so quiet that I have started worrying about him. Lavanya came this evening and spoke to Chandu. He listens to her most of the time. Nayantara and Anshul, accompanied by Chakradev, also came. Then we went out for a stroll. Daksh and Rocky met us near the stadium. So, we went inside the stadium and sat in the stands. We felt the presence of Chaitanya like a whisper in the air as memories of his laughter echoed in the stadium. We were quiet and didn't speak, but suddenly, we all started to cry.

40

Beyond the Horizon

Kolkata, March 2024

They all went in different directions—became Bankers, Corporate leaders, Mathematicians, Archaeologists, and officers in the Central Government. Except for Chaitanya, they all celebrated their fiftieth birthdays, some in 2020 and others in 2021. Mona celebrated a couple of years later. The boys and girls were now middle-aged men and women, yet they remained friends, and the essence of their friendship remained unchanged over the years. Their friendship remained the only constant in their ever-revolving lives. They knew they would always find their way back to each other, bound by memories and an unbreakable bond that would continue to shine brightly in their hearts forever.

Chandan:

That was the story of Chukchuk Nagar and my friends. There are many more stories about the colony, but I am not expected to narrate an epic. So, maybe some other time.

Thirty years have passed since we left Chukchuk Nagar. And thirty years is not a very short time.

How do I start the end? Or how do I end the start? It's difficult both ways, but let me still give it a try.

But first things first. For me, Mona will always be the first. I asked her to help me summarise our days in Chukchuk Nagar for my diary. She said, 'What you write is mine, and what I write is yours. So, you do the job.' And thus, here I am, attempting to fulfil both our parts.

Mona stood first in St William's Convent in her 12th board examination. She didn't make silly mistakes this time, which was quite a relief. She chose Physics, Chemistry, and Maths as her undergraduate courses at Lucknow University.

We graduated in 1991. By 'we', I mean the rest of the gang. I chose to do a post-graduation in Mathematics and continued to attend the University for another two years. But more about myself a little later. Let me first talk about my friends.

Bholanath Sharma was the first one to leave Chukchuk Nagar. The year was 1992 or maybe the beginning of 1993, I don't exactly remember. Though I remember Chaitanya was still with us then. Bholanath's father, a few years before his retirement, suddenly died of a heart attack. Bholanath was then in his final year of graduation. It took him quite a long time to overcome the profound loss. He didn't eat for days. A silent transformation took place, which was quite visible. He was never that fun-loving or easy-going Bholanath anymore. He took the CAT (Common Admission Test) exam and cleared it on his first attempt. He joined the prestigious Indian Institute of Management in Ahmedabad.

A day before his departure to Ahmedabad with his mother, we sat beneath the mango tree where we had spent countless hours laughing, dreaming, and growing together. A sense of melancholy hung heavy in the air even though a gentle breeze stirred the leaves of the trees. We were there for each other since childhood. We had become a habit to each other. And now the time had come for the first to depart.

Tears swelled in our eyes as Bholanath embraced each one of us. While we hugged, he whispered in my ears, 'Thank you, Chandu, for giving me a beautiful childhood. I thank you all from the bottom of my heart,' he said.

We took him to the Dixit shop, where we forced him to eat some *golgappas*. He was initially hesitant, but then he ate one piece. 'Be careful. Dr Chakraborty has retired,' Anshul remarked, and we all laughed. But the laughter rang hollow in the stillness of the moment.

From there, we went to the stadium and sat there for some time. Chaitanya, who was frail and weak and not keeping well, asked Bholanath, 'One cigarette, Bhola, for friend's sake.'

Bholanath put the cigarette between his lips, 'But without lighting it, for friend's sake.'

And we all laughed again.

The following morning, we all gathered at the LPG railway station. We sat on the same bench, which we must have sat on a million times. We heard the train's whistle. Tears welled up in our eyes. We hugged him tightly this time. He boarded the train with his mother. As the train began to pull away, our hands slipped from each other's grasp.

Slowly, Bholanath disappeared into the distance as the train gained speed, its whistle echoing through the railway station.

Bholanath came to Chukchuk Nagar only once during his final year, as his mother had shifted to their ancestral home in Kashi. He had thinned and told us that he now jogs daily. We sat below the mango tree for some time. He told us he had received a job offer from a multinational company and would soon leave for America.

Bholanath now works in an American multinational company and has become an American citizen. He resides in Cincinnati. He is married and has two children, a boy and a girl. He has named his son after me-Chandan. I asked, why? He says that name makes him feel I am still around him whenever he calls his son. He has learnt to cook French and Japanese cuisines. He told me he would like to retire early from his current job and be a chef. I do not doubt it at all.

I asked about his mother.

'How is Aunty?'

'Fine. But age is now catching up. She is with me and has started wearing skirts.'

'Really?' I was not able to control my laughter as I had always seen her in a saari.

'I will send a snap. Mummy is now an American citizen, so she is competing with her elderly neighbours.'

We both laughed.

We are in touch. Thanks to WhatsApp.

Diksha Nair and her parents were the next to leave Chukchuk Nagar six months after Chaitanya's death. I could never imagine how people can get old due to grief. The parents, in their mid-fifties, suddenly seemed to be in their mid-seventies within a few months of their son's death. Their movements had become slow and laboured. They hardly spoke to anyone. They had stopped their evening stroll. Diksha would often come to my place. We would sit beneath the mango tree. I tried to make her smile. Rocky tried, too, with his jokes.

'The house feels empty, Chandu. He was a dumb ass, never listened to us, but still, he has taken away our soul with him,' she said.

Her father took a transfer and left for Cochin, where they had their ancestral home. Two years later, I attended her marriage accompanied by Mona and Daksh. She was so happy to see us. 'Is the mango tree still standing, Chandu?' she asked with a hint of nostalgia.

'Of course.' I said.

'And the monkeys?'

'No. After our Diwali blast, they never came back.'

We laughed.

I met Ravindra Uncle and Parvathi Aunty. I touched their feet. They hugged me, tears streaming down their eyes.

I saw the large, garlanded portrait of Chaitanya in the house. How can someone so full of life be reduced to a mere portrait adorned with flowers? We played many hide-and-seek games in our childhood, but Chaitanya hid himself eternally, completely, permanently. There were those pangs of guilt. Had I done enough, said enough, or been enough for him? I don't know. I wish I could have done more. In the silence of that room, I could hear echoes of our conversations, his jokes, and laughter, in the whispers of the wind, in the gentle rustle of leaves in the eternal embrace of a friendship cut short.

Diksha is now settled in Singapore with her husband and son, Vaibhav. She completed her post-graduation in Economics in Bangalore and then completed her doctorate. She is currently employed with the World Bank.

Whenever we talk, I always address her as 'Doc Saab'. Diksha was always a smart girl. I knew she would do well for herself and contribute much to society.

Rakesh Sood, our very own Rocky, left Chukchuk Nagar in 1994. Rocky surprised us every time. He decided that he would study no more—enough of studies as he had absorbed enough knowledge. After graduating in history, he attempted various examinations, from Civil Services to Banking services to Postal services to Railways and many others. He didn't get a call from anywhere, but he was relaxed and chilled out, spending his time either at Dixit Sweet shop or strolling around Chukchuk Nagar with Daksh, Nayantara, Anshul, and sometimes with me and Mona. Between 1991, after completion of his graduation, and the middle of 1994, he did nothing. Only ate, slept, and strolled. However, one day, he received an appointment letter from the Archaeological Survey of India (ASI). He couldn't recall the date, the month, or even the year when he had taken the exam.

I met him once in a coffee shop at Hazratganj, where he confessed that climbing the water tank was his plan. That day, I received a thrashing after being chased by the bees because of his stupid plan.

'So, how's the job, Rocky?' I asked.

'Bullshit job.' Rocky responded as usual. 'We are continuously exploring and excavating. They don't even allow the dead to live in peace.'

'You mean to die in peace?'

'Yes, right, die in peace.'

'But you must be enjoying the job. You have been working for ASI for a while now.' I remarked.

'Only the research and documentation part. That I like.'

'Why?'

'Free foreign trips. Next month, I will research the Angkor Wat temple in Cambodia with my team. Foreign trips are fun times.'

Rocky had a gift—his wit and sense of humour. He was clever and always spontaneous, and there was never a dull moment with him. He had a knack for turning ordinary moments into memorable ones. It was always a pleasure to be his friend.

Rocky stays in Cuttack and travels abroad frequently, excavating old temples. He is married and has a son, Tony. The other day, I had a video call with his family. Tony did all the talking, and we just listened. As they say, it's all in the genes.

Daksh Chopra and I were classmates on our 12th boards at St William's, along with Nayantara, and we went to University together. Daksh took Physics as a postgraduate and then completed his doctorate at Delhi University. He came back to Lucknow and joined the University as a lecturer. His wife,

Rupa, was my postgraduate classmate. She completed her doctorate in Mathematics and joined as a lecturer at the University along with Daksh. They are now professors in their respective departments. I learned later that Rupa is a distant relative from my mother's side. So, apart from friends, Daksh and I are now relatives too.

We occasionally met and often talked over the phone as he is in Lucknow. He suggested we reunite sometime soon. They have a son and a daughter, Rohan and Devika, and reside in their palatial bungalow on the University campus. The other day, he told me something that shocked and surprised me.

'Do you remember the mangoes? The one we ate and put stickers on?'

'You and the others ate. Mona and I didn't.' I clarified.

'Well, it seems that Mr Bakshi, my father's boss, knew about it. The transfer of my father to the northeast was a punishment.'

'Really? How do you know?' I was shocked.

'Mr Bakshi had shared this with his son. His son is a professor in the Psychology department. We have these departmental get-togethers. So, he referred to that episode one day, though he didn't know that he was talking about my father.'

We were quiet for a few seconds and then burst out with laughter.

Nayantara Iyengar's father retired from the railways in 1999. Her parents left Chukchuk Nagar after his retirement and are now settled in Chennai. Nayantara, always bright and brilliant, completed her graduation and then applied for Standford, Harvard, and other colleges. She received calls from all the Ivy League colleges, including Princeton and Yale. She joined Princeton to study Computer Science, specialising in cybersecurity, data structures, and computer graphics. She married a French guy, Octave Felix Moreao Deschamps, who works on internal security for the United States government and resides in New York. Nayantara is a consultant at Princeton and Cornell University. High-profile couples in a high-profile country!

They didn't want to have kids and stuck to their plan, so I asked why in one of our WhatsApp calls.

'I didn't want my kids to be like me,' she said.

I was surprised.

'Everyone would like to have a kid like you, Nayantara. Every person would like to be in your shoes.'

'No, Chandu. I think I was too overambitious. It takes a toll; we lose the balance. I enjoy my work, as does my husband. But I wish I was calmer. More grounded, I mean. You were a witness to how I reacted when Bholanath topped the class. That's not good.'

I didn't say anything. But then she mentioned something interesting.

'Bhola came to our house last month with his family,' she said.

'Really?'

'Yeah, he cooked the whole time he was here. Octave loved his French preparations.'

'That's wonderful.' I said. 'Find a mango tree there and conduct a meeting with him beneath it. Do send me the videos.' I laughed.

There was silence for some time, and then I could hear the sobs.

'Nayana, are you okay?'

'I miss those days, Chandu. I miss Chukchuk Nagar and our gang. I miss the mango tree. I miss the jackfruit and guava trees. I miss the monkeys. Our bonds, the simplicity of our days. I miss it all.'

We were silent for a few minutes, and then she said,

'Let's have a reunion. Let's again have a grand meeting under the mango tree.'

'Absolutely, Nayana. Daksh and Rocky keep on reminding me of a reunion. I will speak to them right away.'

We spoke for a few more minutes.

'Please tell your husband to shorten his name. It feels more like a French poem rather than a name.' I remarked.

'I will, I will.'

We both laughed and then hung up.

I had not been in touch with Chakradev Gopalakrishnan for a long time. He joined the Vidyasagar School of Arts with Rocky for his 12th board and then graduated from Lucknow University, majoring in Sociology and Political Science. He was outstanding in sports and got a job offer from the Railways in the sports quota. He married early with his childhood crush Priyal, who also resided in Chukchuk Nagar. Except for Bholanath and Nayantara, we all attended his marriage, which was held at the Capital Hall. He was posted on the southeastern railway and resided in Visakhapatnam. Within a year of his joining the railways, his father took a transfer to Hyderabad so that they could be closer to their son. Their ancestral home was in Mysore. Once his parents left Chukchuk Nagar, we lost touch.

I asked Rocky about Chakradev's whereabouts. Rocky didn't have a clue either, but he said he would get back, which he did.

Rocky came up with a piece of sad news. Priyal had passed away in 2012. They have a daughter who stays with Chakradev.

I was shocked. I called Chakradev after Rocky shared with me his number.

'Chandu,' he said as soon as he heard my voice.

'Twenty-five years, Chakra. You have forgotten me.' I teased.

'After all these years, I have not forgotten your voice. So, how can I forget you?' He replied warmly.

I asked about his daughter. She was in Delhi studying at Miranda House.

'Miranda House? That's the best, Chakra.' I remarked.

'Yes, Pooja has her mother's brains,' he laughed.

We talked about Priyal. She died of blood cancer. There were no symptoms. She suddenly felt dizzy and fell one day in the market while purchasing groceries. The final stage of the disease, the doctors said.

'I will retire in 2030. But I am considering taking a

voluntary retirement, going to Mysore, and staying at my ancestral place. Papa and Mummy are there. They are also old now. They need me.'

'Why don't you ask them to stay with you at Visakhapatnam?' I asked.

'They are happy there, though they come here often. Now, with their granddaughter in Delhi, they are not so inclined. And travelling at their age is also a problem. So, I visit them almost every month for a day or two.'

We spoke for a long time. He asked me about the gang.

'Now I have the All India Radio's number,' he laughed.

'Yes, you will get regular updates from Rocky.'

I often speak to Chakradev now. Sometimes Rocky joins in, too, and makes us laugh with his utter bullshit.

Anshul Deshmukh is in Mumbai. He works for a multinational company and manages the marketing department. He majored in Economics and then completed an MBA in marketing from a prestigious college in Mumbai. He lives with his parents, wife, and two daughters in Santa Cruz. I have been to Mumbai a few times for work and have always stayed with him. He never allowed me to stay in a hotel.

'What the fuck! Stay with me. I have a nice home. It may not be as good as a hotel, but it's nice. And there is a mango tree in the backyard.'

I liked Anshul. He knew his capabilities from the beginning and never aspired for anything more than his capacity. He knew he could never compete with Nayantara, Lavanya, or Bholanath, so he never got into that race. He was always sincere and hardworking.

Whenever I was in Mumbai, we sat under the mango tree in his backyard. Deshmukh Uncle and Aunty were always so gracious and welcoming. Even at her age, Aunty would make Misal Pav and Puran Poli, especially for me, as she used to prepare in Chukchuk Nagar more than two decades ago.

Lavanya Iyer always evoked a flutter in my heart. She was my childhood crush. Though I pretended nothing was between us, she was too sharp and understood. She reciprocated, too.

In her 10th board exam, she came second. In her 12th board, she secured first place. At her graduation, she stood first again. During her postgraduate studies, she attained second place. For Lavanya, it was always first or second in her academic pursuits.

After her postgraduate degree in Applied Economics, she appeared for the Indian Economic Service examination and was selected. Her first assignment was in the Planning Commission in New Delhi. That year was 1994.

But before I talk about Lavanya, I must talk a bit about myself to maintain the narrative.

After my postgraduate studies, I was unclear about what I wanted to do in life or what career to choose. However, one thing was very clear in my mind: I had a passion for Mathematics and the desire to remain closely connected to it regardless of the career I chose. So, I appeared for the Indian Statistical Service examination.

I was selected and relocated from Lucknow to Calcutta for a six-month training at the Indian Statistical Institute, which was the opposite of what my parents had done when they moved from Calcutta to Lucknow. After the training, I joined the Calcutta branch of the Central Statistical Organization (CSO). That was in 1995. Calcutta was officially renamed Kolkata in 2001.

As a trainee, my main job was to analyse and interpret data for research projects and government initiatives, focusing on non-linear optimisation, stochastic processes, and combinatorics. I must have done a good job, as after two years, I was promoted to Assistant Project Lead, responsible for projects funded by government and private agencies.

Late one evening, I received a list of five officers from various departments joining us on deputation for two years. These transfers and deputations were common amongst the Indian Economic Service and Indian Revenue Service officers serving in the Reserve Bank of India, Office of the Economic Advisor, Centre for Studies in Social Sciences, and the Planning Commission.

I saw one name that surprised me as I glanced through the list. Lavanya Iyer was second on the list. I knew she was working for the Planning Commission in Delhi, but I was unsure whether it was my friend, Lavanya. The following day, I called the Planning Commission office in Delhi and was told she was on an official tour to Mumbai and would return next week. So, I called home and asked my mother to visit Lavanya's house and get some clarity from her parents, as I could not contain my excitement. Maa said the Iyers' have gone to Tirupati and would probably visit Coimbatore, their native place, before returning to Lucknow. She was unsure when they would return, though she said it would not be more than two weeks.

Next week, I was so busy with meetings and visits to government offices that I didn't have time to call the Planning Commission office in Delhi again. I returned, one day, to my office at around five in the evening after visiting the Office of the Chief Economic Advisor after a marathon four-hour meeting. As I walked towards my cabin, I heard that familiar voice, 'Chandu.' I turned around. She was there, beautiful as ever, smiling at me, adorned in a stunning saree. And the only words that came out of my mouth were, 'What the fu...' I immediately changed it to 'Oh my God!' I was in the office, so I needed to be careful with what I uttered.

She laughed as she always did. And I dashed towards her and gave her a very, very tight hug.

'Don't squeeze the life out of me,' she joked breathlessly.

I loosened my grip.

'You will not die till I am there.' I said.

She said she flew directly from Mumbai and was unaware of my call to the Planning Commission office in Delhi. She would return to Delhi, pack her things, and come to Calcutta for her two-year deputation next month.

She stayed with me that week in Calcutta.

We would go out for dinner, and I asked her one evening,

'Did you know I had a crush on you?'

'Of course. I always knew,' she said, devoid of any expressions.

'And do you know that I still have that crush?'

This time, she looked at me.

'Really?' she asked.

'Absolutely. I hope you are not married.'

'No. But are you now going to propose?' Her eyes widened.

'No, let's keep this short. I am going to marry you.'

'Chandu, I can't believe this.'

'Stop calling me Chandu now. That feels more like a sibling.'

I spoke to my mother, then my father, then her parents, then Mona, then Rocky, then Daksh, then Anshul, followed by Chakradev. Then, I wrote a mail to Bholanath, Diksha, and Nayantara..., to every gang member I mean. And they all knew it. They all knew that I was having a crush on her. What the fu...!

To keep it short, six months later, we got married. The gang was there, including Bholanath and Nayantara, who had flown all the way from the United States. I met Octave and Bholanath's wife, Uma. It was fun. We all ganged up once again. Maa smiled for the whole month. That itself was a miracle.

I am happy with Lavanya and my children, Vedant and Vidya. Lavanya relocated to the Reserve Bank branch in Kolkata from the Planning Commission in Delhi. We bought a house and planted a mango sapling in the backyard for housewarming. Maybe someday, when the sapling grows into a tree, we will again hold a meeting there with the gang.

Lavanya still calls me Chandu. Old habits, what to do?

Maa and Papa stay with me, though they visit their ancestral home often. Iyer Aunty and Uncle are now my mother and father-in-law, respectively, though I still call them Uncle and Aunty instead of Appa and Amma. Old habits! Uncle and Aunty come to our place almost every year. Aunty and Maa spend a lot of time together in the kitchen, chatting and laughing, while Papa and Uncle stroll in the morning and play cards the whole day. Maa chatting and laughing nowadays is a real miracle.

I go on vacation twice yearly with my parents, Lavanya, and the children. Last year, we went to Bali. Apart from other places, we visited the Besakih temple, the largest and holiest Hindu temple in Bali. While leaving the temple, we saw a crowd listening to a man lecturing the tourists with great animation. I walked towards the man to listen to what he was talking about. As I came closer, I almost fainted. It was our dear old Rocky! If I had to write what happened after he saw me, this note would become an epic of at least a thousand pages. So, let's leave it at that.

My Mona, darling, went to Banaras Hindu University (BHU) to study Biochemistry after graduation. Then, she completed her MPhil in Molecular Biology. Then, she fell in love with her classmate, Nirvaan. I was the first one to know. So, I spoke with Nirvaan several times and concluded that she made the right choice.

He told me he had received a job offer from a research-based organisation in Geneva and would leave with Mona after their marriage, if at all that is permitted.

I was the one to break the news to her parents.

'Chandu, if you say he is the right one for her, then it's

right,' her mother said.

'Chandu, if you say he is the right one for her, then it's right,' her father said.

And when Mihir said the same thing, I remarked,

'Change your lines, please; it's not a drama dialogue rehearsal.'

After I came to Calcutta and Mona went to BHU, we spoke almost thrice a week. I had a landline at home, and she used to call from her hostel. Long-distance calls were expensive in those days, so we only spoke for a few minutes. Our conversations mostly revolved around proteins, genetics, enzymes, cellular respiration, metabolism, and many other things, which were more of Mona's monologues. I was, however, more interested in whether she was eating the right food, sleeping on time, taking less stress, or avoiding silly mistakes in her exam. I knew whenever she was worried over something, even in her silence. I knew when she was joyful. I knew Mona like the back of my hand. We never drifted apart.

I took leave for a week and went to Lucknow for Mona's marriage with Lavanya, who was then pregnant with our first child. My parents also accompanied me. As Mona saw me, she came running with outstretched arms and hugged me the same way she used to when she was three years old after I returned from school. She introduced me to Nirvaan, and though I had spoken to him over the phone, it was the first time I was meeting him. He touched my feet. I blessed him. He is a well-bred guy. Mona's choice can never be wrong. I also met her future father, mother, and brother-in-law.

The venue was the Capital Hall. I handled the decorations, catering, and all logistical requirements and coordinated with the pandit and other vendors. Her parents and Mihir had taken care of the guest list and invitations. I went with Mona and Nirvaan to Aminabad and Hazratganj market to select the wedding sarees and sherwanis. Daksh and Rupa came every day and would return in the evening. Rocky, Anshul, and Chakradev came with their family. Diksha joined her husband and son a day before the wedding. Bholanath arrived on the day of her marriage, though Nayantara couldn't make it as she was travelling to Brazil.

The Haldi and Mahendi ceremonies took place beneath the mango tree. That was Mona's clear-cut direction.

On the day of the marriage, we all sang and danced throughout the night.

At the time of the vidaai, Mona bid farewell to all of us. There were tears of joy and sadness. Malti Aunty was inconsolable, but I tried to maintain my composure.

We dropped them off at the airport. They would be in Delhi for a few weeks before flying to Geneva. She hugged me, and tears welled up in our eyes.

'With whom shall I cycle now, Mona?' I murmured in her ear. She wept. I choked. Our embrace felt like a desperate attempt to hold onto those moments of togetherness.

We clung to each other, unwilling to let go. But when the final boarding call echoed through the terminal, time pushed us towards separation.

'Chandu, Thank you. Thank you for everything,' she said.

Then she opened her handbag and showed me something that moved me to tears. It was that elongated metal coin I had placed on the rail and had gifted to her. 'The memento. I will keep it with me always,' she said and then turned away to depart, wiping her tears.

Sitting in the lounge that day, I wept for a long time as I saw her flight ascend into the sky.

Mona's father, after his retirement, moved to Varanasi. Mona comes to India every year with her husband and daughter, Tanvi. After arrival in Delhi, she catches a connecting flight to Kolkata and stays with us for a few days before leaving for Varanasi. Lavanya and Mona have always had that affinity and have shared a strong bond and fondness for each other since childhood, and they spend hours chitchatting. Mona gets a lot of Swiss chocolates for my children. She got Lavanya and me a Swiss watch. She is now a director at Elexis, a top multinational European company that deals with biopharmaceuticals. Nirvaan works for Aunza, another pharma giant.

The mango tree I planted has grown, and whenever Mona comes, we sit beneath the tree and sip our chai—for old times' sake.

Malti Aunty and Jitendra Uncle talk to my parents regularly.

Mona's brother Mihir is a doctor. He is a cardiologist and passed out from Christian Medical College in Vellore. He stays with us whenever he visits Kolkata for a medical conference or seminar. He advises us on how to care for our hearts and the right food to eat. Mihir is married, but unfortunately, I couldn't attend his marriage as I had a meeting, which I couldn't say no to as my presence was essential. But Lavanya went with my parents and the children. His wife, Sagarika, is also a doctor. She is an ophthalmologist. They reside in Vellore with their son, Naveen, studying medicine. He is in his first year.

Mrs Titli Basu settled in Durgapur after her husband's retirement. Her elder son, Monu, joined the Armed Forces, and the younger son, Sonu, works for an oil company. Basu Aunty and my mother talk regularly over the phone. I mean, she speaks, and Maa listens.

Jaswinder Singh and his wife settled down in Amritsar after his retirement. I learned a year ago that Tajinder Aunty had passed away at the age of 90. I am not in touch with Jaswinder Uncle, but I have asked Rocky to locate him. I want to talk to him and meet him. He is one of the finest gentlemen I have ever met.

I visited Chukchuk Nagar in 2018. The colony was celebrating 50 years of Durga Puja at the Capital Hall, so I took a three-day leave and visited the colony after almost eighteen years. I had never been to Chukchuk Nagar after Papa's retirement.

Lavanya was in Chennai for official work, so I took the children, Maa and Papa, to Lucknow. Lavanya joined us a day later.

The golden jubilee of Durga Puja at Chukchuk Nagar was a spectacle of unparalleled grandeur. It was a momentous occasion. The idol of Goddess Durga was up on the stage with her children, and decorations, the pandal, the devotional songs, the evening aarti, the cultural programmes, and the overall ambience was more elaborate than I had ever seen in all my years at Chukchuk Nagar. Generations will remember the golden jubilee of Durga Puja celebrations at Chukchuk Nagar. Unfortunately, the rest of the gang couldn't make it except for Daksh, who resided in Lucknow. He visited Chukchuk Nagar with his wife, Rupa, and the children. We met, hugged, laughed, wept, and then laughed again.

Maa and Papa spent all their time in Capital Hall and refused to come to our hotel before midnight. After Lavanya joined us, we all went walking around Chukchuk Nagar. First, we visited my block, which had new occupants, introduced ourselves, and requested that we see the mango tree. The request was immediately granted. We went into the backyard and saw the huge tree, now with its branches sprawling in all directions. We walked up to the tree and stood at the same spot where, more than a quarter of a century ago, we used to sit and hold our meetings. We sat beneath the tree. Tears welled up in Lavanya's eyes, followed by Daksh's, and I couldn't hold back my own emotions. Our children, seeing us in this condition, were puzzled and amused at the same time. That was not their fault. They didn't know what this mango tree meant to us. I stood up and reached out to touch the jackfruit, and guava tree. I saw some ripe fruits, which made me smile. Daksh would have snapped nearly twenty photos of just those mango, jackfruit and guava trees.

The current occupants offered us tea and snacks, and we spent some time chatting with them, sitting in the same room where I had spent almost twenty-seven years of my life, telling them about our friends and the mango tree meetings.

We went to Daksh's and Lavanya's block. We didn't go inside the quarter but clicked photos from outside. Lavanya had planted a Sheesham sapling in her garden sometime in 1985. That tree, now towering, provided ample shade to the entire block. She was so happy to see the well-grown tree that she reached out to embrace it.

From there, we went towards the water tank. We sat on the cool pipes, listening to the gurgling of the water inside. Now, there were weeds and shrubs around the tank. The man in charge of the Pump House gave us a surprising look after seeing four adults and four teenagers sitting on the pipe. Daksh and I lay on the pipe for some time, just like we used to do as young boys.

'From where are you, Sir?' the man asked.

We told him our story. When he heard about the bee attack, he exclaimed,

'The bees are still there, Sir. Last month, they stung my colleagues who had gone to the top to clean the tank.'

'Bees will be bees,' I said.

From the water tank, we walked to the Cooperative store. None of the shops, including the Dixit Sweet shop, were there. They had all been replaced by new shops with their new owners. But Surinder the *paanwala* was there. He recognised Daksh and me immediately. We embraced and chatted as we savoured the *paan* he gave us. We met Chacha's son. He was following his father's footsteps of selling *laiya chana*. He gave the children chocolates and four full packets of *laiya chana.*

We stood in front of the Polyclinic, opposite the Cooperative store. It reminded us of Bholanath's *golgappa* mishap. That brought a smile.

'Shall we go to the stadium or the *Naher*?' Daksh asked.

'*Naher* is on the other side. Let's go to the stadium. We can visit the *Naher* some other time.' Lavanya remarked.

So, we went to the stadium and sat there for a while. It was the same place where, many years ago, I had pleaded to Chaitanya, not once but numerous times, to give up and stay away from addiction. I believe my inability to persuade him was my biggest failure.

At the stadium, I saw some boys playing football on one side of the ground with neither Guruji nor the Unity Club in sight. I was pleasantly surprised to see some girls playing football along with the boys. Guruji would have been very happy seeing the girls play football. We saw some boys and girls playing basketball, and a cricket match was going on, which I presume was a zonal-level game.

We visited our school. St William's stood steadfast, just as it always had. We met Sister Lucy, and what a meeting it was! Sister Lucy is such an adorable and endearing human being.

We went around the school auditorium and ventured into the 'forest' where Rocky often got lost. The cricket pitch was now well maintained, and I am sure I could have scored a 100 every time if I had such a 'beautiful' well-curated pitch while in school. We went inside the auditorium, stood there for a while, and visited Mr Spoke's room while coming out. Mr

Spoke had retired and was replaced by another PT teacher. In the end, we went to the church. Baby Jesus and Mother Mary smiled at us. 'You have been good kids,' I thought I heard them saying. We bowed to them for their blessings and then exited the church.

We came out of the school gate, met Laddu, and bought some *churan* from him. I immediately clicked some photos of the *churan* and shared them with Mona. Laddu didn't recognise us. We are now middle-aged, and Laddu has surpassed that milestone. So, it was not his fault. We went to Dewalal's shop and bought *samosas*. Daksh snapped some photos of the *samosas* and immediately shared them with Bholanath on WhatsApp to make Bholanath jealous. Dewalal had passed away, and his son was now looking after the shop.

Then we visited the mandir, sat there for a while, returned to Capital Hall, and had tea and snacks in the makeshift eateries. We could hear the beat of the drums and the sound of the *sankh* and watched the evening aarti. After watching the evening aarti and the cultural programmes, we stayed until late at night. The children relished their time in Chukchuk Nagar, gaining a glimpse into their parents' childhood memories. Daksh and Rupa dropped my parents and the children off at the hotel while I hired a car and reached our hotel with Lavanya. Daksh's Tata Safari could accommodate only eight people.

I told Daksh I planned to visit the LPG Railway station early in the morning. He said he would try to come. He invited us for lunch at his house. I was hesitant as we had to catch the evening flight to Kolkata, but then Daksh put immense pressure on me and Lavanya, and before I thought I would burst under the mounting pressure, I said, 'Yes.'

Daksh arrived just as Lavanya and I stepped out of the hotel early in the morning. Considering that Daksh's house was at least 10 miles away, it was quite an effort on his part to be at the hotel so early. The children wanted to sleep, so we didn't disturb them.

Daksh drove us to the LPG Railway station, around a kilometre from our hotel. We entered the station and sat on a bench as memories flooded back from more than two decades ago. We sat there sipping *chai* as a few superfast trains rattled past. The station transported us to our youth as we sat on the bench for quite a long time. After a while, I walked to the station master's cabin and introduced myself to the man in charge, who was sitting on a chair and doing some paperwork.

'I am Chandan Chandola. Are you the station master?' I asked.

'I am the assistant station master. What can I do for you?'

'No, No. Nothing. I was a resident of Chukchuk Nagar. I used to visit the station quite frequently with my friends. Do you know Mr Ramesh Shandalya? He was then the station master here.'

The man looked surprised. He immediately stood up.

'I am Gagan Shandalya. Ramesh Shandalya was my father. He passed away in 2001, six years after his retirement.'

'I am so sorry to hear that. He was such a gentleman.' I

choked and could hardly speak.

'That's what God wanted, Mr Chandola. What can we do against his wish?'

I nodded.

'Wait, are you the Chandola who rescued a boy from being run over by a train? My father often spoke of your bravery.'

'Yes, I am the same Chandola, and it was not only me but also my friend Chaitanya who helped avert that accident. Chaitanya, unfortunately, is no longer with us.'

'I am so sorry to hear that, Mr Chandola. May your friend be at peace wherever he is.'

I thanked him, returned to the bench, and updated Lavanya and Daksh on our conversation. We sat there for a while, left the station, and walked towards the Rasangan shop. It was early, and the shop was closed; otherwise, we could have bought some *rasgullas* and shared the photos with Bholanath again.

In the end, we went to the *Naher*. The water was in full flow, rushing with an unyielding force. We stood at the place where Chaitanya used to visit often. His memories washed over us—overwhelming us. I felt his presence in the gentle sway of the trees.

I suddenly heard his voice, 'Chandu.' I turned around. But he was not here, not there, not anywhere.

We stood there for a long time and finally found comfort in the memories of our beloved friend.

And then, we quietly walked back towards Daksh's car and back to the hotel.

Daksh took us for lunch at his house. Rupa cooked everything even though they had a cook at home. The delicious lunch became more than a meal, as laughter and our stories flowed freely, although we spent considerable time on the mango mishap. Daksh felt guilty that his father was transferred because of his stupidity. We all laughed. The children bonded very well, and seeing them enjoy the company of each other, I felt that all these years had just melted away, bridging the time gap. We had a quick video call with Mona while she was in her Geneva office. She clapped, laughed, and shouted 'Hurrah' many times. After ten minutes into our call, I said, 'Mona, go back to work. I will call you later.' She frowned, not wanting to go, but then, she always heeded my suggestion.

When we left Daksh's house, we left behind the cherished moments of togetherness.

Daksh dropped us at the airport. We hugged, and he touched the feet of my parents. I saw his eyes swell up with tears as he bid goodbye. Lavanya and I both waved at him with tears in our eyes.

On the flight, Lavanya continued to hold my hand from takeoff to landing and whispered a 'Thank You, Chandu' in my ears, smiling from ear to ear as we were ready to disembark. The good thing about having your childhood crush as your wife is that she always remains a crush. So, we fight about silly things, and nothing is serious at home. On top of that, Maa and Papa always take Lavanya's side, and hence, I prefer to remain silent. I wish she would stop calling me Chandu, but I know that will never happen. Which wife calls her husband

Pintu, Shintu, or Dabbu? But my wife calls me Chandu.

But she always cares for and loves me, and I love her—my dearest Lavoo.

I called Mona outside her office hours a day after I reached Kolkata and updated her on our Lucknow trip. Her excitement was palpable as she listened to our Chukchuk Nagar adventures.

'I wish I were there, Chandu,' she remarked.

'Don't worry. We will have a reunion soon. Rocky is working on it.'

Then she spoke to Lavanya; as always, their 'discussions' continued for a couple of hours.

The entire week was spent answering calls from my friends. Every gang member called me for an update on our Chukchuk Nagar visit, and the calls concluded in the wee hours of the morning.

Anshul had called, and though we were discussing our work and other things, we strayed a bit when he asked me, 'Chandu, why did you never consider Mona a potential life partner? You both have been inseparable since childhood.'

I smiled at that question.

'Mona is the extension of my soul. With your extension, you cannot fall in love, whatever love means traditionally. We didn't realise it then, but I know we have always had a spiritual connection. Our relationship cannot be defined.'

'Okay.' Anshul remarked after a long pause. However, I understood from his 'okay' that he didn't understand what I was trying to say.

We spoke for a few more minutes, hung up, and then I went to sleep.

That was the start of the end of the story—or maybe the end of the start.

That was the story of my friends—the story of those carefree days spent side by side at Chukchuk Nagar chasing dreams, dogs, mangoes, monkeys, and whatnot. With us, we carried the joy of youth and innocence. We carried that unbreakable bond formed in the simplicity of childhood. And above all, we carried love.

Life has taken us on separate paths, but the warmth of our bond remains. As we get older and each moment slips through our fingers like grains of sand, it is not possible to reclaim those old times, those teenage years, and those moments that define who we are and how far we have come. Yet those bonds of friendship continue to offer shelter and comfort as we celebrate the joys of life together.

As I look up at the evening sky painted in orange and gold, thinking about those spicy moments of our friendship, I whisper a silent thanks for the priceless gift of our bond, our story of childhood Curries, Colours, and Chaos; we carry a piece of each other in our hearts- a treasure I will cherish for a lifetime.

Long Live the Gang!

Rocky sent a stupid joke, which he usually does, followed by a video to our WhatsApp group today. It's of Jagjit Singh, the famous ghazal singer singing,

Yeh Daulat bhi le lo,
Yeh shoharat bhi le lo,
Bhale cheen lo mujse meri jawani,
Magar mujko lauta do bachpan ka saawan,
Vo kaagaz ki kashti, Vo baarish ka paani.

(Take away this wealth, take away this fame,
Even if you can take away my youth from me,
But return to me the rainy season of childhood,
That boat of paper and the water of the rain)

Seconds later, he sends a picture of a Mango Tree laden with ripe Mangoes!

And a message, 'Reunion being planned in January 2025. Details will follow. Get, Set, Go!'

More Books By Suman Mukherjee

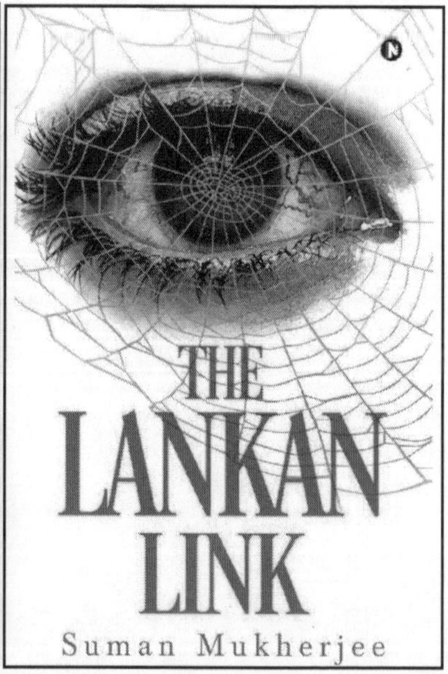

"An pulsating ride that promises a lot of twists & turns....."
- S. RAHUL
(Author of the bestseller 'Left Me Broken')
The
N.G.
CODE
SUMAN MUKHERJEE
FERNTREE

Jhimli B Saha is an artist born in India and lives in England.

Painting and writing have always been her ways of expressing herself in the form of colours, prose, and poetry.

She participates in solo and group painting exhibitions in and around London.

She has done a course on creative writing in London.

She has published short stories online and in a 'journal of women's Tanka.'

This is Jhimli's first fiction book.

Suman Mukherjee worked in a multinational company before becoming a writer. His creative works encompass different genres...from crime investigations to political thrillers, love stories, horror short stories, and the spiritual genre.

When he's not writing, Suman indulges in his love for travel and food. Exploring new places and cuisines is a source of inspiration for him. Reading has been his lifelong passion, along with his other love, cricket.

Suman loves being around children and believes that children are the best storytellers as they can make us laugh and cry, either through their words or their actions.

This is Suman's seventh book.